SPECIAL EDITION

THE SPY WITHIN

Book 1

Ж Calm Collected And Controlled Meets Fiery Sassy And Wild Ж

By

Lavinia Dasani

Plumitif Press LLC

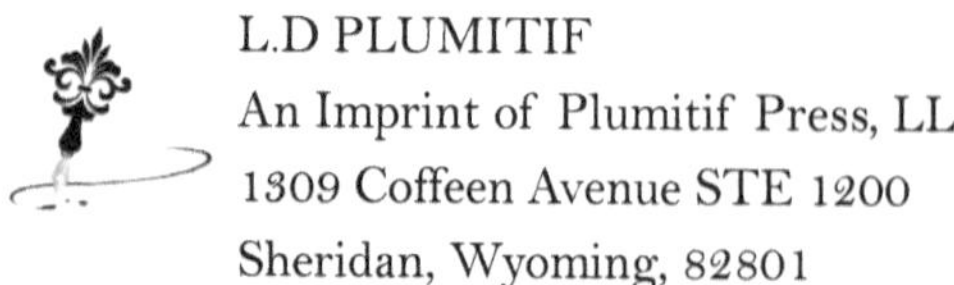
L.D PLUMITIF

An Imprint of Plumitif Press, LLC

1309 Coffeen Avenue STE 1200

Sheridan, Wyoming, 82801

ISBN (pbk): 978-1-7339857-8-9

ISBN (ebook): 978-1-7339857-9-6

ISBN (Hardcover): 978-1-965147-00-9

ISBN (Pocket Book): 978-1-965147-01-6

Printed in the United States of America

THE SPY WITHIN REVIEW

"The history line reminds me of a bold and sensitive woman. Career and family women in the world of man. A MUST read to raise strong girls." — Deborah, Amazon reader.

"Super love the book. Hope you guys give this story a chance because it has a new approach and a lot of humor, family, comedy, domination, action, love all in one book. You will be hooked and have a feel good moment once you start to read the story." — Beta Reader.

"The Spy Within is a page-turner and jaw-dropping book. It is a book that won't disappoint. Every page holds new surprises. It will keep you on edge, but in a good way. I promise you that this book will not disappoint you. It is such an amazing boom you won't want to put it down until you are done." — Rachel M. Cordero, Goodreads

WARNING

The following material contains S-ensuous contents. These are described as containing graphic romantic details that are not as explicit as an erotica novel would. Then again, like any romance novel, be it action or not, expect love scenes. However, I will give a fair warning that there might be some gruesome details within the literature.

This ROMANCE book is entirely an entertainment literature and you've been warned of its potential 'dangerous' contents in advance. Keep out of reach of children.

Proceed with caution — Not for the faint of heart.

ACKNOWLEDGMENT

For this special edition of The Spy Within, book 1 of Tame Series, I want to say thank you to all the readers that have given me critical feedback so I could make this version better. And despite all the problems I encountered throughout this long process of re-editing this novel, I'm grateful for all who supported me and guided me.

Keeping true to the 1st edition, I would like to say a special thank you to all my readers from Wattpad. I started off on Wattpad and got a lot of valuable critics and reviews. You, wattpaders, are great and a blessing. Thanks for supporting me throughout my rollercoaster of a journey, especially with all the grammar mistakes in the first version of the Tame Series.

Additionally, I'm dedicating this book to my mother. She has genuinely supported me through my writing journey and has always let me know I can do it no matter what happens in my life.

A big thanks to my family and friends throughout the years while this book was in the making.

All of your support has meant a lot to me.

CHAPTER 1
LIFE AS USUAL

PHOEBE

Swiftly leaping up from my seat like a coiled spring, my leather chair almost toppling over, I fitted my concealed earpiece, "How are you even a part of my agency!?" In a low voice capable of rumbling the ocean, I rebuked the spy.

"I'm sorry ma'am, it's just-"

Cutting through whatever he was about to blabber and checking my surroundings to make sure nobody was within earshot, I whispered, "You are pitiful! How did an agent from D.S.I allow an essential package to be intercepted by a gang as lowly as the one you were assigned to? Explain it to me!" Stentorian and commanding, I was ready to crush the man with fiery insults and verbose punishment.

"I apologise once again, ma'am. But you should know I'm already working on rectifying my errors. I'm currently attempting to capture the person who first intercepted the package." Quickly saving his ass from my current wrath, he gave me a briefing of his plan.

"I want that package delivered to its assigned destination by the end of tomorrow night! And if you need to put a bullet in your little girlfriend's gut for not cooperating with this mission, then so be it." Ruthless and emotionless, my order was definitive—one which he couldn't dare to violate.

I could literally hear the horror and fear in his voice as he jumped to his feet. "But… Ma'am…" he whined.

As if his whining would change my mind. Ha. It seems like he is just now accepting the fact that the warnings he received during his training season about how heartless I am, almost like a monster, were completely true.

Going back to my seat and making sure my voice was still low but powerful, I firmly stated, "My patience is wearing real thin, agent! Do what needs to be done before I show you what disappointing me brings upon you and your family. Also, I require a full report about your mission from start to end. Send it to Pierce upon completion. I will check on it, two days from now."

"Yes, ma'am." He answered meekly just before I hung up and cautiously took out my earpiece. The last thing I wanted was for stupidly curious people in the office to notice I had something inside my ears.

I swear, lately I've been wondering how the agency has been handling their hiring process. If this guy was the product of our new hires under Pierce's control while I was lying low and under the radar, then my agency was in deep shit.

"Miss Smith! Instead of idly sitting in the office, bring me the document for the new business proposal on the oiling company. Now!" Frostily declared my boss, making me jump in my seat. I swear, if this jumping trend continued, I would soon have to nail my chair to the floor.

"Yes, sir. I'll get to it immediately, sir." I voiced out through the phone with clenched teeth.

Oh, how I hated it when my boss, *'The Great Mr Federick Ashton Archer,'* ordered me around and treated me like crap. If I sat around, as he so kindly put it, his business would literally fall apart. Yet, here I was, dealing with His Highness.

Knocking once on his office door, I walked inside when I heard him lowly grunted, "Come in."

I showed no reaction to his crudeness and confidently walked to his desk. Placing his *'oh so important'* paper in front of him, I made it clear he couldn't intimidate.

Eager to leave the sight of him as soon as possible, I haughtily inquired if he required something else. When he said *'no'*, I nearly bolted out of his office, but then I remembered I had to notify *'His Highness'* ahead of time about me going out for lunch today.

"Mr Archer, I won't be available for lunch today. If you require anything during my lunch hours, I will be back two hours from now."

He continuously stared down at his papers, swiftly nodded his head as if saying, *'It's okay'* and murmured a low "Hmm". After receiving his *'gracious response'*, I happily left his office.

Usually, I would grab lunch at the office canteen and immediately walk back to my office to continue with my work. The reasoning is simple. Mr Federick Ashton Archer. He apparently doesn't know what *'break time'* means. If I don't inform him whenever I go out for my lunch, he will inevitably seek me out for some trivial paperwork that can easily be put off — as he oh-so-routinely does. And if he can't find me during these *'crucial'* moments, then all hell breaks loose.

The moment I left his office, I let out a sigh of relief, solidifying my point about my inability to tolerate him and his arrogance. Unfortunately, my fellow gender and I did not mutually share this feeling — as far as they were concerned, the reality was an entirely different story. Every one of them had unashamedly thrown themselves at his feet, begging for Mr Federick Ashton Archer's divine attention. It's like they had never seen a 6'2" tall, dark-haired, grey-eyed man with 8 packs abs and a 9 o'clock shadow. The entire world basically treated him like a Greek God; worshipping the very ground he walked on. Then, there was me, who saw him as the perfect description of a man whore and a playboy.

How do I know you ask?

Well, let's say, despite being the head of several departments, I also get the pleasure of being Mr Playboy's own personal executive assistant. Consequently, I have frequently arranged his many 'dates', handled calls from countless women, and even stumbled upon him doing the nasty with his 'dates' in his freaking office. It is pretty disgusting.

Then again, unlike other executive assistants, I've taken upon more roles than just overseeing Federick's work and arranging meetings. I've created a sophisticated filling system for the company and constantly come up with great ideas to push the company's reputation and prosperity further. In all actuality, my excess responsibilities put me officially at about the same level as the great Federick Ashton Archer, and unofficially, at the same pay.

Thankfully, the finance and accounting department is under my wing with little to no direct supervision from Federick, making it easier for me to blend my actual income and hide it from curious eyes. Leaving all technicalities aside, let's just say, *'Archer & Associates'* has a few secret investors with high voting power — investors whom Federick Archer has been dying to meet face to face for the past two years.

Luckily for me, I have rules and self-respect, unlike women like Lucy

Braton, the office go-to-bitch. There is no way I would allow myself to feel remotely attracted or lustful towards someone with such a big ego and ass-hole-ness level as Federick Archer. Not to mention, I vowed years ago that I would never date someone I worked for or with.

But let's forget about the person whose life's goal is to make mine impossible and difficult. Instead, let's talk about the people who continuously make me smile. People who help me forget about the bad days and turn them into good ones. Basically, the two people I love the most — more than anything, even life — for them, I will do anything.

Those two dudes are why I needed a two-hour lunch break. My sons — the two most important men in my life — are so sweet. They saw how stressed I was from work and scheduled a lunch date for us to bond and relax. Thankfully Federick Archer didn't bother asking why I was taking such a long lunch or what I was doing, because I would've had to lie my ass off. What most people, including my boss, Mr Federick Archer, didn't know was that I was a mother with two sons. For the people at the agency, and at Archer & Associates, I was single and without kids. Only my best friends, who are also a part of my team at D.S.I., and my kids' grandparents, knew the truth about my life.

You may ask yourself; how?

The simple answer is that I've been with the company for so freaking long — even before Federick Archer took over from his dad, Joseph Archer — that I escaped having my personal information go through the new systems.

Now many of you may ask, how come Federick Archer hasn't yet looked over my files?

Let's just say Joseph Archer and I have a special bond that even Federick Archer himself doesn't know about.

Plus, I have my ways of feeding Federick as many lies about me as I want. Obviously, as a promise to Joseph and Alicia Archer, I try not to take advantage of the benefits I have over Federick. I am, after all, assigned to protect his arrogant ass whenever necessary, and only keep things which need to be kept secret from him, for his own protection and safety. What you don't know can't hurt you, right?

CHAPTER 2
MATCHLESS TRIO

PHOEBE

Best friends since kindergarten, Mia Luc, Damien Ambrosh, and I, Phoebe Ziva Smith, aka Angel in the spy world, were the most badass trio of our times. We were what every team envied and aimed to achieve.

Together, we were unstoppable and an epic typhoon despite our significant age difference. With Damien being six years older than me, and Mia being five years older than me, we indeed made an odd and peculiar group. Even though we all originally connected in kindergarten, I had known of Damien since I could walk. His father and mine were business buddies. Mia, however, was transferred to my private school from the orphanage because of her exceptional intelligence. They were relying on her intelligence and potential to bring influence to their orphanage. The two of us immediately clicked on the first day of kindergarten after she stood up for me and trashed the kid that was bullying sweet little me. Ever since that day, she had been the big sister I never had. So much so that even my dad ended up accepting her as a second daughter.

Rounded brown-hazel eyes, long brown hair, tall, lean, with an athletic build and reddish perky lips, Mia Luc was nearly the picture-perfect version of me. The fundamental difference was that I had pure brown eyes, slightly curvier and about an inch shorter than her.

Damien Ambrosh was such a guy. Muscularly built, about 6'2, he had sharp blue eyes, thin rosy lips, blond hair, and a chest worthy of praise. His 6-pack at the young age of 15 was a sight for my 9-year-old self.

As a team, we were always pushing each other beyond our limits. We helped each other improve, but most importantly, had each other's backs, no matter the situation or circumstance. Not only were the three of us known for our top performance as spies, but we were also known for our devious yet hilarious pranks. The coolest part was that with me being next in line, we couldn't get into trouble for pulling our infamous devilish pranks on other agents.

My father, Robert Smith, was a single parent. He was my role model. He was powerful, successful, ruthless when needed and extremely loving toward me. His attitude, together with his propensity to always push me to be better than him — to be perfect in whatever I do — was what made me the powerful badass agent and the woman I am today.

Despite my requests for my dad to train and treat Damien and Mia the same as me, he was adamant about making me work harder and longer. We had recurrent private sessions at senseless times of the day. The harshest ones were the aggressive and intensely dangerous workouts and occasional training sessions at 2 in the morning. As a teenager, I highly prioritised my sleep over everything else — but getting my father to understand that was an almost impossible task. And so, whenever he was present — and not gone on one of his many long trips — he would make me give up on my precious sleep.

But now, I can proudly say he showed me how to always go for the best — even when my mind tells me I can't handle it. Thanks to him and my life experiences, I learned sacrifices were part of the process to achieve or gain something of significance in life. It was harsh but reality and it all contributed to my success.

In the dangerous world I grew up in, being engaged and married at an extremely young age was no shocker. So, when Damien asked for Mia's hand in marriage when she turned 15, after officially dating each other for two years, it was no surprise. Those two had been in love since middle school but were too stubborn to ask each other out.

All it took was for me to inform Damien that Mia was asked out for the annual Homecoming dance and that the guy planned to deflower her on that night. The jealousy and anger in his eyes made me believe in true love. It was something the young, ignorant, and stupid me wanted. But that wasn't my reality. For business' sake, my father betrothed to someone I didn't particularly like.

Unfortunately, a few months before their wedding, my dad sent Mia out on a *special* long-term case. But they didn't allow me — the leader of the team and future head of the agency — to know the details. Then again, I wasn't one to take no for an answer. Even though it took me 2 years, I never gave up. I remained persistent, and as resourceful as my father, until I uncovered Mia's special mission and the evil dark shadow that was Cole Vanderwill.

Ignoring my dad's wishes, I fearlessly threw myself into the lion's den once I realised my dad gave Mia a mission intended for me. I refused to let Mia be the sacrificial lamb and the vengeful target of one of my kills' sons. Regretfully, my rescue mission went south, and the devil himself gave me the front seat to watch him cold-bloodedly slice Mia's throat open with no remorse or hesitation. The same woman who, in the meantime, had become the mother of the monster's two children.

To this day, I still detest this cursed, never-ending mission. Mia was only 20 years old when she died and endured the sufferance that was supposed to be mine. Not even being kidnapped and tortured for several months after witnessing Mia's death by the author of my tribulation made up for the loss that Damien and I felt. There isn't one day that goes by when I don't miss Mia Luc; her smiles, her cockiness, and the role of big sister she played in my life.

However, I am also grateful for what she left me on her way out — the one thing I know I couldn't get on my own. Mia gave me something to live for again. It was something new, and once I learned its value, it became just as important as my life. She left with me her two wonderful sons, Wyatt and Teo, making me an instant mother.

With Mia's death, the matchless trio was incinerated. Damien lost the true love of his life and, till today, has loved no one as much as he loved Mia. Like me, he too turned frigid — colder than Antarctica. He was a living corpse, killing mercilessly. For the longest time, he pretty much only talked to me, the author of *his* destroyed life. To this day, I am still in awe of how Damien could look me in the eye, talk to me, and work with me for years before taking off to Rio for a long-term mission. Since then, he's been a ghost to me.

Following my rescue from Vanderwill's den, I spent months in a pitiful corner, incessantly crying my heart out until the mental anguish became physically unbearable — worse than a gunshot wound would. Full of hatred and an aggressive need for vengeance coursing through my blood, I craved to avenge Mia's death. Blinded and constantly seeing red, my decision-making skills significantly waned. My anger and pain destroyed my ability to care about others, even my father.

All I wanted was to painfully and slowly kill Vanderwill. To rip his heart out of his chest while staring directly into his eyes. I craved to see the fear growing, and the light dimmed in his eyes. Cole Vanderwill has been the monster and shadow stuck to my ass like a second skin ever since I infiltrated his gang to rescue Mia.

The worst part is that he vanished into thin air — off my radar — after he effectively stripped me of my stress-free life and immediate family. Because of him, at the shy age of 16, I had the blood of the two most important people in my life on my hands. Because of Cole Vanderwill, Wyatt and Teo never got to grow up with their mother and grandfather. Those lovely kids missed having Damien as their dad.

While Mia was still Vanderwill's mistress, she made me vow that if something happens to her, I should adopt Wyatt and Teo, and never reveal to them she was their mother and Vanderwill their father — unless it was essential. And around ten years ago, when I became Wyatt and Teo's legal parent, I held true to my promise. In the beginning, I hated it, and wanted to hurt them with the truth, thinking it would hurt Vanderwill. But I refrained for Mia. With time, Wyatt and Teo wormed their way into my heart and became my most prized possession — my world and the reason I started feeling again.

Fortunately, I can now say they feel the same toward me. Throughout the years, their abundant love, the glint of pride whenever they talk about me, and the respect they've shown me changed my heart. To where I now find their over-protectiveness sweet and don't mind them holding me to a high standard. With time, they've successfully cast away my doubts about their feelings and intentions towards me. They showed me their loyalty and that I can trust them.

Although Wyatt is more built than Teo, people almost always perceive them as twins, even though Wyatt is 16 years old and Teo is 15, only one year younger than his brother. Even more strange is that Wyatt and Teo sometimes would have this somewhat twin-telepathic moment. Most of the times, it was hilarious. But these two troublemakers knew how to use this ability to annoy me or get their way. Nevertheless, they have been a blessing to me as a family, especially after the tragedy and loss caused by Vanderwill. But no matter how much I loved my sons; I was more than thankful that they both looked more like Mia than Cole Vanderwill.

Honestly, the way both these boys turned out baffled me. Yes, they bicker a lot and are mischievous and childish at times. And I would love to not have to deal with their continuous efforts to sneak out without security. Keeping up with their teenage boys' secrets sometimes is a pain in the butt. Then again, after having spent 10 years of my life worried and scared that they would turn out like their father, I was happy to be proven wrong. Long story short, the idea of not raising my kids in a good way was beyond terrifying to me. But, overall, they've turned out pretty much perfect.

As the years went by, I noticed I was becoming more like my father. Without realising it, I started repeating the same things he used to tell me when I had too many questions for my own good. Luckily for me, my kids turned out to be far more understanding than *'child-me.'*. The privilege of mothering and raising them was not lost on me, especially after experiencing years of guilt in the beginning for not being able to provide them with a father. However, as time went by, I realised I had done my best as a single-working parent.

Other than my presence when I would be gone on countless peculiar work trips, my kids have missed nothing in their life. In fact, when they turned 12, I gifted both with their own unlimited bank cards. They handled their expenses under the brief supervision of their grandparents and nanny while I would be on one of my many trips.

Wyatt, Teo, and my relationship didn't follow the usual norm. Yes, I was their parent, and I held them to a standard. But I was also easy on them. Along with being their mom, I was also their best friend and confidant. To the world, I was cold, harsh, and unattainable, but to them, I was warm, carefree, and open. I had no hesitation openly joking with them and sharing parts of my private life with them. We had no filter in our family. On occasions, I would openly joke about Wyatt's sex life and all his embarrassing moments at school or out with his friends. I would listen to them express how they are feeling about someone or a situation or talk about the people in their lives. When needed, I'll share how annoying a specific person at Archer & Associates was or a brief about what's going on in my life. Honestly, ever since they became my reason to live, all I wanted was to fully enjoy every single moment I get to spend with my boys.

Then again, all this pampering might have had something to do with the guilt I felt, knowing that I had been deceiving my family and going against the explicit rule of no lies or secrets. But I had no choice. I had to break my own rules to protect my kids. They may find me elusive and strange, and at times my words may not align, but I am resolute in my mission to protect my family from any danger. I had long come to term about my propensity to suffocate my loved ones in a silk cocoon; so, no rules in this world were going to stop me from overprotecting my sons.

All I can do is try my best, even when it gets irritating, frustrating, and exhausting. I must continue being cautious and on my guard. And as tiring and straining as it is, I just can't stop myself from acting the way I do — not when I have so much to lose and have been on my own for so long.

Thankfully, I got a good deal for a beautiful family home by the beachside. With a few discreet modifications, the house now caters perfectly to my needs, all while maintaining the facade of its original design. The best thing is that it's not too far from my agency headquarters and Archer

& Associates. Having both so close to me has been a blessing for my family and me.

The little dark secret about Archer & Associates is that it ran deeper in my veins than anyone could ever imagine. Since its origination, Archer & Associates has been Angel Agency's covert ally. Angel Agency, now known as Delta Special Intelligence, aka D.S.I, was my pride and where I truly belonged. And Archer & Associates actively worked as a shield in the shadows, masking the true extent of D.S.I's operation.

Fortunately for me, no one from my either work knew where I exactly lived or who I truly was. To everyone outside the spy realm, I lived in a New York City apartment and was the Executive Personal Assistant to the cold, ruthless and heartless Mr Federick Ashton Archer, and I intended to keep it this way for as long as I could.

Given my childhood and my complex surreptitious background, I had learned to like normality and the simplicity of a normal life whenever I could get it — which, to my great displeasure, was only possible at *'Archer & Associates.'*. This was one of the main reasons, despite despising being pushed or ordered around, I was still working as *'Mr Cold Grey Eyes'* executive personal assistant. That asshole was the only person who could push my buttons with a snap of a finger. And damn him for being so tall. I hated how, during a confrontation, he could easily topple over my average height and stare deep into my soul.

When Mr Federick Ashton Archer first moved back to New York after university, he immediately assumed I was a decorative presence, lacking substance and purpose. Like one of those bimbos who does little other than being pretty and sitting idle. Yet, throughout our two-year of working together, I've joyfully shown him how wrong he was on multiple occasions.

Nonetheless, this didn't stop him from continuously belittling me, as if I had done nothing worthwhile. Yet, I knew deep down he had long acknowledged I was worth much more to the company than what he showed on the outside.

Heck, I directed the entire company in his absence. I knew everything there was to know about this dang company… from the inside out. I, for sure, knew more than Federick himself did. For once, any person who searched well enough about *'Archer & Associates'* would see that the company deals with establishing businesses property, authenticating, shipping, buying, and selling of materials and objects provided by diverse companies, countries, and branches, such as cargo, airplanes parts, food, artifacts, spices, arts, clothing, among several other things.

But they won't find out that I secretly owned half of the company. The most they could find is that I've been working for the company for a long time. And maybe, just maybe, with extensive and purposeful search, they could find out I've been working as the executive personal assistant for the past nine years and a half. First to Joseph Archer, Federick Archer's father, and then to the jerk-face himself. And they could search heaven and earth, but they would never find my face or name under the partners and associate search on the web or company records.

It was Federick Ashton Archer who was the face of this multi-billion-dollar global company. Yet, the arrogant bastard didn't even know that his own company dealt with the import and export of military weapons and newly designed tech behind closed doors, under my supervision.

CHAPTER 3
LUNCH DATE

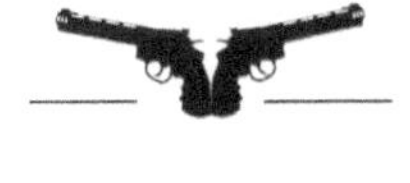

PHOEBE

~ Flashback to the beginning of the day ~

"Sweetie, are you sure you don't want to go out with your friends or the girls at school? You know, instead of taking your old mother out, who has to go to work," I jocularly commented, with a smile.

They both laughed. "Mom, you are not old, and the answer is yes, without a doubt. We want and would prefer to go out with you, not our friends or some girl at school," Wyatt, my outspoken boy, responded.

"Are you asking me out, baby boy?" Swallowing my laughter with great difficulty, I sheepishly inquired. Unfortunately, I did not do an excellent job of hiding my smile. They saw right through my façade and played along.

They exchanged a knowing glance, then offered a respectful half-bow in my direction. "Yes, indeed, my lady," Wyatt and Teo simultaneously replied with a respectful nod. It was like they had practiced this line a thousand times before ambushing me this morning with their request.

"It'll be our honour to go out for lunch with you. Say yes, and we'll pick you up this afternoon." Wyatt continued with gentleness.

On queue before I could utter a word, they both grabbed my hands, raised it to their month and gently kiss the back of it. As cute as all of this was, their unison and twin-like behaviour were creepy and annoying sometimes.

As a mother, I couldn't help but feel an overwhelming sense of sweetness and pride, knowing that I had raised two remarkable and well-mannered young men. But considering the current situation, I couldn't hold it anymore and burst into laughter.

Several minutes passed before I could release my grip on my stomach and regain my composure. Grinning from ear to ear, they were happy that their attempts to make me laugh and relax had paid off. I have a knack for hiding my emotions. And I try to keep my stress and frustration away from them. But seeing how hard they were working at making me happy told me my perfect façade had cracked. With how hard Federick was pushing me lately, it was no wonder my face painted my stress. This civilian life was trying to take me out.

Covering my grin with a semi-serious expression, "I must head to the office and catch up on my work if I want to join you boys for lunch. And if you end up waiting for me, please do not talk to any strangers. Or ask for me from the people in the company."

The boys gave me a familiar look, one that I've grown accustomed to recognising all too well lately. I could tell my odd remarks intrigued them whenever they offered to meet me by my work. But over time, they learned I would not provide them with a direct response, at least not in the way they expected.

~ Present ~

I felt a tinge of sadness, imagining the expressions my sons gave me after I gave them another complex and cryptic instruction with no logical explanation. Despite my career choice, I didn't like lying and hiding things from my boys. And sometimes, when I couldn't come up with a good enough excuse, I gave them my infamous *'stop asking questions'* look. But, with them growing so fast, even that move sometimes failed to deter their questioning, leaving me no choice but to lie to their face. I might hate every second, but there were dangerous people out there who only lived to ruin me. And my family was the only way to destroy me.

Actively pushing all those dark thoughts, I dug into the pleasant memory of what had happened this morning and I felt much happier. I hurried down to the office's lobby, knowing my boys were always punctual for me.

Considering the last time the boys visited me at work was about 2 years ago, before Federick took over, I was undeniably worried about what this new batch of people would say if they saw me with the boys. What unpleasant comments they might make in front of my kids that would undoubtedly make me snap? Or worse, what if they flirted with them?

My sons were gallant, and they would take advantage of looking older than they were and flirt back. Which would only cause more problems for me. At age 16 and 15, they could both easily pass for 20 years old, if not a bit more — especially with all the bodybuilding they've been doing. This was precisely why I wanted to be at the entrance at least five minutes earlier.

As soon as I walked out, I noticed them parking in a 'no parking' zone in front of the building and waving at me excitedly, as if the red Mustang wasn't already attention-grabbing enough. Smiling, I lightly shook my head in slight amusement as I strode toward them. Leave it to my sons to break the law outwardly. Much to my surprise, as soon as I reached them, they embraced me in a bear hug, puissant enough to crush me, lifted me up, spun me around, and planted kisses on my cheeks all at once. Furiously blushing at their open affection, I didn't dare to look around. I was sure people were looking at us, thinking we were weird.

"Seriously, boys," I said with a headshake and a grin as I hopped into the car. "Where are we going this fine afternoon?"

"Oh, nowhere fancy. There's this small but awesome Mediterranean restaurant near the park. Let's have lunch there, then go for a walk, and you will be free to go back to work after — stressing out and making us some good money to spend. While we, the youngsters, will go to our friends for some fun and games."

They once again shared *'the* look'. Clearly, there was more to their plan than what they were revealing. But I dropped the subject and smirked back, showing I knew they were hiding something from me but would not press, to which they responded with a reassuring smile.

"Ok, boys, let's start this adventure. Wyatt makes this baby roar, and please don't be drive like a grandma... We are impatiently waiting here."

"As you wish, woman, you asked for it," he declared with a smirk as he wheezed to the New York City Park.

As promised, we reached the restaurant in record time. I ordered myself a plate of fresh pasta, and the boys ordered their burgers and sodas, which were typical of them.

"You know, if you boys continue eating so much junk food, you will soon be like mister over there." Softly teasing them, I pointed behind me at the obese guy eating burgers.

Facing the boys, I added, "Remember what grandma said, *'you are what you eat…'"* gesturing toward their food with my forefinger I attempted to hide my smile and put on a serious face.

"Seems like I'll have to go all motherly on both of you. What do you say?" I lifted an eyebrow as I devilishly and proudly smirked.

After staring me in the face for a few seconds, they erupted into fits of laughter, their boisterous cackles filling the room. For them, this matter was too trivial for me to go into full-on mother mode on them. Any other day, I would agree, but I couldn't give them this win — not so easily, at least.

"Well, my dear sons, your health isn't a trivial matter to me, as you've so eloquently suggested. So, if I must, I will go full-on mother mode on you two. What do you guys think about that?" Inquisitively raising both my eyebrows, I explained in a sweet voice and an *'I won'* smile.

That sure did the job of shutting them up. Gulping and smiling timidly, they shifted uncomfortably in their seats. Their behaviour was so hilarious that I burst out laughing after watching them for a few seconds. If I were to venture a guess, I'd say they weren't fond of my controlling, motherly side. It was truly scary sometimes, that I must admit.

~~

"**W**ell, boys, I had a wonderful time, but I should get back to work. Make sure you both are home before me."

We had already taken our walk around the park and were joked around as usual. However, my two hours were almost up, and I still needed to make my way back to the office.

Since my dearest boss loves taking every tiny opportunity to irritate me, my five minutes lateness was perfect for him. Not wanting to get caught by him, I sped-walked to my office. Luckily, yet surprisingly, Federick Archer was not in his office, meaning he would not know of my lateness. I wasn't one to take my rare luck for granted, so I strode the rest of the way to my office in case he was lurking around.

Regrettably, for me, the stars weren't in my favour. Mr High and Mighty was nowhere else but in my office, looking unhappy and impatient for my return.

Who was I kidding?! This guy was always angry and on edge. I was pretty sure these were the only feelings he knew. Hum, I wondered how he didn't get bored with himself or with his lack of expressions and emotions. Heck, I doubt if he knew how to smile and laugh. His face was like a plain granite structure that continuously emitted negative emotions and expressions. If I'm asked, Federick was a creepy, angry, and cold guy. And that's coming from someone as emotionless and frigid as me.

"Good afternoon, sir. How can I help you and—"

"Cut the crap, Miss Smith! Why are you this late? And you better have an excellent explanation."

Was he seriously getting all worked up over such a petty matter? This dude gravely needed a life, mainly one comprising not annoying the life out of me. On the plus side, his reaction was funny and totally laughable. However, I kept my humour to myself and gulped. With my reservoir of excuses dry, my attempt to think of a good enough explanation was taking a toll on my brain.

Silently standing in front of his majesty, I stared at him, pondering what I had done so wrong for him to be acting so alarmingly. Alas, I came up with nothing. Five minutes late was never such a big deal before. Well, if I couldn't come up with an appropriate excuse, I might as well accuse him of being absurd. Not that it would significantly affect him. His entire face was an absurd joke.

"What happened, Miss Smith? The cat finally got your tongue. Or is it you don't have a good enough explanation this time around?" The great Federick Archer derided with his infamous smack-worthy smirk, which was both rude and devious.

Suddenly, he took a single step towards me, and something shocking and unimaginable occurred. I took a freaking step back. And let it be known, I've never ever taken a step back. I was one of the most ferocious cold-hearted killers, after all.

Federick's eyes widened in surprise, mirroring my astonishment at the sudden step back. Locking my gaze with a hint of intrigue, his usual stand-offish and neutral look was long forgotten. However, I was so furious that I didn't bother to notice his strange looks, nor did I let them get to me.

My anger was at both him and me. I was irked I didn't have an answer to his stupid question, and for letting him talk to me so disrespectfully. And my reaction when he stepped forward was beyond infuriating. This was a substantially unreal and absurd surprise for me, but also the cherry on top of the annoyance cake.

I knew if I spoke up in that moment, I would lose control and explode. So, I zipped it for once in my life. I didn't want to say or do something that I would undeniably regret later or create too great of a scene for the entire office to watch. That will just make my day worse. As such, I let Federick Archer talk his stony heart out.

But the asshole kept quiet. Boring into me like he was trying to read my soul, Federick captured my gaze for what felt like hours. Since he came back and took over his father's company, this was the first time we actually looked into each other's eyes for this long, and that too without a word between us. This moment was so weird and uncomfortable. I almost wanted to run out of the office. Then again, I would not break first, and let him win. No… not when I was actively striving to hide my anger and not snap at His Highness.

In the end, once he had collected himself and recovered from the initial shock, it was he who finally spoke up, breaking the silence. Frankly, part of me wanted to know what he was thinking. But the man was too complicated, and I had no intention of spending my precious time on him.

"If you don't want to spend the night in the office with me, get to work right away. I want all the documents I had asked you to prepare earlier. Or should I wait longer, so you can get out of the phase you are in?"

It might have taken me a few minutes, but I eventually got out of my dazed state at the realisation that he had asked for some documents. "No sir, I'll immediately get them for you." I finally responded while going around him to my desk.

Still quite confused and irked, I lightly shook my head, attempting to get out of whatever sorcery I was under. Without realising it, I had bent over my table to get the folder, just like I usually do when he's not present. I swear, that jerk was such an asshole and a pig. If I could, I would have kicked him right where the sun didn't shine.

He dared shout at me, insulted me, and showed no respect for me or my privacy. But the moment I bent over my table to get him the documents he needed, he gawked at my ass. His eyes lingered as if I was the most scrumptious dinner ever. Indeed, he was a big jackass.

I was relieved that the rest of the day passed with no more incidents. Luckily, I finished everything I needed to do before heading home, feeling completely drained. All I got to say was that Federick Archer sure was extremely angry at me that day. And with no apparent reason or me having to push his buttons, might I add.

His royal assholeness dumped an overwhelming workload on me, insisting I completed them by the end of the day, even though I knew most of the tasks had no urgent deadlines. I had tacked the required documents for the next day a long time ago. But no… I had to do next week's work as well.

Mr Archer did all this intentionally. He couldn't deny it. He knew damn well I avoided bringing work from the office back home. Obviously, he never knew the exact reason behind it. But he sure took advantage of that knowledge today by giving me all this unnecessary work.

He even told me, "It's a lot of work. If you can't finish it by your end of day, take it home with you," accompanied by that damn smirk … selfish, arrogant bastard.

I had him eat all his comments by the end of the day. I completed all the work given to me, even if it meant staying at the office later than I usually do. His facial expression as I dropped everything on his desk was payment enough. It was too damn hilarious. But with great effort, I refrained from laughing at his face right in front of him.

Instead, I happily went home to my sons, indulged in a luxurious one-hour bath, and savoured a glass of chilled red wine as I relaxed in the night's quietness by the beach. I felt extremely satisfied knowing that all my hard work paid off in the end.

CHAPTER 4
THE PHONE CALL

PHOEBE

These past two weeks have been weird and shrouded by an air of mysteriousness. It was like Mr Archer had made it his business to attain a new height of rudeness and dictatorialness toward me. If I did not know any better, I would have thought it was me who was the problem. That he always behaved so annoyingly rude toward me because I am too *'me.'* But working for him for the past two years made me realise it was he who was the problem, not the other way around.

In the beginning, Mr Federick Archer was tough to figure out, especially with that mysteriously enigmatic and powerful aura around him. Which, I must admit, under normal circumstances, would attract someone like me. And if he were someone else, I would undeniably want to discover more. But Federick wasn't someone else. He was someone I couldn't get close to, and trying to understand him confused me way too much for it to be healthy.

Consequently, I did what any reasonable person would do in my position. I stopped caring about his endless mood swings and emotionless ass. Mainly for my sanity, but also because I had far more important things to worry about than him. Heck, if I were to see a shrink, I bet he too would advise I keep my distance from Mr Archer, unless I wanted to end up in a looney-ville. Federick Archer was insubordinate and didn't deserve my extra effort. That stony man was in the category of annoyingly cold-hearted people I pay zero attention to.

Having insight into Federick's past self, I knew he didn't care about people or their emotions. I would even go as far to say he despised anyone he couldn't control and manipulate. All he cared about was himself — and possessing everything he oh so desired or wanted. Given what I know, his aloofness during the past two weeks shouldn't have bothered me as much as it did. However, not knowing the reasons behind his actions bugged me more than I expected.

Despite all my wise reflections about the 'Great' Federick Archer and how much I shouldn't care; I couldn't help but worry about him. I even took my precious time to ask myself continuously what was truly wrong with him. Some days were so bad I actually had to repress myself from asking Mr Archer whether he was doing alright. I had to remind myself to mind my own business, do my work, then go home to my wonderful kids and relax.

With the planets aligned against me, it was no surprise that by the third week, the tension between Mr Archer and me had intensified. We constantly clashed about anything and everything. On the flip side, I started to feel something unusual and peculiar in our arguments and the odd atmosphere between us. However, I dropped that strange feeling and concentrated on maintaining my cool, so I would not kill his majestic assholeness.

By taking a step back three weeks ago, I unintentionally added fuel to the fire and exacerbated the tension surrounding us. Much to my dismay, I couldn't unravel why I behaved so stupidly and impulsively. It left me feeling frustrated and perplexed, resulting in heightened unease and countless sleepless nights.

Despite my confusion, one thing was clear: I was far from thrilled about it. I wanted to bang Mr Federick Archer's sweet and handsome head hard against a wall, followed by mine. Fortunately, for both of our sake, it hadn't come to that point yet. So far, we've been acting like the incident in his office three weeks ago never occurred.

But the Friday of the third week was when *'Mr Annoying'* really dropped the ball and infuriated me to the point of no return. On a daily, this devil-child put me through hell, and I've been incredibly patient with him. The only thing I can say is that Federick Archer should count his blessing on my gained ability to control myself and my emotions. Past me would have caused a havoc without thinking twice about it.

In all reality, all I wanted to do was beat the living shit out of Federick's arrogant ass, and then I would have seen who would have been sorry. He had dared threaten me and my job, evidently not realising his threats couldn't harm me or my contract with the company. Despite those facts, threatening me was the worst way to go and too much for me to take. The way he spoke, responded, and acted towards me was a first in my life. It's no surprise that I was caught off guard.

Our whole outburst began when Mr Arrogant asked me — no, not asked, he fucking ORDERED me — to go abroad with him for the weekend. I understood it was for business reasons, and any other time, I would have chalked this order as trivial and not make a big scene. But after nearly three weeks in a pressure-filled, anger-arousing atmosphere, it was no wonder I cracked.

Besides, it was not all my fault. Mr Archer could and should have given me a week, if not three days' notice, to prepare and take care of everything at home. My contract clearly stated that he must give me a minimum of one week's notice before asking me to travel abroad with him. If he failed to comply with these terms, I had the full authority to decline.

I had a family to look after, for Christ's sake — not that he was aware of this minor fact. Still, he knew I had way more responsibilities and commitments than him. But this wasn't the only part that pissed me off. After he so kindly *'told'* me to accompany him on his trip — which was four hours away from New York by PLANE — he went crazy and ballistic on me after I nicely refused to accommodate him.

My rational mind closed on me. All I wanted was to hurt him. Bringing up the sweet terms of my contract, leaving out the part where he couldn't fire me, I stung him right where I wanted. His irate face tasted like victory. I wanted more, but I knew I couldn't reveal the fine prints of my contract just yet. Someone as close-minded and stupid as Federick wouldn't understand it.

The sight of Federick Archer grinding his teeth in sheer annoyance and demanding an explanation for the second time was absolutely hilarious. Unfortunately, Federick Archer cut short my good mood by demanding an explanation for the second time, causing me to avoid once again making direct eye contact with him. I absolutely hated it whenever he scrutinised me with his arctic gaze, as if he was trying to penetrate and search my soul — to figure me out.

Considering I was not in the best mood, nor was I going to find some ideas in my throbbing head, I merely let him know I couldn't go because of some personal reason. However, it seems, *His Highness* was not very pleased by my answer.

One minute he was withering the life out of me with his mere sleeted glare, and the next, he was accusing me of stupid nonsense. As per his majesty, I allegedly had a string of boyfriends without whom I couldn't spend one weekend. Not only that, but he also accused me of being selfish, unprofessional, irresponsible, unable to make sacrifices, and unconcerned about the importance of my job.

All the while, I kept wondering, *'What the heck was he even talking about?'* or *'Where did he ever get such an absurd idea?'*

He continued to ramble incessantly, like an insane person, pretending he knew me to the bone. But he couldn't be farther from the truth. He was oblivious to my personal life, the people I held dear, and the countless sacrifices I had made and continue to make. And I would stake my life that in this regard, he fell short.

Yet, here he was, standing in front of me, intently glaring at me and accusing me of the utmost foolish things. But hey, what could I expect from such a stupid and arrogant guy as himself? Someone who fucks every single woman that crosses his path. Honestly, I don't think there's a single woman, besides his mother and myself, who hasn't fallen head over heels for him, idolising his every move.

On Friday, I had already decided not to go to that damn meeting with Mr Archer. Especially after the way he had treated me. But when the darkness of the night surrounded me, I was much calmer and changed my mind. I decided to accompany him, but not before checking with my sons about their plans for the weekend.

Given that they were both occupied with sports practices and spending time with their friends, my absence from town wouldn't really be a problem. On the plus side, I'll would prove to Mr Archer how responsible I was by coming to work and leaving my *'boyfriends'* for the weekend — not that I cared what his assholeness thought of me.

For some odd reason, I never cleared myself not having a boyfriend, much less, several boyfriends. It didn't seem important enough. After he finished barking at me like the dog he was, I left his office. Upon reflection, it was definitely the right decision, considering I could potentially leverage his confusion to my advantage in the future when I need to take unexplained absences.

Then again, it seems fate had another plan for me. Way too early the next morning, I got a phone call from someone else, prompting me to cancel all my plans. Since Mr Archer already thought I wasn't coming, I didn't bother informing him of my new weekend plan. Not that he didn't try continually calling me over the span of 30 minutes, right before his flight took off. The upside of this surprise phone call, however, was that I didn't have to see Mr Federick Archer's face for the entire weekend.

I bet his face was beyond hilarious, as I ignored all his calls. Simultaneously, I felt a sense of dread knowing that come Monday, my laughter would be non-existent, as his overwhelming anger would consume him. As I was not as cruel as Federick Archer, I reluctantly reached for my phone and called my assistant, asking her to assist Mr Archer through the phone if he needed anything.

As I instructed what she needed to do and how long she would have to assist Mr Archer, I could sense a whirlwind of emotions crossing her face. She was upset having to work long hours to complete some of my easiest jobs, but also thrilled that she would get to be in the presence of the *Almighty'* Mr Federick Archer.

However, I didn't care about her feelings. I just needed my job done properly. She was not the perfect assistant for me, but she was all I got right now. At the time I hired her, I had a small pool of candidates, and I desperately needed an assistant but had little time to choose. As such, I picked the first one who had the best resume and could do the essential parts of all my work and assist with the non-confidential things as needed.

What matters is that she respects and fears me and is a great help whenever I am not around. Given my tendency to take numerous days off, sometimes for extended periods, she can generally adapt to the inconsistent scheduling and varied responsibilities. One more advantage I get from her besides paperwork being done is that she has a way of angering Mr Archer with her usual *'flirting'* and inefficiency. Adding more fuel to the fire, Mr Archer knows damn well he cannot do anything about the situation except endure it. The reason once more being my contract term, which unsurprisingly always infuriates him to no end.

Considering Mr Archer and my history, I knew he was going to conclude I did not accompany him merely to infuriate and disobey him. To show he had no control over me. That he couldn't order me around as he does to everyone else. And maybe I would, or wouldn't... heck, who am I kidding? I would definitely do such a thing. This time, however, I honestly had a much more important and pressing work to attend to.

When I woke up later that morning, the boys were still home. It seemed like they were surprised because I had informed them the previous night that I would be gone for the weekend. Conscious of the opportunity presented to me, I clarified to the boys that Federick had changed the departure and arrival time of our flight.

In a firm yet nurturing manner, I told the boys, "I need both of you to be home at a reasonable time while I'm away. If I'm not back by Monday, grandpa will pick you guys up around noon. I already called to let them know about the situation. So, make sure you both a ready to go by noon. And please, listen to your grandparents and don't create any problem for them. It's a direct order, gentlemen."

I maintained my serious mommy's face. "Have I made myself clear?".

Since this exact scenario of me unexpectedly changing plans and sending them to their grandparents had been happening since they were toddlers, they had long stopped asking questions after the 5th or 8th time. Nevertheless, even after 10 years, I could still see the confusion and curiosity in their eyes as they silently nodded.

"Look, I love you guys a lot. You know that, right?" I gave them time to nod their head prior to continued.

"Good! Just always remember, my love for both of you will never waver, regardless of anything. Your safety is of utmost importance to me, and I will do anything to ensure the latter. Don't you guys ever doubt my love, or me, for that matter! Always and forever."

I enveloped them in a warm embrace, planting gentle kisses on their foreheads, expressing my love through this simple gesture. They were looking at me as if I had just announced I was going to die any minute now. But before they could ask anything, I smiled and sent them off to their practices.

Ever since their toddler selves burned their everlasting place in my heart, I began bidding my goodbyes a bit dramatically whenever I was off for over two days in a row. It had proven to soothe me, knowing if I die while being away, they had something to hold on to.

Then again, today was more intense than usual. Since receiving the phone call this morning, I have had a weird feeling in the pit of my stomach. I couldn't quite explain or shake off. As usual, I went with my instinct — they haven't proven me wrong yet.

CHAPTER 5
BEGINNING OF ANGEL

PHOEBE

After my surprise phone call with Pierce Hitch in the morning, I found the perfect escape from Federick Archer's unexpected trip demand. Pierce was an interesting character. As the executive director of my agency, Pierce oversaw the agency during my absences. He knew the risk and challenges that came with sitting on the leader's seat, and he joyfully took it.

Pierce's primary concern was maintaining the agency's safety, privacy, values, and honour while I was on a break from leading the agency and major missions, for the sake of my family. That was if he wanted to keep his head attached to his shoulders. The man knew it was difficult and dangerous to work under my direct supervision. But he was high-strung in power and blinded by greed. He probably thought I wouldn't interfere with his directive. The combination of that misconception and the idea of partial control over the agency, thus basically controlling half of the world, was motif enough for Pierce to put up with my coldness.

For these reasons and my lack of trust in Pierce, I had one of my agents secretly monitor him and provide me with detailed reports. And guess what? I was totally right. Allegedly, Pierce had been taking immense pleasure in being in charge and ordering strange missions when I was not around. Besides his relentless ambition, he was constantly striving to gain greater access to the agency and uncover its myriad secrets. Even though I could still kick him out if I wanted to, I also wanted to be fair to him. Mainly because he had been with this agency since my father opened it. Meanwhile, my strategy was to be more cautious when dealing with him and not believe everything he says without question.

Besides, Pierce's presence on my chair helped me step down from my high horse to sort through a few things in my personal life — to retake better control of my life. It enabled me to take care of my other company, grieve properly, be a mother to my kids, and create a better and more stable lifestyle for all of us. Even though I was a mother who was rarely present and had a lot of secrets, I was still a mother. One who could now proudly say she had taken better responsibility for fulfilling her role.

Instead of being out on long-ass cases several times a year, which sometimes required me to be gone for half the year, I now worked less than 5 cases a year. I changed my life so much since my boys turned 9 and 10 that my previous life now seemed like a completely different world, where my good days meant something utterly different. Yes, I was still frequently absent for extended periods, but I made it a point to never be away for more than one month at a time. Despite all the changes, one thing was for sure; my past life never bothered me. Instead, it made me happier and carefree. I welcomed, embraced, and lived for the danger and uncertain adventure.

This mother role I stumbled into and the new life I created limited my spy life to only critical and dangerous field cases deemed necessary for my attention. That's why Pierce's phone call intrigued me and made me a little uneasy. I was unsure if the reason behind his call was for a fresh case or my personal vendetta cold case. One which was an immense and disastrous failure 10 years ago. A case that I had obsessively been working on in my personal time, hoping to find a new clue.

I was more than ready to raise all hell to turn this cold case hot again. To make damn sure I won the war between Cole and myself — even if it meant being absent more often, risking suspicion, or retaking control of my agency and my other company. Honestly, I've been toying with the idea of regaining control of my agency for a couple of weeks. Although it was only a thought, if I didn't achieve the desired results and the situation became excessively complex, I would be left with no alternative but to execute my idea.

In contrast to what Angel means, I was anything but an angel, especially when I didn't get the results I desired. Well-known and feared in the underground world, my name alone made people pee their pants. And uttering my name was akin to inviting death to your doorstep. Except for a selected few, the people who knew me as Angel didn't have a clue that I was also Phoebe Ziva Smith, or a mom with two sons, and vice versa.

Spy, Secret agent, Assassin, Angel of Death — call me whatever you want — it was all my job description.

My agency or I did not work for the government. However, we often collaborated when needed. We were all a group, an organisation that cleaned up the street for the safety of others. My agency expertise in drawing the unlucky number for those criminals the police and other government branches couldn't get their hands on — be it because of time restriction, legality, jurisdiction, clearance level, border, or simply because it was none of their business. I must say, coldly and gruesomely, killing and eliminating all those dangerous criminals and murderers who make it on our naughty list has been one of the most pleasurable tasks within my agency.

To put it simply, we dealt with underworld gangs, soldiers-gone-rogue, mafias, drug dealers, drug lords, fugitives, dangerous psychotic rapists, killers, kidnappers, terrorists, and situations that could cause real chaos within the public. Over the course of my 26 years on this earth, I have eliminated so many of these individuals that I can no longer keep track. Fortunately, I had never once looked back and felt bad or sorry for their families or them, not even a bit of compassion or sadness.

My father was the proud boss and creator of the agency. And 2 and a half years before he died, he passed it all down to me. Through this, I naturally received all his wealth and everything he ever owned. From then to now, I can say I've spent millions, if not billions, making both my agency and life better. Pondering over it, there's no way my family treasury will ever face a dry season. Not when I have my own millions religiously coming in every quarter, on top of the heritage passed down from my father.

My father once worked for another intelligence agency where he was the best agent, which helped make our agency's name more valuable, famous, and robust. However, upon discovering that he was going to become a father, he left the agency and establish his own company and spy agency. From what I remember hearing as a child, the agency was once called 'The Smith Group,' but then changed to 'The Angel Organisation' after I got trained to take over the agency.

Obviously, this organisation is unfamiliar to most people, except for a select few individuals such as our partners, allies, high-ranking government officials, and police officers who have high enough clearance to be aware of our existence. Those who are aware of our agency only know our company name, not the exact location of our main headquarters, giving us an advantage over other agencies. Furthermore, we never reveal our true identities. We all go by nicknames for our own safety. Only my team members and I have access to the real identities of everyone. Even Pierce doesn't have complete access to all the vital information.

When I took over the agency, I started a new and utterly different reign. The way I ran my company differed from when my dad was in charge. I made damn sure everyone was giving their best, keeping the competition among us fun, but still very much alive. As a matter of fact, my agency was the pure definition of a hierarchy. We housed the best scientists, fighters, shooters, trackers, undercover agents, soldiers, weaponry experts, hackers, plan and strategic makers, and geniuses. And even though we encouraged everyone to succeed and acknowledged it, only the best among us gets prominently recognised in the infamous Escal-Board, situated in the middle of the milieu, for everyone to see.

Each of us is assigned a unique team based on our expertise and the specific needs of the missions. Then again, I would occasionally merge teams, fostering a sense of unity and cooperation to tackle specific cases or situations effectively. However, sometimes I would purposely combine them as a test to prevent the team spirit from fading away. This proved to avoid conflicts or the creation of barriers within the agency and helped prevent animosity between the teams. Even though in the beginning, this strategy caused a lot of dispute and tension within the agency, I had to do whatever it took to grow my agency — to become the top and the best among all.

Although my agents were highly competent in their assigned tasks, I continuously upheld my status as the best among the best worldwide. There have been a lot of agents who have tried to break mine or my dad's record, alas, to no avail. On second thought, there was one guy who reached the same level as me. Franco Ives — another thorn in my side.

He and I were constantly clashing, be it in meetings or conferences. Thankfully, we no longer had to meet in person, because that would invite the next world war to our doorstep. As a matter of fact, for the safety of everyone and his own sake, he now lived all the way across the world — far away from me.

My proficiency in this field directly resulted from the countless hours I've devoted to training and battling my way into the realm of spies, starting from the age of 5. Since my father was considered the best, I had to put in extraordinary effort just to make it onto the newcomers' list, let alone achieve a score close to his prime. Franco and I had to break the entire record to achieve his final score. I was the first to do so at the mere age of 9. Franco reached it when he turned 20, about 11 years after me.

All in all, I had my father on my side, a guiding light in my life, always ready to teach and inspire.

~ Flashback ~

"**D**addy, why are you going again?" In a small trembling voice, my eyes were full of tears, near the point of crying.

"Sweetheart, don't make it more difficult than it already is. I really must go to this meeting… it is imperative."

With hardly audible sobbing, I stopped him midway through his packing for a split second.

Staring at me, a sad look in the depth of his beautiful eyes, he said, "Look, baby, I know you are upset and angry at me right now, but I promise I will make it up to you once I'm back."

My cheeks turned red with the bloom of anger. "No, you won't." I said with a small, definitive voice.

"Yes, I will. I promise…" He responded calmly.

"Then bring me with you… it's just a business meeting like the others. I will be nice this time, I swear." I stomped my feet as I made my case.

"Hey, sweetie, don't be like this. I cannot bring you with me this time. Or tell you any more than I already have. You are too young for these sorts of business or explanations. Just go to sleep, baby girl. I will see you in the morning before I leave." Gently walking me to my room, he put me to bed and kissed my forehead.

"But dad, it's just a stupid business meeting with Uncle Joseph, plus I have been at your company several times already. I'm sure everyone would love to see me again."

"Baby, please, stop being so stubborn. I don't want to be harsh to you the night before I leave. So please listen to me and behave… Plus, you don't want to meet Federick again, right?"

My dad could see my anger right through my eyes, but I merely nodded my head in agreement because I really didn't want to see Federick Ashton Archer ever again in my entire life. He was older than me by four years and was the most horrible human being to ever walk on this planet. That jerk-face was never ever nice to me, always making fun of me in front of his friends and enjoying making me cry. Last week alone, he ripped my most favourite pink ribbon from my head and ran away with it. He hadn't given it back since. That was the last straw between us.

Being a spoiled brat at five years old, nearly six in nine months, I was already used to having my way, just like freaking Federick Archer did, which was one of the main reasons we always fought. I always got everything I ever wanted with no restriction whatsoever, unless my father was home; then, there was some restriction. After all, I was a sweet little kid who was too damn curious for her own good. I was a stubborn child who did not swallow defeat in an argument. But right now, I was a kid who was tired of her father being away yet again with no proper explanation.

Not wanting to fight with him before he left for God knows how many days — or better months — I complied with his request, but not before huffing a long breath to show my annoyance. To top it off and make him feel even guiltier, I went to bed without giving him our usual goodnight hug.

"Good night, father. Thank you for letting me know when you will leave. Close the door on your way out." I coldly and standoffishly muttered.

Seeing as he wasn't making a definitive move to get out of my room, I instantly shut my eyes, pretending to be asleep. After a few beats, he finally figured I would not be easy on him this time around, so he did as he was told and closed the door on his way out, leaving me with my wild thoughts and a bad mood.

Feeling restless, as if something was restricting me from falling asleep, I sat up on my bed and hugged my knees to keep myself warm. Dropping the notion of sleep, I began thinking of a way to either stop my father from going or convince him to tell me what he was hiding from me. I might have been a toddler, but I was no fool. I knew he was lying and hiding something from me. It was clear as daylight on his face.

While sitting on my comfy bed, trying to plot something in the middle of the chilly night, I heard strange noises outside my room. The sound appeared to originate from my father's room, yet it also felt as if it emanated from a deeper place. I realised it wasn't possible as there was no other room besides ours on the floor we were. Then again, my outstanding hearing was the talk of the town.

Do I or do I not trust these fantastic abilities of mine?

After a while, though, I ruled out the noise as mere fiction from my over-imagination, especially since I was staying up past my usual bedtime, and not to mention I was in a bad mood. However, when I heard the noise again, I just couldn't let it go. The more time passed, the more my curiosity grew, leading to a multitude of scenarios in my mind. I was really curious to uncover the source of the noise, so I silently left my room and crept into my father's room to avoid startling whoever or whatever was inside.

However, when I was inside, I felt disappointed. At first sight, everything was normal — no giant bunny or beautiful lost princess for me to take in. The only odd part was a missing father, whose voice I could clearly hear in the distance. Suspicious, I couldn't help but wonder if a giant dust rabbit abducted my dear stubborn daddy, so he wouldn't leave for his trip. Or whether a troll kidnapped him as her food or, worse, to marry him.

After that unsettling notion, I had to battle my overly imaginative thoughts to regain some common sense. Once I regained control over my brain, I started thinking and looking around like any rational person would, not a five-year-old child. And there it was... the wall behind my father's bed was completely unaligned with the side wall. It was mid-open, for Christ's sake... not a standard wall indeed.

CHAPTER 6
A DISCOVERY

PHOEBE

~Flashback continued~

As I glanced back and forth between the mid-ajar wall and the door behind me, I found myself in a silent decision-making stage. *Do I step toward my exit or toward the odd wall?*

Steeling myself with a final breath, I cautiously stepped into the secret room, only to get the biggest shock of my five years of existence. The wall to my right was a formidable display of weaponry; guns, swords, knives — each varying in length and design — alongside an assortment of medals and other lethal weapons whose names eluded me in that moment. On the opposing side, an imposing array of mid-sized monitors dominated half of the wall space, their flickering screens casting an eerie glow across the room. In the centre, a big brown mahogany table stood, with its chair rolled sideways. A lone computer rest atop it with several piles of file scattered around. Positioned behind the desk stood a bookshelf, its shelves filled to the tooth. Directly across the table, a large black Tv screen spanned the length of the wall, its imposing presence commanding attention.

Dumbstruck, I scanned the room with wide eyes and an agape mouth. No wonder my father was always bored when watching spy movies with me. He was living in one. To double-check I was not dreaming, I pinched myself hard. Instantaneously covering my mouth, I muffled my cry of pain, fighting to stay calm. Indeed, it was far from a mirage.

My father, completely unaware of my presence, hurriedly packed his bags with unfamiliar weapons while simultaneously conversing and yelling at the person on the screen, occasionally pausing to explain certain plans. Amidst all the discussion, I remembered him mentioning how he hated lying to me, upsetting me, hurting me, or shouting at me for no real reason. He said that seeing me in the condition I was today, upon discovering he was going to leave me alone for yet another one of his eerie trips, hurt him.

However, the most memorable moment was when he informed the peculiar man on the large display that his disappearing act wouldn't fool me for long, as I'm not foolish and will eventually uncover the truth. Carefully listening to every word, I was beyond happy and flattered to know my father thought so highly of me. He recognised I was not an ordinary child, but rather exceptionally intelligent for my age, and he loved me so deeply that he would sacrifice his work.

Too scared my father would see me and stop whatever he was doing, I stood still, not daring to move the slightest bit. Their conversation had me completely engrossed and fascinated. I'll admit, I was quite surprised at first. But after wrapping my mind around the fact that my father was a secret agent who went on several real adventures to save the world, I was excited.

Idolising my dad at that moment, I finally knew what I wanted to be when I grew up — unlike the times I wanted to be a dancer, a horse rider, or a pilot, only to end up hurting myself and firing the instructor. Or better yet, the time I wanted to be a hacker after having watched a movie only to end up destroying my personal laptop; or that one time I tried to be a carpenter, only to end up breaking the lavatory and burning the fuse, putting the house in utter darkness for at least a week. This time, I knew from deep within what my destiny was. The glint in my eyes and the excitement I felt rushing through my veins were utterly different from the rest of the times I knew for sure what I wanted to be. It was so powerful and felt completely right.

As my father turned to grab a document, he saw his adorable daughter smirking at him, with arched eyebrows and arms crossed. That specific moment was so hilarious, I nearly crack up. But with great restraint, I kept myself collected. His eyes widened in terror, as if he had just witnessed a ghost ready to drain his life force. He knew there was no going back to where we were. He had no choice but to answer my multiple questions with absolute honesty.

Ending the video call, my father silently and gently picked me up in his arm, closed the secret room door behind him, and sat me carefully on the edge of his bed, readying himself to be questioned. He was a little resistant in the beginning, but after I pressured and pestered him for a short while, he agreed to talk to me openly.

He recounted how he constructed and started the agency from scratch when I was born, what his job demanded of him and how the other company he owns with Uncle Joseph is mostly a cover-up so people would not question us and our wealth. Part of me was silently hoping he would at least mention my mom in this summary of his life. Alas, I was left wishing. He didn't once mention her, as if she never even existed, and an airplane brought me into this world.

As my dad spoke, he paid close attention to my facial reactions, searching for any cue to cease. As he so consistently pointed out, my eyes were the window to my heart and soul, mirroring all the emotions I might be feeling. To his surprise, I was utterly immersed in his story, not missing one bit of what he was saying, with only pride and admiration for him in my eyes. Even though I knew he wasn't telling me everything, as I was still a five-year-old with nightmares, I trusted him completely.

After my father explained what his other job was all about, where he was exactly going the next day — in as few details as possible so I wouldn't get frightened and horrified — I went to my room, happy not to be in the utter dark any longer. As I glanced back at my father that night, he appeared elated and relieved after finally confessing everything. As such, I didn't bother him with the idea of me wanting to be a part of this secret and dangerous life.

Aware just how overprotective my father could be, I realised he wouldn't accept this choice of mine as readily and would do anything to keep me safe. I had to find the right time and method to give him this shocking life-changing news. I wanted him to agree without causing a commotion, as I relied on his help to encourage me and reach my full potential.

In the morning, before my dad went to work, I made him a glass of juice and gave him a bowl of fruit salad that I had prepared with the help of Maria, our caretaker, as a symbol of trust and good fortune. Hugging him tightly, I ignored the car that was insistently honking, as if someone had died in its backseat. I rarely showed my affection, but at that moment, I felt the sudden urge to let my father know how content I was with him. I just couldn't let him leave without letting him know I was proud of his work and the difference he was making in this world.

"Thank you, sweetheart. I needed to hear this from you. I don't know what I did so well to have such a wonderful and understanding daughter like yourself." Instantly overwhelmed by how emotional he suddenly became, I tried to look anywhere but straight at him.

"I think it's time for you to go, dad. Unless you want to be late and have that honking car bust in and break everything in its way." Pushing down my awkwardness and shyness, I responded with a cute smirk.

"Why do I feel you are trying to push me away, love?" Searching my eyes, he voiced out playfully to hide his suspicious side.

"I would never! Rather, dad, I want you to kill all the bad guys and come back to me safe and sound." Kissing him on the cheek, I realised I had just addressed my father as *'dad'* out loud for only the second time in my whole life. Looking up at him, I witnessed the shock and happiness overflowing my father's eyes and face before he engulfed me in his embrace.

"Dad, I am happy too, but I need to breathe." Attempting to take a deep breath within his bone-crushing hug, "Only 5 and a half remember." Tapping his shoulder gently, I breathed out with a smirk.

"If you are trying to sass me, it won't work. I am too happy to get mad," he retorted, finally releasing me from his death grip.

Giving me an honest, bright, and cheeky smile, he walked out to the furiously honking car. The last thing I heard before the front door closed was, "I am the happiest man on earth. My daughter just called me dad… If I could leave this damn mission, I would right this second."

"Don't, Dad!!!" I shouted back, almost as loudly as him.

He would not be back for at least a month, giving me the perfect opportunity to implement my plan from the night before. The moment his car disappeared down the driveway, I wasted no time. I purchased several videos and online books on fighting, self-defence styles, and methods. Maria tried to talk me out of my craziness — as she so elegantly put it — but I had made my mind. Making the most of my exceptional talent for self-learning and keen observation, I trained myself into as good of a fighter as I could within a month's time.

Days in and out, I dedicated most of my waking hours to learning and practicing, working harder than ever before. I wanted to show I had what it took, so my father couldn't reject my offer. Once I felt confident enough with my skills, I didn't worry about closing the gym door. And with my father's return expected in a few days, I had no concern about being spotted. Then again, mother nature had another plan for me.

Sat on the mat in the gym, I deeply exhaled and grinned at my handiwork. Finally, I had achieved two successful rounds of throwing 3 daggers at the self-defence dolls around me and followed it up with a back-kick on a big pink bounce-back doll. Shortly after beginning my training, I discovered hidden talents and fighting abilities I never realised I had. Frankly, my endurance impressed me. Particularly after those days, I almost gave up. Learning all these moves in such a limited time was painful, but as I sat there breathless, my target achieved, it was all worth it. But my joy was short-lived. As I turned around, I saw my dad standing at the threshold, stunned yet impressed. His sweet and innocent daughter was no more.

"Pick up those daggers, place it on the table, and join me in the kitchen." With sharp eyes, my father sternly ordered. I felt a tremble in my core as I watched a wave of anger and pride dance in his eyes.

"And Phoebe Ziva Smith, you better have an excellent explanation for all of this." Pointing at the dolls, knives, swords, wooden staffs, and all the other training materials I had bought online, I knew I was in deep trouble.

I mustered up courage and timidly approached my father in the kitchen to reveal my idea and desires. As expected, my father was not too fond of my excellent idea of a career path. Apparently, my chosen career path was way too complicated, and I didn't know what I was getting myself into. Yet, I was perfectly aware it was no movie. Absolutely rejecting my request to give my idea a shot, my father kept going on about how he wanted me to have a normal childhood.

Normal Childhood — my ass. I had anything but a normal childhood. But I made the wise decision to keep this comment to myself.

"Daddy, I want to do this… You can't deny me this… It's my decision and dream. I'm your only daughter — heck, your only child — and I want you to be very proud of me. Why won't you let me do this? Don't you love me anymore, daddy?" I pleaded with big, glazed eyes.

As I stared at him, I could sense his hesitation and doubt, so I made the bold choice to retort with a comment that had the potential to hurt him greatly. But I had to do it for the sake of my future spy life.

"And what normal childhood are you even talking about? You are barely ever here because you are a SECRET AGENT and have as much chance of dying as I do." Raising my tone, I was near crying.

"Baby, I love you with all my heart, and it hurts every time I leave you. Don't you ever doubt this! Your safety is my priority, angel. Look, if you want to make me proud so much, study business and take over the other company I built for you and the Archers? It is a much better choice. And as my only child, your work there would help keep the cover for my agency."

Since he showed to sign to budge, an alternative approach was in demand. "But, dad, you don't understand. Being your only daughter is why I need to protect myself. You won't always be there for me, to protect me from all the dangers in the world. Not to mention, it would be much safer if

I take over the agency after you than a partner or an outsider."

"Which is why you have so many bodyguards watching your every step, love," he simply responded.

Refusing to let the issue go, I employed my best puppy eyes to ensure he couldn't ignore me. "You know, during your absence, I realised I have what it takes. It was like I was discovering my destiny. And I want to learn more about fighting and your spy life. Most importantly, I want you to help me with all of it. I want your support, daddy. You are the best daddy, teacher, and mentor. Please, daddy… Please don't deny me this… I know you saw me practise. What I could do at this age impressed you and made you proud. Admit it."

"I will accept you have shown potential in the gym. But baby, understand what you are feeling right now might be another one of your flavours for the month. I cannot afford to expose you to the violence of my life at such a young age, for only this much."

Locking eyes with him, I could tell he was close to caving to my demands. That was if I kept pushing the right buttons. I quickly went through any ideas that might be handy in this delicate situation. Then, just like magic, I realised only compromising would work for me.

"Okay, you may be right, but let's compromise. Then both of us will be winners." Most definitely stunned by my comment and suggestion, he merely nodded his head in agreement, waiting for me to continue.

Taking a deep breath, I continued, "Since you want me to take over the company instead of the agency, and I want to be a spy like you. I say, let me do both, just like you. Train me to take over both companies. I will study business whilst training to become a fighter and an agent. Like that, if the spy thing doesn't work out, I will be skilled to concentrate on making the other company billions."

I sat quietly, giving my father the chance to weight everything. "You are very stubborn and know how to manipulate others into agreeing to any kind of situation—whether or not they like it. You're an intelligent one. Then again, you are also too curious and soft-hearted for your own good." Pausing for over a beat, he gazed at looked at me, and said something that shook me to the core.

"You are becoming more and more like your mother. I just hope you will be wiser than her."

Throughout my entire childhood, this was the first time my father brought up the topic of my mother. The sight of sadness in his eyes, even for a fleeting moment when her name was mentioned, shattered my heart instantly, leading me to vow to never broach the topic of her, no matter how much I yearned for information. His beautiful blue eyes turned into a big black circle of sadness, ready to consume and envelop him in a blanket of sorrow. Not knowing what exactly to do to console him, I merely hugged him hard and cracked a joke.

"I know I'm good. Even Uncle Joseph says I could persuade a lion to do my bidding if I put my mind to it." As I smiled at my dad, I could sense his relief from the change in topic.

"So, are we going to train today or later?"

With a smile on his face, he tousled my already dishevelled hair before standing up and walking towards his room in silence.

~End of Flashback~

I often wondered what it would have been like if I hadn't changed the topic that day. Would I have known who my mother was, or would my dad have stopped himself from letting out too much information? Then again, it didn't really matter anymore. The secret hope of ever finding out who my mom was died when my father passed away.

Despite all those *'What ifs,'* I trained so hard, I surpassed my father's scores and became better than him — automatically making me number one among all the spies. In the end, not only did I become the proud owner of a successful agency and half-owner of a billion-dollar company, but I also maintained the number one title on the 'Escal board' of agents across the world.

My success was so great that even the entire criminal underworld knew Angel. What really got to these dirty bastards was their complete ignorance of my true identity. It made them tick. Although some had a vague image of *'me'* and heard snippets of information on the streets, there was no solid verification of its accuracy. In fact, they were so scared of me that there has been a price on my head for years.

CHAPTER 7
REOPENING OF OPERATION COUPLES

PHOEBE

"**P**ierce, do you have any new insights on this damn case!? Any reliable updates, addresses, or something remotely important?"

Inside my spacious floor-to-ceiling bulletproof 6-inch glass walls office, I sat on my tall executive white leather chair. Surrounded by white and grey themed furniture, I blatantly questioned Pierce. No immediate answer from him pissed me off. "You better have a good explanation for pressing me to cancel my weekend plans!"

Astonishingly, the moment I brought up cancelling my plans, Federick Archer's handsome yet vexing face and intense grey eyes mentally attacked me, causing me to lose focus for a few beats. It was so bizarre. I could see and feel his cold, piercing grey eyes on me even though he was not present. It knocked the breath out of me.

"Ma'am... Ma'am...!" Staring up at Pierce, I was utterly unsure what had just happened. Pulling myself together and taking back control, I did what I did best and pushed the thought of Federick Archer at the very back of my head.

"Actually, Ma'am, I called you because we finally gathered enough information to reopen *'Operation Couples'* officially. We have a feeling Mr Vanderwill will make his reappearance soon. I received a report that Mr Vanderwill has been making his moves around the city. But we still need to confirm with the *'Insiders'* to ensure the rumours are correct and not pure speculation."

"What are the rumours?" Purposefully ignoring that Pierce had addressed Vanderwill as *'Mister'* twice in one sentence, I abruptly interjected. This matter held lower importance compared to what was possibly ahead.

"The word on the streets is that there will be a celebration to announce Mr Vanderwill's official return. At the event, he plans to bring his recently acquired partners and followers from various countries. It's rumoured that he's intending to reopen his factories for drugs, weapons, and smuggling various items. We've also heard of him launching a new clandestine business. But we know little about it yet. The underground is also discussing Mr Vanderwill's affirmation that he will let no one stop him this time."

"As if!" I interjected with defiance, my disgust for Vanderwill rising.

"Um… Ma'am…" Pierce hesitantly continued in a low voice, almost like a whisper. Thank God I had an excellent hearing, otherwise, I would have had to get even closer to him.

"Will you speak already!?" I was already angry at the limited information about Vanderwill's reappearance, and Pierce was acting and speaking as if my office was being tapped.

"Uh… Um… I'm not saying it's true, but there's another whisper going around… um…. Apparently, Vanderwill is still in love with Angel. And he will do everything to get Angel as his own. Or kill her if he doesn't succeed." Pierce hesitantly spat out.

"The Fuck!" I was going to kill someone. I could feel it in my blood. Giving Pierce a death glare, I made him want to crawl under my table and hide until I was gone.

"These details about Mr Vanderwill and yourself are plain rumours, Ma'am. We can't entirely be sure what was exactly said and done." Pierce attempted to reassure me, but his apologetic gaze only fuelled my anger further.

"How are you still not sure, Pierce!? It's your fucking job to find out these things!! Have you been sitting around and eating peanuts all this time!? Tell me! I really want to know what you've been doing so far?"

"I… Umm… I…. Ma'am…"

Taking a deep breath, I quietly unclenched my fist before proceeding. I couldn't afford to be angry or lose my cool. "So, let me get this straight… We've been trying to track down one man for the past few years to still have no result. We've been trying to get some kind of hint of where he is situated right now or where his future location might be to still have no result. Then you tell me you have some information about Vanderwill coming back but, yet again, do not know what he is exactly planning to do. The cherry on top of this wonderfully delicious, layered cake of no results is that you have at your disposal the best teams, our agency's intelligence, and basically have control over the reign of my empire!".

When Pierce didn't make any move to respond other than to stare at me like a deer caught in headlights, I couldn't resist throwing all diplomacy and etiquette out the window.

"Am I right or not!?" I thunderously and fiercely shouted back at Pierce, only to have him scarily nod his stupid head in agreement.

"Has our agency become so dense and worthless in your leadership that you can't even get a correct and accurate detail about Vanderwill or his fucking plans? You are really making me contemplate retaking full control over the agency and firing your ass! What do you think, Pierce?"

Gulping his spit, Pierce was not only afraid of losing his job, but also his life. I tried to be restrained and diplomatic, but I couldn't hold back. I was furious and my remaining patience was dwindling in this godforsaken case. It had, after all, been 10 freaking years since Vanderwill slipped from my hands, destroying my life, and leaving me broken. He had single-handedly turned me into the worst cold-hearted person to ever walked the earth. Even Federick Archer would be considered an angel compared to me, and that's saying something.

"If you want to keep your job and a head on those shoulders, I suggest you move your inefficient ass and get me the result I want. This is my last warning, Pierce. Get it straight in your damn thick head!"

Vanderwill wouldn't get the better of me again, no way. This time my kids were on the line — my only reason to live and my only chance to experience love. The time, effort, and energy it took to build this new family and life was borderline exhausting. I was determined to protect it from any trouble, and Vanderwill was beyond trouble. He was a disaster waiting to happen. Fuelled by this refresh incentive, my mind raced with ideas and tactics to unearth Cole Vanderwill from the hole he's been hiding in. This time, we had to try harder than we had been under Pierce's supervision. I was beyond tired of this never-ending hide-and-seek game between Vanderwill and I.

I knew Vanderwill was attempting to manipulate me again by publicly declaring his return to the criminal world and vowing to complete unfinished business from years ago. So, I had to come up with something insanely wild if I wanted Vanderwill gone once and for all. Considering my history with Vanderwill, I must confess he was anything but stupid. He was deviously intelligent and cunning. Knowing him, he must have already strategized his defences and attacks, customising it from our previous encounters and my known moves from his associates. Little did he know that throughout the years, I'd become a hundred times wiser and didn't act as spontaneously as I used to.

My personality, as well as my reaction and demeanour towards complicated situations, had taken a 180-degree turn over the years. I now thought twice before attacking and, if possible, planned well ahead of time and contemplated the cause-and-effect of my every decision. I made it a habit to use my brain more than my core strength during my missions. The best part was that Vanderwill hadn't realised the past Angel didn't exist anymore — she died 10 years ago with her family.

Understanding that Vanderwill wanted me to come find him and start another round of disaster, I deduced I had to find a way to provoke him intensely. I had to compel him to leave his lair on his own. Comfortably sitting on my big cosy white leather chair, I spent some time silently reflecting on a plan before buzzing Pierce back inside my office. The man was wise and knew I would vent my frustration at him if he stayed in front of me with no result to show, so he had stalked out of the room at the first opportunity.

"Contact the spy who informed you about Vanderwill and arrange a videoconference with them, team 1 and the Elite team. Also, we are going to put our intelligence to extensive use, so have the lab and weapon department ready for us. And if my team can't make it here on time because of distance and time difference, don't worry about it. We'll video them in during the conference. Arrange everything and have it ready within the next 6 hours… no exception."

"May I ask what the plan is, Ma'am? For us to be calling the Elite team and all the best agents from team 1?"

"We are going to stop waiting around for Vanderwill to make his first move. I'm done being surprised by him. It's now my turn." I declared, before dismissing Pierce to handle the tasks.

After six hours, everything was in order as requested, except for two members of my team who were still en-route to New York City on my private jet. As instructed, Pierce placed them on video call as they waited for this abrupt meeting to start. Initially, my team was not too pleased about ending their much-deserved holidays, but they were determined to complete this God-forsaken mission, even though this didn't start with them. This was one of the many qualities I loved about my team. Their honesty and loyalty were unwavering.

"Okay, guys, I'm not fond of repeating myself, so listen up. I've called this meeting because we have something of the utmost importance coming our way, and we must be ready and prepared for it."

Directing my gaze at teammates, first at Matt and Xylan who were attending via video call, then between Talon, my right-hand man, and Logan, my second and brother from another mother, "Sorry to put a damper on your fun, but the agency needs you."

As far as for everyone else in the room, I couldn't care less about them. They were all under my reign and had no choice but to do as ordered, or there would be hell to pay. Growing up in this challenging world, I learned to not quickly feel emotion for others or get attached. So, being a standoffish bitch was second nature to me. Then again, with my sons, it was a different story. With them, Phoebe Ziva Smith was in control while in here, in my agency, and with my agents, Angel, the cold-hearted monster, was in command.

"We have little so far. But it's enough to reopen *'Operation Couple'* officially. And this time, we are going to make our moves first. We are no longer waiting on Vanderwill to surprise us. Based on the Intel we've accumulated throughout the years, we can easily find some of his men. The plan is to locate some of Vanderwill's men and associates, kill all of them except for one each time, letting them crawl back to their master to report." Stopping, I gave them time to ask a few clarifying questions.

"Excuse me, Angel, but don't you think this plan is extremely risky and out of our usual protocol?" One agent from team 1 inquired with confusion and hesitation.

"Given the new protocol going around nowadays, it's a good question. As you've mentioned, agent, it will be the pure definition of poking the bear, which Vanderwill will not expect from the new me. This will simultaneously anger him and decrease his people and businesses count."

"So, why do we want to anger someone with his infamous reputation again?" Another agent from team 1 asked in bewilderment. Either this agent was an absolute idiot, or he was looking for a premature death by comparing my reputation to that of Vanderwill. I clearly was more feared than the despicable piece of shit that was Cole Vanderwill.

"First off, my reputation outranks Vanderwill's reputation by far greater length. So, if you are going to tremble at someone's name, it better be mine and no one else. Got it!"

"Yes, Ma'am… Sorry Ma'am…" the same agent quivered in an almost low tone, not daring to maintain eye contact with me anymore.

"Adequate… The goal is to anger Vanderwill so much he will have no other choice but to confront me, after which I will eliminate him like the disgusting insect he is," I clarified in my usual cold, standoffish tone, my mind already savouring at the idea of having my hands covered in Vanderwill's blood.

"You make it sound so simple. Yet I know it won't be," Matt from my team added through the video call.

"You're right… It may seem simple, but believe me, it won't be. You are all excellent at what you do. That's the reason you are even standing in this room right now. But the truth is we will end up with some injuries — heck, it could be me for all we know. And I'm the best of you all." With no remorse whatsoever, I explained in a monotone.

If any of them got offended or felt humiliated by my words, then they did their best to keep it to themselves. Until their dying breaths, they were all my assassins, but my concern for their emotions was irrelevant.

Turning towards our Insider Spy on the screen, "I.S., give us every tiny detail and information about the whereabouts of Vanderwill's influential and vital people close to here. I want to know the type of business they are handling right now, along with the weapons and technology they are currently using. And if you remember or hear more information about Vanderwill later, immediately communicate it to Talon."

Directing my sharp gaze towards the fidgeting members of team 1, "Team 1, your team captain will divide you into groups depending on your strengths. Whoever ends up in the weaponry section will get the information about the adversity's weapons and their known tactics, after which you will meet me in the lab to prepare and modify our own weapons. Talon, as my right-hand man, the lead tech specialist, expert searcher, sniper, and hacker, I want you to compile all the information from our I.S. resources and do your thing. Ensure we have the land plans, mapping coordinates, underground route, blueprints, and air direction for our planes." Glancing around, I gave them time to digest the instructions and for Talon to note everything down.

"This mission is already risky, as some of you have pointed out. As such, we cannot take any chances of foul play. Those who will be on Talon's team, investigate the nearby locations — like what we can use to our advantage and where our disadvantage lies. I also want to know what type of gadgets our targets have, the possible hidden spots for them during an attack, and statistics of how many men we are expecting to kill."

Turning my head to the two agents on the screen, "Xylan, being our sniper and shooting expert, take some men from Team 1 and find the best spot where you will have a good view of our surrounding, but also have a good shot once the mission starts. Matt, as my fighting expert, tracker, and someone who's agile with the knowledge of how to handle several guns simultaneously, you will be behind and beside me. Logan, as our best silent killer, fighter, and leader, you're second in line. You will inevitably direct part of the team to other sections of the building. The rest of team 1, you are to do your best job and take the position instructed to you by your captain and members of my team. Also, if you have problems or questions, make sure you see my team before we leave."

"Um… Angel, what if they cannot answer our question? Should we come to you, then?"

"It's highly unlikely, given their status as the Elite Team. But in the rare case they can't, they will report back to me so I can provide a helping hand. Howbeit, if you have any problems on the battlefield, don't hesitate to approach me, but know I will be quick with the explanation."

"Understood!" Team 1's captain exclaimed.

"Excellent… I expect everything I requested to be prepared when I return in the evening. Be sure to be in 'Garage E', prepared and ready to go. We will strike at night. Mission 'Strike-First' is on agents! There's no backing down. Go start on your assignments." In a full pitch and clapping my hands twice, "Go… Go!" I emphasised my point and command.

As I supervised and assisted anyone who needed it, I made sure that everyone meticulously adhered to my instructions. The last thing I needed was some screw-up in our weapons, their mechanism, or even our plans. By evening, all of us were good to go, and two of my men had finally arrived, bringing with them their goofy smiles. All we had to do was wait for the darkness of the night to enshroud the city and then officially launch mission *'Strike-First'*. Step one in *'Operation Couple.'*

With a serious atmosphere between the teams, everyone knew they couldn't joke around with this operation. The entire agency knew I desired Vanderwill's lifeless body at my feet. Once again, my instincts proved to right. There was a high possibility I would not return home by Sunday.

CHAPTER 8
STRIKE- FIRST

PHOEBE

As the night fell, an eerie darkness swallowed the city, setting the stage for the commencement of mission *'Strike-First'*. This mission had three targets. Our first stop of the night was a deserted box factory. As we neared the dilapidated facade, an unsettling feeling washed over us, causing our spines to tingle with unease.

"Alright, guys," I warned, "If you don't want to end up dead in this shitty place, be careful and stick to the plan. Follow my orders to the letter and don't do anything stupid."

"And miss out on seeing the other two creepy places… Heck no!" Xylan interrupted with his funny comments.

I shot Xylan a quick glare, "Alright then… Time to get going… Everyone checks your comms, we need to stay in constant contact, then get to your assigned positions. It's going to be a long night, so try not to have all the fun here."

Standing in the front line as planned, I silently observed my targets' body temperature through my wristwatch as they foolishly played cards, drank, and smoked to the point of filling the room with thick clouds. We had planned to launch a simultaneous attack in every section, so precise timing was crucial. Lightly tapping my wristwatch, I whispered, "One… two…" to the others who were surrounding this section of the factory.

As I counted to three, I swiftly emerged from my hiding spot and took a commanding stance in front of them, pointing my gun directly at their face. Saying they were shocked would be an understatement. After all, they weren't expecting to be disturbed, much less by her almighty Angel. But I knew that the other two locations wouldn't be as astonished as this petty party in front of me. Such news travelled at extraordinary speed in the underworld business.

"Hello, sweet cheeks. Did anyone invite the Angel of Death?" Staying on guard, "Cause here I am… ready to collect." Slowing approaching them, I thunderously voiced out with a sweet menacing smile.

"I will give you the choice of dying the easy way or the hard way… Although I would prefer the hard way…" My huge grin threw them completely off guard.

My years of experience proved there was usually one idiot who arrogantly thinks they are stronger and smarter than the attacker and fire first, thus having the privilege of dying first. Playing right into my hand, a guy to my right pulled out a gun from his back and fired at me. Unfortunately for him, I saw it coming, ducked, and rolled on my side before the bullet could hit me. This jolted everyone out of their stunned state, prompting my men to emerge from their hiding places and start the real fun.

Running full speed towards the foolish guy, I was ready to unwind from all the stress I had been feeling lately. Anyone could tell he was scared when he began shooting in all directions, yet couldn't hit the intended target. His emotions, even if it was only fear, were going to be the end of him. This was the reason I had two distinct personalities, one as Angel and the other as Phoebe. They occasionally play hand in hand, but most of the time, the Angel part of me was void of any emotions.

Unable to shoot directly at my fast-approaching zig-zagging figure, the guy whom I'd named crazy shooter number 1 remained defenceless and rooted to the ground. Dodging his shots, I delivered a powerful back kick to his chest, causing him to fly back and fall unconscious. With a slight tilt of my head, I stared at his motionless body on the ground, pondering why he was here when he clearly lacked any fighting ability. Honestly, Vanderwill must have fallen low if he is hiring these amateur guards.

Seeing more guards approaching out of the corner of my eye, I shifted my focus entirely to the present and patiently waited for them to come closer. Using a variation of Makki techniques, I blocked most of the attacks, and followed by throwing a few punches, knocking some of them off their feet. Running towards another group of men, I sprung off the ground like a compression spring and threw a spinning hook kick, dropping them like dominoes. Doing a back-flipped to get back into fighter position, the brutal violence satiated me. Smashing skulls, bashing heads against walls, and fracturing bones, I cleared the west wing in record time.

"Later asshole… Heck, I lost count which number you were… It doesn't matter anyway…" With a sarcastic smirk, I brought my knee up to my stomach and forcefully stomped the deep crimson sole of my black thigh-high stiletto boots onto his head, causing his skull to crack and blood to seep out, leaving a dark stain on my beautiful combat boots.

Just as I was about to join and support my agents, two men from the west and east wing suddenly appeared of nowhere. With a tight grip, the guy from the west wing held me firmly, preventing me from using my arms while his partner from the east wing closed in.

I was excited about what was going to happen next. I wanted them to strike me so damn hard that both Vanderwill and Federick would vanish from my thoughts, if only for a moment. This would give me a reason to hit them ten times harder, thus helping me release all the pent-up frustration from the previous weeks.

"I would not hit me if I were you…" Compelling them to attack me, I taunted in a sweet voice.

The east-wing guy did as I predicted and ignored my advice — which, believe it or not, could have majorly helped him in the end. Connecting his fist to my left cheek, he chose a painful death… a wise decision, indeed.

Faking a small whine and cry of pain for effect, I pushed him to hit me even more. "What did you say I shouldn't do if I were you?" he imitated a high-pitched girly voice while throwing punches at me.

"Oh, come on… is this all you can do, princess? I am disappointed."

"Oh, you asked for it, Angel." Allowing my sarcastic remarks and teasing to affect his judgment and fighting reactivity, he took pleasure in repeatedly punching me in the stomach to assert his masculinity. Then again, I was Angel. I hardly felt anything. Yet I entertained him. But after the twenty-eff of him punching me while his friend was restraining me, I had had enough of playing with those two morons. I needed some new toys to play with.

Surprised and confused by my smirk, the guy who was hitting me stopped. Right before he could ask why I was smiling, I swiftly squatted down as much as I could with the other guy clinging to me, and flung my head backward, hitting the other guy in the face. Using his falling body as leverage, I fly-kicked the guy in front of me on the stomach, propelling him backwards, gasping for air.

"BITCH! You broke my nose!" He screeched.

Turning around, I met the beautiful sight of him clutching his bleeding nose and grunting in agony. porting my notorious Angel of death smirk and dripping with sarcasm, I quipped, "Compliments will not get you any-where, love…"

Completely ignoring the blood oozing out of his nose like a red river, I laid a few more punches on his face for my satisfaction and stress relief. As I weakened him, I crouched down and retrieved my unique engraved dagger from its holster on my thigh. Grabbing the guy by his hair, I swiftly sliced the dagger across his neck. With my Angel's initial etched on his neck, I released him and watched as he tried to stop the bleeding before his eyes gradually went dark and he succumbed. Turing my gaze towards the other asshole, who had taken pleasure and pride in punching me, I glared at him, unhappy about being hit by such a flimsy insect.

"You should have taken my advice… but most importantly, you should have hit harder. You hit like a grandma.". Provoking his masculinity made him act impulsively, without considering his alternatives. I predicted his attack, dodged left, and countered with a back-kick, sending him flying.

Faking a bow, "Another free flying lesson for your dear highness." I mused. "You ought to feel happy and thankful towards me. So, what should you be saying?"

"Go to hell, bitch!"

"Oh, thank you for the invite, but no can do! Can't say I didn't give you a chance, though!" Proceeding to pick up my dagger from the ground, I aimed for his back, and 'boom,' he slumped forward, face-first, not moving.

Staring at the two bloody dead bodies in front of me, I was not even tired or breathless yet. I wanted more, so I stood in the middle of the east and north wing with an expression of almost boredom, waiting impatiently for the many footsteps I could hear approaching. I swear I could have sat on the ground Indian style, waiting for my undeniable attraction to drag them to me.

As per our plan, Logan's team and mine gathered at the predetermined spot after an intense two-hour fight. Acting as if we did not know about the lone survivor listening in, we openly and loudly planned our next move and discussed the target location. The original plan was to hit the next location that same night, but as soon as the survivor hopped away, I was told some agents were too tired or hurt…. *And then they call themselves the best team. I call complete bullshit.*

I wasn't pleased about pushing part two of mission *'Strike-First'* to the next day. I was ready to go tonight, itself. This inconvenience, however, could still be used to my advantage. By arriving later than they planned, we could drop a bigger surprise on them. Either way, they would wait on us all night long, if not till the next night, arm to the teeth. The last thing they would expect would be me showing up in the early hours of the next morning.

~The Next Morning~

Since the next location was in a cold and dark part of the country, leaving around 3 am seemed perfect and advantageous after everyone had rested. Fully prepared, we headed to the forest in the pitch darkness, where our next targets were on high alert and impatiently waiting for our grand arrival. I was eager to learn about their plans for me and hopefully have a more thrilling fight than last night. Besides, it would help distract my mind from matters that would only anger me — matters such as Federick Archer and his infuriating self.

"Alright, agents, let's stick to the same plan as yesterday. But be more careful. Our enemies are waiting for their death with guns ready to blaze through your skins. So, do them the honour of taking more guns, bullets, and ammunition with you." Stepping out of our vehicles, we marched through the forest, swiftly infiltrating their basements and building while eliminating the welcome party at each entrance.

Announcing my arrival as I did with the first targeted place of mission *'Strike-first,'* I got less of the *'I just saw a ghost'* bewildered look. In all reality, I got the *'finally…you are here'* look, nearly cracking me up. Then again, I had to maintain my professionalism as Angel and not burst out laughing like a maniac.

The first team paired with me blazed everything up with no care in the world. Not even stopping when mountains of powdered cocaine poured out of thousands of boxes. At the end of the fight, though, I was once again left disappointed. Perhaps it was because of the early hours, and they were tired of waiting for Angel to make her grand appearance. Despite their inability to better prepare themselves, I would hand it to them; they were better at helping me pour out my anger and frustration than the first group.

I waited at the meeting point for the other agents for over thirty minutes, but my patience ran short, propelling me to head to their assigned part of the building. It would be a pity if hikers came up this far and stumbled on a bunch of people shooting and fighting amongst each other. I would have no choice but to eliminate them, too, as no witness was one of the agency's crucial policies.

"Humm… Angel, don't be mad, but we've got a few problems." My pointed look compelled the lead agent from team 1 to spill out.

"We had to take down all the targets… so no one is alive to deliver the message."

"WHAT!!" Squinting dangerously, I propelled all of them to back away from me.

Staring at me, as if I had just transformed into a gigantic monster, one of them piped up, "Not to be disrespectful, Angel, but there were a lot of them, and we are not as good as you. To stay alive, we kept killing all of them, thinking one of us could keep one alive."

"Well, this is a first from my agents… a complaint in a praise… but don't let me stop you. Tell me more about what else you guys messed up."

"Truth be told, I propose we wait the whole day before attacking target 3 since some of our men were unlucky enough to get hurt. On top of that, Talon got shot on his right arm. He's the one with all the data, and he still needs to map out the exact location of our next target. We also need to connect with the rest of the team to prep plans for part 3 of the mission. I'm sorry, but given the situation, I would advise to wait at least until tonight, if not for tomorrow," Logan jumped in with a better explanation and plan of action to save the other agents' sorry asses.

Glowering at the row of well-trained agents in front of me, I had to take back my compliment of them. They most definitely were not as perfect as I had initially thought. It was beyond evident they were a bunch of incapable assassins with problems following my orders to perfection. This was my result of assembling a team of arrogant leaders primarily focused on impressing me, but only ending up making foolish errors and acting like animals.

"Thank you, Logan, for jumping in and being honest with me in front of all your comrade… I appreciate it to a certain level." With his mouth slightly ajar and his large green eyes popped out, my response shocked Logan.

I raised my hand in a stop gesture and shook my head slightly at Logan, signalling that I still had more to say. Understanding speaking right now, especially in front of everyone else, would mean disrespecting me, Logan shut up and prepared himself to get bellowed at. Funny enough, the rest of the agents followed his queue like little kids.

"Don't worry, Logan. I won't reprimand you, yet… Trust me, if I had to, I would have already done so, and you don't deserve to be shunned… do you?"

"If you say so…" Logan softly added.

With a serious expression, the Alpha in me took over as I looked over my agents. "However, next time, I want ALL of you to give your best, beyond your limits even, and with no excuses. I don't know what the fuck is wrong with you guys, and neither am I interested in knowing. All I want is for my agents to follow my orders to perfection and not act like some dumb, lost puppy… GOT ME!"

"Yes, Angel." All the team members swiftly responded.

"Adequate!!" I declared. "With no messenger to send back, and considering Logan's opinion, we'll wait until this evening to see if Talon and the others would be in good enough shape to fight. Otherwise, we'll have to wait until tomorrow to continue with part 3 of the mission *'Strike-First.'.*" Glaring at team 1, "Pray this part of the mission hadn't been a waste of my time, and news of us attacking this place somehow reaches Vanderwill and his other alliances…"

Directing my focus to Logan, I instructed, "Logan, please ensure that Talon is brought to my room once he finishes in the infirmary."

"Of course, Angel. I will send him right up to your room, even if I need to drag him up for that. Don't worry about it."

"You realise when people say do not worry, it's then that I get more worried." Keeping my voice low, I muttered solely to Logan.

"Sorry… I know," Rubbing the nape of his neck, Logan sheepishly muttered back.

"Let's get going before it gets too bright out here…" Matt hurriedly voiced out behind me.

Giving Matt a *'thank you for rescuing me'* glance, I jumped in the car with him, Logan, and Xylan while the rest of team 1 and their associated agents drove in separate vehicles. Yes, the other agents were secretly jealous of the Elite Team, but my teammates have fought to be where they are. Little did the others know how perilous it was with the extra hours, the responsibilities, and the maturity levels needed to put up with my every crap and secretive ways. It was not all jokes, privileges, power, and being best friends with Angel.

Frankly speaking, the Elite team was family to me. They were the most fabulous best friends any girl could ever ask for. Every single member of this team has worked their butt off to reach this level in the agency and had to work even harder to gain my trust. So yes, when it comes down to them, I am soft-hearted and indulgent, especially behind closed doors.

Heck, aside from a few trusted security details within the agency, the Elite Team was the only ones who knew my real identity and life situation. However, when the need arises, I can be standoffish and cold like I am towards my other agents. I am only forgiving to a certain extent, after all.

CHAPTER 9
LOSING LOGAN

PHOEBE

Happy to be walking the halls of my agency after an excruciating morning, I spotted an annoyed Talon. Grumpily sitting among the other agents in the infirmary, he was mad at himself for getting hurt when I had explicitly ordered him to be careful. Now he had to pay the price for his carelessness.

Leaving Talon in the expert hands of our doctors, I headed towards my room to sleep off this new day. Since I had been awake since the previous morning, I needed to rest my eyes and mind before strategizing the next part of mission *'Strike-First'*. And this time, I had to factor in issues that arose at the second location. Like making sure there was at least one survivor. We also needed to improve our exit strategy to avoid being ambushed again, as we were when we left the forest. Our targets knew the hideouts and area better than us, and as we were leaving, they jumped out of trees and thicket. Already injured and tired, my men left it to me to rescue them. On the plus side, though, I finally gratified my fighting urges from these past few weeks.

"Hey Angel, wait up!" Turning around to the familiar voice, I saw Logan running up to me.

"What do you want, Logan?" I inquired with a lazy smile.

"Where are you headed to?"

"My room, to rest… Why?" Cocking an eyebrow, I quizzically questioned, curious why he suddenly sounded unsure.

"Um… If you don't mind, can I speak with you in private?"

"Can we do that later? And why are you whispering?" I responded in a whisper.

"It really can't wait; it's something personal… But why are you whispering?"

Letting out an exhausted breath, "Because you were… Come on, let's discuss this in my office."

"Okay…" Logan let out a large sigh.

Closing the office door behind me, I invited Logan to sit on the couch with me. "So, tell me, what's so important it couldn't wait until later?"

Logan sat in front of me, stared, and popped his mouth open like a fish multiple times, saying nothing before letting out several exasperated sighs. Both curious and worried about why he was acting this way, I took the first step.

"So… Are you going to say something soon, or am I just going to sit here and watch you polish your talent of how to imitate a puffer fish?"

"Yes, right… Sorry. So, as I was saying, I have something critical to tell you." He stopped once more, wearing my patience thin by the seconds.

"As you were saying?" I pressed.

"Look, you know who I am deep down and how I've always seen you like my baby sister. I love you so much and would never take advantage of your kindness or our friendship, but…"

Feeling anxious after this quick speech, I expressed, "Before you make your case any worse, Logan, tell me what you did this time around. How did you and the others mess up this time?"

Abruptly looking up at me, he finally gave me his utmost attention. "No! No! It's nothing like that… It's just that…"

"Just what?" A tad bit impatient, I interrupted. With every second he was losing, stammering in here, the less likely I could clean up their mess.

"Just don't be angry or at least think about it with a cool mind before you take any rash decision, but I -…"

"Who did you kill?" I abruptly interjected, only to have him laughed at my face.

"Why are you laughing like a maniac?" Scouting slightly away from him, "Did you finally lose your mind?" I carefully inquired.

"No… it's nothing like that," Logan uttered between dying laughter.

"That's what they all say." Cautiously staring at Logan, I waited for him to regain his cool.

"As funny as this was, what I have to say is way more serious than killing someone." I almost asked if he had abducted the president or any royalty, but I held back and bit my tongue.

"You remember the girl from Italy I was dating about a year ago?" I nodded, not seeing where this was going or where the critical part was.

"Well… I forgot to mention we never broke it off. The reality is we've been seriously dating for the past year."

"I don't see where this is going?" I voiced out my confused thoughts.

"The thing is, she moved in with me about three months ago…"

"Oh… I see why this is so horrible. You don't know how to break it off with her and want your talented baby sister to help you get rid of her."

"NO!" Logan nearly squealed like a cat being strangled to death.

"Wow, calm your horses! What is it you want, then?" Raising my hand in surrender, I calmly pointed out I meant no harm.

"Look, I don't know how to ask this without appearing like a betrayer and an abuser of your kindness…"

"Just ask already! Or I'm out of here." Frustrated, I was in no mood to play the guessing game.

"Imgonnaaskhertomarryme…" He speedily declared in a single breath.

"What the heck did you just say?" I asked in total confusion.

"What you just heard."

"Either you picked up gibberish as a new language, or I need to have the whole agency and you drug tested… So, if you would clarify what just came out of your mouth, it would be greatly appreciated."

"I said, I'm going to ask her to marry me next week. I know this is bad timing, but her work visa at the place she currently works ends in two weeks."

To say I was shocked was an extreme understatement. I was beyond the simple word 'Shocked.' Feeling myself about to hyperventilate, I took several deep breaths before speaking again. And by speaking, I mean continuously muttering 'wow' for a few beats. Logan, being ever-patient, waited for me to re-compose myself before delivering his next blow.

"I know this is a shock to you, but I have another bad news. She doesn't know about my spy life, and I wish to keep it this way as long as possible. Which is why I'm here asking you... no, begging you to please accept my resignation as your agent. It was an honour to serve by your side. But I'm not growing any younger, and I really wish to have a married life. I will still assist you for this week, but after this, I really can't... I'm so very sorry."

Shaking my head in bewilderment, "You are just fabulous, Logan!" I sarcastically snide. "So, if I understand correctly, you've been keeping your serious relationship a secret for a year, even though our team has a policy against lies and secrets. You've purposefully hid things from me, of all people. Then, you dump all of this on me while I'm in between this whole Vanderwill shit. And announce you're leaving me when I need my team, and you the most. To top it off, you're freaking getting married!"

Bowing his head down, "Pretty much," Logan ashamedly proclaimed.

"Look at me when I'm speaking to you, damn it!!!"

"Phoebe, I just..."

"Do you realise the situation you've put me in? The one way to fully get out of this business is through death, damn you! If I were my old self or even my father right now, I would immediately give you a death sentence, regardless of our close relationship. What was your goddamn brain doing when you were making those stupid decisions!?" My mind going a thousand miles an hour to come up with a solution that would save him, yet not break the rules of my agency, I was itching to smack Logan.

"Phebes, I understand your situation. I'm very sorry. But you are neither your father nor as heartless as your old self. You are so much more compassionate, our leader and owner of this agency. You can change any rules you desire — even the old ones implemented by your dad. I wish there were another way. But I'm so in love with this girl, and I can't let go of her or put her life in danger by continuously working here. I know you are upset and disappointed in me, thinking about how I could get myself into such a mess as love. But, believe me, sis, I tried for months not to love her, but it hurts too damn much not to. Heck, it hurts more than the time I took a bullet in my lower back and chest at the same time."

"I'm beyond upset with you right now... But not because you got yourself trapped in this love mess when you knew better, but because you've hidden such an important detail about your life from me. Imagine if our enemies had got a clue about this little secret of yours and used it to blackmail you to get to me. Clearly, you don't trust me enough, and now you are leaving when I need my team the most."

"Don't say this, Phoebe. You literally are my only family, my baby sister, and I trust you with my life. Nobody could ever change this or turn me against you. I just wanted to cherish the moments I had with Nadiya, with no one knowing, because I had intended to leave her after a few months. But there is this light and aura around her — I just couldn't resist. And before I knew it, I was in deep. I apologise for the timing, but you could always make your secret protégé a permanent official member of the team. He deserves it. He has potential, and I wouldn't doubt if he took my place in no time."

"I'll take your recommendation into consideration," Helping myself to a much-deserved glass of water, I kept it simple, despite being touched by his brief speech.

In all truthfulness, Logan's recommendation was right on point. My protégé, a boy who holds a special place in my heart, and my kids' best friend, along with their undercover protector, possessed knowledge surpassing that of any agents not part of the Elite team. In my mind and heart, that kid was already like my own. About six months ago, the agency officially recognised him as a D.S.I agent, and despite his lack of experience, his performance was impressive, even jaw-dropping. In contrast to others, he could fight for a longer time, and although he could use more practice, the talent and potential within him were more than evident.

"So…?" rubbing the back of his neck, his big green eyes filled with expectation, Logan anxiously waited for me.

"So, did you inform the rest of the team about your unfortunate departure?"

"No. They were next on my list."

"Well, good luck then…" I muttered as I started towards the exit door.

"Why?"

"Because they will either be much harder on you. Or if you are lucky, be happy for you and tackle you to death after congratulating you."

"Oh…" Logan simply responded as an afterthought.

Opening the door midway, "By the way, Logan, you're fired. You have one week to say your goodbyes and enjoy pure freedom before I pull all your credentials and access from the agency's system. Take that time to collect all your belongings as well. I'll see you at Archer & Associates this Monday. Wear a neat suit and clean up. You'll be interviewing for a high-level position. And if this girl of yours says yes, you have my congratulation and blessing. All I request is to meet her to see if she's a good fit."

Closing the door behind me, I left an astonished Logan. For sure, he wasn't expecting my offer or my calm reaction. Heck, I was surprised by how well I handled the situation. Despite my initial frustration, the love in his eyes for that Italian girl pushed me to look beyond myself. After all, I've learned from life that waiting for the perfect time is an endless wait.

Therefore, I quickly realised that my big protective brother, who has always been there for me, ready to sacrifice his life during my worst times, deserved a happy ending. I was no love-sick puppy, nor did I believe in such bullshit. But I was pleased one of us was finding happiness in such a disastrous moment. If Logan believed in a surreal thing as romantic love, then so be it… I would support him as the loving baby sister I have been to him since Damien left. That's the least I could do for someone who was a light in my life, and who stubbornly picked me up every time I fell or lost myself.

Entering the sanctuary of my room, I indulged in a luxurious, soothing bath in my Jacuzzi. After taking my time to dry off, I wrapped the towel around my chest and sank into the softness of my king-sized bed, providing relief to my aching back. Gazing up at my ocean-blue ceiling, I stared out into the vast nothingness. I cherished my snippet of alone and quiet time, revelling in the serenity and stillness around me.

The universe, true to its nature, interrupted my perfect moment by sending Talon to shatter the peaceful silence. Talon persistently knocked on my door until I finally gave in, feeling like he could break down the door if it weren't made of double-layered oak wood.

"Come in Talon… How many times should I tell you? Just knock once when you know I'm alone in this room to inform me of your arrival, then come inside."

As Talon shut the door, I raised my head from the bed and saw him smirking at me, his eyes fixed on me peculiarly. Surely that couldn't be lust in his eyes. Observing Talon for a few beats, it finally hit me. I was still laying with a small towel around my naked body.

Heavily blushing, I averted my gaze. "Talon, will you please stop eyeing me like I'm your next new toy? Come, lie beside me, and tell me how you are feeling. How bad is your wound and how much it hurts? I need to know how much harder to hit you for getting yourself so stupidly injured when I explicitly ordered you to be careful? Our mission counts on you, dumbass."

"Phebes, you realise you are half naked, if not completely naked? This towel barely covers your thighs. Less and your wonderful ass would be under exposition. All I feel is jealous of how it gets to wrap itself so tightly around you."

"Last I checked, Tal, this is exactly the job of a towel — to wrap itself around someone's wet naked body. But please, don't refrain from keeping your eyes to yourself," I sarcastically muttered with a straight face.

"Sweetheart, I don't know if I can take you seriously when you dress like this. In fact, I can't even control my wandering eyes or hands. See, it's coming towards you like a super magnet attracted to its opposite pole."

"Stop! Don't you dare come any further, Tal…" rolling over to the other side of the bed, I tried getting away from him. Despite that, he persisted and continued walking towards me, intent on tickling me, fully aware of how ticklish I was.

"Talon, stop, please…" I couldn't help but laugh out loud. "Okay… I give in… I'll change, so my, oh so striking, beauty does not torture you." Finding it hard to breathe evenly through our laughter, I finally let him win this round.

Doing as promised, I walked to my closet with a smile. "Enjoyed yourself?" I voiced from within my massive walk-in closet.

"Very much so… you have no idea how pleasing and relaxing it is to see you squirm beneath me."

"You know I'm still your boss, right? Better treat me good and stop taking advantage of your cute innocent boss," I mused while slipping into my P.J.

Settling in, Talon laid on my bed just like I had been earlier, with his right arm bandaged and propped up with a supporter from his neck. Stepping towards him, I lifted his unharmed arm and positioned myself next to him, resting my head on his chest while he casually embraced me with his uninjured arm.

"Believe me, Phebes. You don't want me, Logan, Matt, or Xylan to behave like those other freaks we have here. Agents who would do and accept anything and everything you say simply to make it onto your good list. They are like creepy lost puppies in search of too much attention. They will even screw over their best friends or families if you ask them, just to be on your good side. I will bet my life on it."

"You're probably right… I wouldn't like it," I uttered in reflection, shuddering at the mere idea.

"I know I am… I'm your right-hand man, after all."

"Cocky much?" Raising a brow, I looked up at his smug self.

"Just stating the fact…" Talon teased with a simple shrug.

"Oh, don't be too proud. Your only advantage here is that these people sometime irritate me with their excessive dependence, confidence, and pride when I'm around. Truth be told, I like my team as it is, despite each of you driving me crazy. Although I love being respected, obeyed, and feared. Still, I wish they would learn to do things correctly when I'm around, tone down the showing off, and avoid exaggerating everything… Then again, my absence might have contributed to their behaviour. I own the agency, but for the past 10 years, it's been mostly Pierce and sometimes you who have been controlling and directing this agency."

Talon said nothing, but his locked gaze and fast heartbeat spoke volumes. The sharp pickup in his heartbeat told me he didn't entirely approve of my last statement. Nevertheless, he chose not to cross a line and kept his opinions to himself. Conversely, his ocean-blue eyes exuded understanding, compassion, love, and respect.

Being prone to ranting when stressed, I was the one who broke our peaceful silence first. "Tal, I might not have fully spelt it, but you are a major key in this entire operation and in my life. So, will you please be more careful in the future? Promise me I don't have to worry about you being so careless going forward."

"I promise to try my best not to get shot at next time, Phebes," he exclaimed with a small smile. Looking up, I searched his eyes for any doubt or anything which would contradict his promise.

"I couldn't show any emotions in front of everyone earlier, but when I heard you got yourself stupidly shot, I nearly had a minor heart attack."

"Oh, you were worried about poor dear me? This humble servant of yours is beyond flattered, your majesty," Talon joked to lighten the air.

"Yes, you asshole. I sometimes worry about you and the other guys. I'm unfortunately not that great of an emotionless bitch," I jested back at him.

Not deeming it necessary to respond, Talon offered me his genuine smile, which he never showed to anyone other than our team and me. He kissed my forehead, closed his eyes, and peacefully fell asleep, with me doing the same shortly after.

CHAPTER 10
VANDERWILL SHOCK

PHOEBE

Waking up with a start, I almost hurt an injured Talon.

"What! What happened? … Did you have a nightmare, Phebes?" Half asleep and half-closed eyes, Talon groggily inquired.

"Matt and Xylan happened!" Regaining my normal heartbeat, I paused for a breath.

"They scared the shit out of me!" Trying my best to ignore Matt's camera flashes and Xylan's constant jumping on my bed like a five-year-old. "Could you please make them stop?" I whined to Talon.

My team and I often shared beds during missions or sleepovers, so these two morons knew Talon would be in my room, especially since he got hurt. Unlike the gentleman that was Talon, these two behaved like they were raised in a barn and never cared to knock. Now, I don't know what would have happened if I had been naked.

"What the fuck, man!? I'm hurt. And we were fucking sleeping. The mission will have to wait until midnight or later. Go disturb some other poor souls. It's still early for us to wake up, anyway."

More stupid flashes, "Ugh!" I mentally screamed while Talon shunned them.

"Matt! Quite snapping those damn pictures! Or your sweet camera will see an early death. Phoebe hiding under the blanket from your stupidity proves how annoying you are." Biting back at Matt, Talon nuzzled the side of his face over my covered head to avoid the continuous flashes.

"You're no fun, Talon. Xylan, tell him," Matt protested.

"Yeah, you're no fun! Party pooper…" Xylan pinched in a singsong voice before letting Matt retake the lead.

"You two are cute. The way you were sleeping, hugging each other, arm in arm. Phebes must be under the cover, admiring your abs and blushing like crazy. You know how she blushes a lot."

"Hey, FYI Matt, I'm right here and only under this blanket because of your crazy flashes and Xylan, who is STILL jumping on my bed. Now, back off or come join us."

"As much as we would enjoy lying down and relax, we'll take a rain check, considering it's already 6pm. You two slept in all day while the rest of us slept until 3 or 4 o'clock. We already completed our assignments. We only need Talon's work, and then we will make some readjustments before executing part 3 of the mission '*Strike-First.*' So, I would highly advise you to get up. Remember, you got a mommy call to make," Matt recapped and teased at my forgetfulness.

"We are so going to print these cute pictures of you two and mail them to your place." Snickering, Xylan planned his devilish idea out loud.

Ignoring Xylan's Machiavellian plan, I ran to the far end of the room to find my phone, which Xylan thought would be fun to hide. "I will get you back for this, Xylan," I mouthed my threat, making Xylan give me the '*come-at-me-bro*' stare before breaking into a fit of laughter.

With immense patience, I did my best to explain to my kids that my busy and loaded schedule was preventing me from getting back on time and that they should follow the plan to go to their grandparents. After I assured Wyatt and Teo about my health and that I would not die of exhaustion, they were satisfied and finally ended the phone conversation. Heading back to bed, I faced the three idiots lazily laying on my bed and laughing at my misery. What a team we were, really.

"Boys, get up and stop acting like children. We got a job to do! In 30 minutes, I'll be ready, and you all better be ready to go by then. And don't tire Talon too much. He will need all his strength to sit in front of all his monitors and work from the office while the rest of us will have fun on the field."

"Now, mommy, don't be too hard on us. We've done nothing wrong. It's all Talon."

Talon, attempting to change my mind with his puppy dog eyes, instantly switched gears when Matt and Xylan accused him of their childish behaviours.

"Hey, why me? I did nothing wrong. It was all those bad guys. We should go beat them up, and I will need to be there for more protection. Remember how my hug was protecting you while we were sleeping? … I'm the nice one, not them!" Talon whined with a baby voice.

"Stop pouting, boys! You guys whine more than my sons." Waving them away, "Now, shush, I need to get ready. And Talon, I was serious when I said you are not fighting today. You are going to direct us from your office."

"But Phebes…"

"No, buts! This is a direct order, Mr Talon Carver." My Angel side showing its tail, I made myself clear before heading towards my bathroom. Hearing Matt and Xylan mocking Talon like elementary children, I lightly shook my head at this playful, raw version of them.

~~

Completely absorbed in his tracking and hacking duties, Talon was busy on the phone with his source, finalising last-minute coordination for the last target. As I observed the busy work happening around me, I carefully devised my plan for tonight's mission. After all, I didn't want any unpleasant surprise like the last time. While I admit it was a good fight, the mission remained unfinished. I just hoped my message made it through the right channels as intended. After all, we gave our opponent more time to get ready — almost a full day, for crying out loud.

Our next and final target for the mission *'Strike-First'* was *'Surprise, Surprise'*, an old abandoned one-story kindergarten school. I swear Vanderwill needed lessons in originality. Using the same entrance tactics as in the last two locations, I found myself slightly surprised by how smoothly it went. Mercilessly fighting and killing those worthless pieces of shit that worked for Vanderwill, I internally thanked the almighty Lord that my assassins were finally following my instruction. It looked like they were actually trying to preserve a man's life.

As I was fighting, however, something was not sitting right with me. With the time the opposite party had to prepare, this fight felt almost too easy. As if on cue, the instant I eliminated my last target, a loud clapping sounded behind me. Confused, I turned around and came face to face with the one and only Cole Vanderwill.

Grinning widely, his perfect set of white teeth on display, Cole Vanderwill stood in all his grandeur. In a simple black t-shirt, blue jeans, brown leather shoes, and the same black leather jacket he wore ten years ago when he disappeared, it was like I was seeing a ghost. After ten years, being so close to that bloody despicable son of a bitch stole my breath. It was as if an invisible force was choking the life out of me.

Shuddering, I felt an involuntary chill run through me to my core. A chill mix with anger, hate, vengeance, disgust, regret, and sadness. Without realising it, I froze on the spot, like a stone statue — the surrounding people long forgotten. The only person in the room for me was Vanderwill. My breath hitched as I stared into his bright blue eyes, memories from over a decade ago flooding my mind. It was as if a film was unfolding before my eyes; replaying our first meeting, my infiltration into his business, witnessing him slice Mia's throat, being held captive by him, the constant cat-and-mouse game between us, and seeing him shoot my father.

For Vanderwill to emerge from hiding and stand before me amid a fight, risking his life, showed the effectiveness of my plan. I was itching to beat the shit out of his sorry carcass. But then I noticed the beginning of a devilish smirk, making me think twice about my action. Knowing how I reacted in the past, he anticipated I would immediately launch myself at him, violently pummelling his pitiful body, especially considering the threat I made ten years ago to end his life if I ever see his despicable face again. But I was not that same dumb and impulsive person anymore. Those ten years of suffering, searching, and scavenging taught me patience and restraint.

Locking eyes with Vanderwill, I pondered the motives behind his presence at this specific moment and location. For sure, he didn't suddenly develop a death wish — especially after all those boasting about his plans in the underworld. Unfortunately, even after what seemed like forever, I remained confused and clueless.

One of my agents noted my frozen composure, and the shock written all over my face. Following my line of vision, he found himself drawn to the almighty Cole Vanderwill, standing in his Grande splendour. Without pondering twice as I did, he ran towards Vanderwill and tried to roundhouse kick him. Unfortunately for him, he was yet to be introduced to Vanderwill's actual strength.

As much as I wanted to puke while admitting this, Cole was skilful at what he did ten years ago. And I, for one, didn't doubt that his abilities and strength had increased just like mine throughout the years. After all, there was an excellent reason Cole Vanderwill had remained undefeated and my nemesis for years. As if reading my messed-up mind, Vanderwill's face pulled into a smug smirk and proved my point in a blink of an eye.

With astonishing speed, Vanderwill evaded the agent's attempt to make contact. In one fluid motion, he grasped the flying foot, twisted it sharply, and forcefully pushed back, causing the agent to be propelled backwards with a leg injury. Given my shocked state, I silently watched with wide eyes, not being able to do anything. I wasn't frozen like an icicle because of what he did to one of my men in a matter of seconds — oh no, I could replace that foolish, impulsive agent in an instant. For me, it was the surprise of seeing Vanderwill alive and in action, making this whole thing so real.

Even though I had been trying to get to Vanderwill for a decade now, a big part of me thought I would never see his cursed face again. Yet, here he was, devilishly smirking at me with his dark aura like a second layer of cloth. As Vanderwill and I continued our intense staring contest, the surrounding people remained completely quiet. To assert his dominance and make a statement, Vanderwill smirked arrogantly as he pulled out his gun and aimed it at my agent, who was writhing in pain with a broken leg.

Never once breaking eye contact with me, he cocked the gun and shot my agent in the head; the bullet going through his skull as his lifeless body dropped. Despite feeling nauseated and sick by Vanderwill's cold and ruthless action, I pushed myself not to back down. He never intimidated or scare me, nor could he start now.

In the corner of my eyes, I noticed Logan, Xylan, and Matt slowly approaching towards me. Even though I knew they would not fight Vanderwill as my now dead agent had, my heart still raced with fear for their safety. I understood that their intention was to be here for me, offering the support and comfort that friends and family provide, but I didn't want it at the moment. Where Vanderwill was present, friendship didn't exist, that I learned a long time ago.

Cole Vanderwill was a cold, murdering bastard, and so was I. I knew how he took advantages of relationship. Which meant my team's simple act of comfort and support could have serious consequences, especially for Logan, who was about to start his own family. So, I raised my left hand to halt their progress. Thank God they understood my signal and silently did as I instructed.

"Cole." I standoffishly and stridently spelt.

"Angel… I see the years have done you wonder. Not only have you grown into a gorgeous woman, but you've also become clever. Ten years ago, you would have already pounced on me by now."

I continued to stare blankly at Vanderwill, his voice disgusting me and bringing back more painful memories. As my anger and the urge to harm intensified, I realised I had to act, despite the difficulty of controlling my emotions.

"Of course, I have. But please don't let my beauty and strength stop your false praises. Why don't you instead do all of us a favour and tell me why you are here? I'm not stupid to attack you right here and now. Surely, you don't have a death wish, so why throw yourself into the lion's den?"

No answer, just a smug smirk and a disgusting, lust-filled gaze.

"Stop your damn creepy smirk, you psychopath… and answer my damn questions!!" I demanded, the anger within me boiling to the verge of explosion. I recognised I was seeing red, and I had to regain absolute control over my emotions. Actually, emotions weren't a luxury I could afford at that point. I had to be like Federick Archer — implacable, cool, controlled, calm, and composed even during tough times, where the adversity was waiting for the slightest drop of emotion.

Sweeping his lecherous and calculating gaze over me, Vanderwill made me sick to my stomach. After a beat of silence, he turned on his heels in the direction he came from. However, right before he vanished, he uttered something so horrendous that it sent a chill down my spine and brought Logan, Matt, and Xylan to my side in a split second. I knew they wanted to offer me comfort but couldn't because of the people around us. As such, they took the best course of action, grabbed my arms, and guided me out of that terrible shithole. Already disturbed and in a trance, Talon's voice in my ears sounded more like shouting than soothing or encouraging.

Once I was back at the agency, I did what I do best in life and pushed away all the people who cared for me, aka, my team, and beeline to my room. Locking my doors, I took a quick shower and then went straight to bed. But by 4 AM, I still couldn't sleep despite tossing and turning the entire time. Every time I closed my eyes, Vanderwill's lustful eyes appeared in my line of vision, and the words he dared to utter before disappearing echoed and replayed in my head. This time, I felt genuine fear.

CHAPTER 11
WEEKEND AFTERMATH

PHOEBE

Around ten in the morning, I woke up with a start, my body drenched in sweat. Needing to cool down, I immediately headed for another shower. Like a broken record, Vanderwill's words kept playing in my mind, the sound of his voice stressing the hell out of me.

Since it was already Monday and the first mission of *'Operation Couple'* was done, I had no choice but to go home to my *'normal'* life. As I returned to my bedroom after taking a long, cold shower to clear my mind of Cole Vanderwill, I was surprised to find my four best friends huddled together, whispering, and waiting for me. Reading their faces and eyes like an open book, I knew exactly what they were discussing. Instead of addressing the situation like a normal person, I resorted to my coping mechanism, and put my wall up — concealing what I was really feeling.

Not giving them the chance to speak, I plastered a small smile on my face and acted like I had everything under control. "Guys, I'm fine. No need to overreact or worry about me. I've been in this business my whole life, and I can handle threats and myself properly."

"Phoebe…" Not taking my bullshit, and his big, overprotective brother cape on, Logan began voicing out his concern.

"Look guys… I admit Vanderwill's words creeped me out and made me anxious, but I assure you, I'm fine. I will handle this issue and complete all necessary arrangements by end of day. But I should really head home to catch up with the boys and Joseph before they head out. And thank you for your support and help, especially for prioritising my problems over your holiday. I honestly appreciate it." Nodding in appreciation, I picked up my baby blue duffle bag and got ready to leave.

"No worries, Phebes. We'll always have your back." With a newfound sense of reassurance, Logan finally spoke after studying my face intently.

"Phoebe, we're family. We'll naturally worry about you and the boys. This Vanderwill guy is crazy… loco… Which is why we've all agreed, including Logan, to stay as long as necessary, even if it means another year or two without a break. We'll catch that son of a bitch and put him six feet under — only then will we be able to take a holiday." Matt announced with compassion. But as I open my mouth, he teased, "You go home and have as much of a normal life as possible with your *'annoying'* Mr Archer.".

Matt's sudden mention of Federick Archer was clearly intentional. Federick was yet another asshole in my life — but less dangerous and far more attractive than the crude individual that was Cole Vanderwill. Matt had intended to distract me, and it worked. However, not the way he had envisaged. Just the thought of Federick Archer had me scrambling for excuses. One for ditching him during the weekend, and one for not showing up to work today. Then again, he couldn't really blame me for the weekend part — he should have informed me earlier than he did.

"We'll uphold this fortress and contact you if we have any new leads. Everything about Vanderwill will pass through us from now on, and we'll always be in touch." Talon, with a confident wink, informed me as the others gave me a smile that was both supportive and sweet.

"Guys, I'm grateful and admire what you are all doing." With a gentle smile, I revealed.

Turning my attention to Logan, "But Logan, you stupid ass, I forbid you to change your wedding plans for me. Problems are always going to be part of my life. I want you to be happy and to have a normal life with Nadiya. So, get your ass to Archer & Associates next Monday for a job interview with me, and please don't fuck things up."

"But Phebes… It doesn't feel right to leave you during such a predicament. I want to help."

"If you land the job I'm thinking of, you'll majorly help me and significantly simplify my life." Smiling back at my best friends, I engulfed them in a hug before ushering them out of my room. Locking the door behind me, I set off to meet Joseph and my sons.

Fortunately, I made it home just in time to see my boys welcoming Joseph before they had to go to his house. Noticing my car approaching at full speed, they all halted and waved like crazy people until I breezed by them to park in my garage. With wide smiles, all three of them engulfed me in a tight hug and gave me a peck on the cheek as I approached my front door.

"Thank goodness I caught you all before you left." Relaxing in their hugs, I uttered. "Joseph, I'm sorry for making you come all the way here, but my business trip finished sooner than expected, so the kids won't need to stay at your place this week. Raincheck?"

"It's okay, sweetheart, less worrying for me," With a gentle smile, Joseph jokingly answered.

"With that being said, I need to speak with you in private. If you want to stay for dinner, you are more than welcome. But let me give my sons a proper '*I missed you hug*' before we head out." Still smiling, I stated with a hint of seriousness.

"Sounds good to me," Joseph smiled back.

Fully turning to my sons, I gave them my utmost attention. "So, how are my babies doing?"

"Doing fabulous," both simultaneously answered.

"Joseph, don't you agree they've grown up a lot? Every time I leave and return, it feels like they've grown even more... I've missed you guys so much." I gave them another hug and playfully tousled their hair, knowing they disliked it when I did this in public. Adding to their embarrassment, I planted kisses on their foreheads as if they were still my ten-year-old.

"Mom. Stop...!" In unison, they chimed in a loud pitch, clearly embarrassed. Mission accomplished if you ask me.

"Why? Did you not miss me?" Pouting, I faked hurt.

"Of course we missed you. But this doesn't mean you're going to treat us like babies on the front porch where everyone could see us, especially our friends. Remember... not good for our school rep," Twining up on me, they jokingly added with a tinge of seriousness.

"See, Joseph... I was right. They've grown up so much where they feel embarrassed by their mother's affectionate treatment after she's been away for an entire weekend. Their friends' views are more important to them than their poor, hard-working mom... I'm hurt." With a whining tone, I placed my hand on top of my chest, pretending to be hurt.

"Mom, we hold you in such high regard and love you so much that our friends can't compare in importance."

"You quickly got back on your feet there, Wyatt. Good one. Anyway, you don't need to convince me. I know my sweet breath-taking boys love and respect me more than anything in this world."

"How did we get so lucky, Teo? To have such a wonderful mother — sometimes it feels surreal." Wyatt theatrically proclaimed.

"I'm the lucky one. You both are so wonderfully understanding. However, for now, I need both of you to go inside and lock the door behind you. Grandpa and I are going for a walk and a little chat. Love you both!" Nodding on cue, both took off and did as I instructed.

Albeit Joseph was smiling, his eyes were flowing with questions. Joseph, a retired spy, my father's business partner, and best friend, knew everything about me. Sadly, he also became ensnared in the web of love, resulting in a swift marriage and the subsequent arrival of his child. After this, his career as a spy was pretty much over. Alicia, his wife, wasn't particularly fond of our overly dangerous lifestyle. She wanted a stable life alongside the love of her life, free from constant worrying. The daunting thoughts of whether her husband would make it home every day, or if someone would attack her family while they were sleeping, quickly became too much for her to bear. This left Joseph stuck between both worlds.

Since Joseph was my godfather and the only one who truly knew my dad, he quickly became a huge part of my life. He was the only remaining person from my childhood that I could still call family. And as the best godfather in the world, he was always there to help me with anything I needed. Additionally, he possessed a wealth of knowledge about the agency, its past, and Archer & Associate. That expertise has helped me so many times throughout the years — particularly with building that special contract to shut Federick up and hide my name as the co-owner.

"Okay, Phebes… spill it!" Taken aback, I looked up at Joseph.

"Uh?"

"What happened? You seem anxious. Did the mission go well? From your face, it looks like you saw a ghost. And that's stressing me out," Joseph worriedly interrogated.

"How did you know? I thought I…"

"Don't worry, you did an excellent job of hiding your authentic emotions. And if I hadn't known you from the time you were in your mother's womb, together with witnessing your drastic change over the years, I wouldn't have guessed. Your fake exaggerated humour gave it all away," Joseph interjected, knowing full well where I was going with my stuttered question. I swear, this man sometimes emulated my father, creating a peculiar blend of closeness and distance within me.

I jokingly remarked, "I can now see where your son gets his intense, soul-searching demeanour," to ease the tension I was feeling deep inside.

Silently, arm in arm, we roamed the beach as I searched for a way to phrase my words properly. Alas, I couldn't find a right way to begin. In exasperation, I plumped down on the warm white sand. Following my cue, Joseph sat beside me. Resting my head on his shoulder, I took comfort in his presence. Wrapping his arms around me, Joseph reassured me he was there for me no matter what — just like my dad used to do. Deeply inhaling, I decided spilling out my heart without sugar-coating anything for the man.

"Vanderwill showed up during part three of mission *'Strike-first'*... and you know what I did? ... Nothing at all... I stood frozen! I couldn't say or do anything for the longest time. And you know what the most frustrating part was?"

Finding solace in Joseph, I looked at him for confirmation to continue, as if I were a kid again, facing some imminent crisis. As he nodded, I turned my gaze towards the vast ocean horizon, seeking solace in its mesmerising beauty as I attempted to bury my anger, sadness, and confusion within its depths.

"I've been preparing myself to confront Vanderwill for years now; and when we finally crossed paths, I couldn't do anything except stand like a stupid gawking statue and take in all his words and disgusting looks. I guess I wasn't as prepared to see Vanderwill's face as I thought I would be.... All the memories I had successfully buried deep in my mind came flooding back to me. His eyes were still as I remembered them — shamelessly wandering over my body, as they always did... the lust in his eyes and his devilish grin were unmistakable. Heck, he didn't even try to hide the fact that he was mentally undressing me. Xylan, Logan, and Matt had to physically pull me away from there and... and... he said something that still troubles me greatly before vanishing once more."

"My God, Phebes... thank God you are safe! Understand it's normal to react the way you did. Some would have handled it worse, but you, my dear-...." He halted and gently lifted my chin, his eyes fixed on mine, capturing my attention.

"Believe me when I say you're a strong one, and I'm proud of how you handled this situation. As I'm sure your dad would be. You're indeed the pride of his heart and lineage. Remember, it's been ten years since we've last seen or heard of this Vanderwill fucker." Joseph tightened his grip around me, his gaze fixed on mine, making me feel more at ease for a short period. "But what exactly did he say?" Joseph asked as I breathed out the lump in my throat.

"Before yet again vanishing, Vanderwill said, and I quote, 'Wyatt and

Teo have grown up to be quite dashing. According to their grades and reputation at school, they are exceptionally intelligent and heartbreakers like their daddy. Good job at taking care of what's mine. If you think their trust and love for you will keep them away from me, think again, Angel. Soon, everyone would know the truth. And once this happens, your world would shatter. Oh, my dear Angel, be prepared to not only feel lonely, but to actually be alone. I'm beyond excited about what's ahead.'"

"Did he give any more details?" Joseph inquired with great concern, his spy instincts heightened and on high alert.

"The asshole played it close. He made his threat and disappeared before I could do anything. If he dropped any hints of his plans, I didn't capture it. My mind was racing and blanked out everything around me. All I could think of was that he must have seen Wyatt and Teo and had been doing his research on them for a long time. I had spent a good decade doing every-thing to protect those boys, but it seems I failed at that. It's just…"

With suspicion guiding me, "I'm puzzled. How did Vanderwill find out about *MY* kids? I had hidden everything pertaining to their existence. And the more I'm thinking about it, something is not right, and I'm sure of it."

"I'm sorry, Phebes, but I genuinely believe your sons deserve to know the truth, or at least part of it." Ready to butt in, Joseph instantly stopped me by placing his index finger on top of my lip. I swear this guy's ability to read minds was beyond frustrating sometimes.

"Listen to me, babygirl. You should be the one to tell them the truth first. Vanderwill will not wait around like you, and if your sons find out from him, it might turn out horrible. The boys have so much trust in you. I'm sure they would understand once you explain everything to them, with-out Vanderwill's word-twisting ability and influence on them. Trust me on this one… I know you are afraid and think I don't know what you are going through, given my son knows nothing about this life of ours. But you also know the only reason he's not part of this life and your team is because of my wife. If I had it my way, I would have told him everything long ago. But Alicia doesn't want him involved in the spy life unless it's vital."

"This didn't escape my mind, Joseph. But if I carefully plan everything, I won't even have to tell Wyatt and Teo the truth. I'll do whatever it takes to stop Vanderwill's plans. Because like Alicia, I don't want my children to be part of our world, and revealing the truth would lead to that, which is a risk I can't take. While you may think they should know everything, I disagree. They are so young and innocent. They deserve to have as much of a normal life as possible. Besides, Vanderwill was right about one thing. If they discover the truth about their real parents, they'll only despise me for lying all these years." I responded with complete seriousness, refusing to back down. I disliked the idea of telling my kids the truth, let alone considering it as a last resort.

"Do you realise you sound just like your father?" Joseph gazed at me with a fatherly expression and asked.

"We should head back… Come on, old man, let's walk back to the house, or I'll leave you stranded on this beach." Breaking the stressful air around us, I jocularly added after a small staring competition.

"I honestly don't know what's with you, women, and not letting your kids know the whole truth." He added with resignation while holding onto my hand to get up. Without uttering a word, I linked my arm with Joseph's as we headed back to the house.

When my father died, Joseph, being his best friend and my godfather, naturally took my father's place, and Alicia became the mother I never had. Despite all the jokes and stubbornness amidst us, I've always treated both with respect, as any kid would to their loving parents. Thankfully, my sons have accepted them as their grandparents despite knowing none of us were blood related.

"I'm not an old man, young lady… Be careful with what you say. Someone might mind."

Laughing as Joseph tried to hide his smile, "Like who? Your thirty-year-old son?" I replied, emphasising his kid's age.

"Exactly."

"No offence, but I don't give a damn about him. You have an asshole for a son. It's like you guys birthed him to make me suffer and make my life miserable."

"None taken, Phebes. I know how much of a man-whore he is. You can kick him, beat him, date him, sleep with him or marry him. Do whatever you want with him… I don't care as long as you don't break his heart… Although I don't think Alicia will approve of you beating the shit out of her sweet darling boy and putting him in the hospital, even if she thinks like me about his character. As we have always said; the problem you two have with each other is just between you two. Us parents are only here to watch and enjoy the show. But if you want, I can speak with my son about you taking a leave this week and not to disturb you."

"No thanks, Joseph. Regardless of my problems, I'm responsible enough to make it to work. I just have to come up with a reasonable excuse for ditching him this weekend."

"Just tell him you were home and sick."

"Oh, I forget to mention he's furious at me right now, and that too, without reason. Not unusual, right? … He's always so pissed off when I'm in the picture. Maybe he realises I'm way better than him. Who knows with the block of ice of a son you have?" Partly joking, I winked at Joseph.

"How I wished you were really my daughter. You are the best kid a parent could ever ask for. Unfortunately, my son is not as good as you, yet. Perhaps consider teaching him how to be more responsible, like you."

"Thanks, but I'll have to kindly decline this generous offer. You're awesome, Joseph. But I really don't want to get any closer than what I already am to your son, much less teach him anything. Your son is good as he is…"

As I smiled warmly at Joseph, I shouted for the boys to say their goodbyes to their grandfather before he headed home.

CHAPTER 12
UNLOCKING SECRETS

FEDERICK

Day by day, my annoyance towards my executive personal assistant was increasing — not that it made any difference to her. She was way too self-absorbed, and as far as she was concerned, without fault. Oh! Who was I kidding? Besides her exasperating attitude towards me, Phoebe Ziva Smith was the dictionary definition of perfection.

Throughout the years, I'd silently observed her smile and talk as nicely as her personality allowed it to others, but never once to me. If she as much as smirked at me, it was as if God himself showed me some grace. Granted, those smirks would surface whenever she made a snarky remark or felt annoyed or angry. My favourite is her unique *'piss off'* smirk. I've never seen someone smirk so beautifully when pissed. Even I, Federick Archer, couldn't pull off this charm from a mere smirk.

But even that bewitching smirk would not save her when I see her again. I was at the tipping point of my annoyance towards Phoebe. Her actions were completely unacceptable. She dared ditch me at the airport, defied my direct order to attend this weekend's important meeting, and flaunted her unbreakable contract to my face. The absolute worst thing was Phoebe assigning her extremely inefficient assistant to assist me during the weekend, fully aware of how much I loathed her.

On Monday, as I marched to my office, I hoped to see Miss Smith. She owed me a reasonable explanation for her stupid and unnecessary rebellion. But her useless assistant was still there, grimacing at me like a monkey who just got out of the zoo. If she thought the face she was making was alluring, I had massive news for her. Contrary to her intentions, her smiling, flirting, and heavily caked face had the opposite effect. Thank God I had experience dealing with these types of women… gold-digging lying bitches.

"Is Miss Smith here yet?" A part of me knowing the answer, I curtly inquired whilst keeping my distance from her.

"No, but I am—"

"If you think I'll be fucking you today, it won't happen. Focus on your job and only do as you're told. Now, is Miss Smith even showing up today?" I coldly cut in, her fake sweet voice sounding like a shrilling witch to me.

"I don't know, Mr Archer, sir. Miss Smith will either be late or not come in today. She wasn't sure if she'll make it for the rest of the week either." Disappointment washing over her and surprised at my bluntness, the assistant uttered.

Angry by the assistant's obtuse answer, I icily glared at her moronic self, driving her to squirm in her seat. Boiling with heaped-up fury, I stormed off to my office, my arctic silence speaking volumes.

"Okay… don't show up today. But you'll eventually have to come back and confront me!" Mentally promising vengeance, the idea of torturing Phoebe brought a devilish smirk to my face.

But it would seem karma had taken a liking to me. Not before long, my morning was brought to a halt and my work interrupted. Why you ask? Well, Miss Phoebe Ziva Smith was holding the file I needed hostage. According to her stupid unique contract, she had the privilege of working directly with me on all our important clients, and she had more access than anyone else in the company. Because she handled most of the work on this specific confidential file that I needed, all the recent information and documents were still with her majesty. To top it off, she was not even answering her damn phone.

"Why does she even have a cell phone when she doesn't even care to pick the damn thing up? Only she knows!". My annoyance reached a new height as I tried her cell for the sixth time in the past 30 minutes. I was ready to destroy something.

I hated losing time, especially in business. And this entire process of tracking down Phoebe to gather the information needed to finish the contract scattered on my table was a prime example of time wasted. Exasperated, and as a last resort, I paged her assistant to search Phoebe's office for the files I required. Alas, she called back less than five minutes later, informing me she couldn't find it. The reason for her inefficiency was that everywhere she looked, it was locked.

Filled with disbelief, I entered Miss Smith's office to find only a few stacks of documents on her table, and most of her other files and folders locked away in drawers. Using the master password, I logged onto her computer to access the files I needed. But then surprise, surprise! Nearly all the folders within her network were encrypted and wouldn't accept my master decryption code. It baffled me. The reason for all this secrecy was beyond my understanding. I was the owner and CEO of this fine establishment, and my computer and office were not as locked and secure as hers.

Marching into Miss Smith's annoying assistant's small office, I was on the verge of exploding from my frustration. I mustered as much patience as I could and bluntly demanded for Miss Smith's address, only to be rewarded with a vague answer. How the hell could she be working as Miss Smith's personal assistant and have no idea where she lived was beyond me at this point?

Forced to search for Miss Smith's information on our company database, it shocked me to discover that all her data was from 5 years ago— around the time she began working as my father's PA. Nobody has made any updates on her profile or done any reports on her performance or work responsibilities.

Intrigued and clueless where to find more about Miss Smith, I delved deeper into my system, but hit a roadblock with a resounding *'NO ACCESS. PRIVATE INFORMATION'*. As I continued scrolling, my confusion grew upon encountering a *'Password Required'* box at the bottom of the page. Growing peculiar, I searched for Phoebe Ziva Smith online, but to no avail. Almost every link I found in my search turned out either redundant to what I already had from my company's database, broken, deleted, or inaccessible. With no digital footprint, it was as if Phoebe Ziva Smith barely existed. My exasperation mixed with my curiosity and confusion, which made it hard for me to wrap my head around this unsuccessful search. This was indeed a strange and unique emotion.

"Was she some fucking spy, an undercover government agent, or what?" I laughed at my foolishness, realising that she couldn't possibly be a spy or government agent — she didn't have it in her. Still, the mystery that was Phoebe Ziva Smith increased my curiosity.

Intrigued to know where Phoebe currently resided, I drove to the address that my database marked she lived at five years ago, only to discover my company had incorrect and insufficient details about her. The white building before me was far from an apartment, as described in the company database. The house in the city was not overly extravagant, but its grandeur clearly showed it was for the wealthy. Since there was no bodyguard at the gate entrance, I buzzed in but got no response. Proceeding inside as if this was my property, I knocked on the door twice before a middle-aged woman stepped outside to greet me.

"Do you live here, Miss….?" Letting my phrase hang, I gave her my usual arctic businessman look.

"Mrs Grey. I'm the house caretaker… Why are you asking?"

"Do you know a certain Miss Smith?" Gawking at me with eyes near-ly popping out of their socket as if I had suddenly grown two heads, Mrs Grey became overly cautious. Not-so-discreetly sliding her hand behind the door, she appeared to be reaching for something.

Tired of her staring and unwillingness to make a move or speak up, I took it as my queue to continue. "Her name is Phoebe Ziva Smith. She lived here about five years ago?"

"And who would you be, Mister….?" With heightened alertness, her eyes wide with fear, as if I had spoken the name of the forbidden one, I understood the urgency of my next move. Covering my quizzical sense with an air of coldness, I had to stop myself from asking this woman whether Miss Smith was once married to the owner of this house and got divorced because she did something wrong. Having been working with the eerie, strong-head, and over-confident woman that was Phoebe Smith, I wouldn't put it past her.

"Oh, I'm sorry, Mrs Grey. Where are my manners? I'm Mr Archer, Miss Smith's boss. I have some important and imminent work for her, so it's necessary for me to know her current address." Once again, Mrs Grey's eyes bulged out for no apparent reason as she started stammering like a crazy person.

"BOSS-SS…? I'm real-lly sorry sir… I did--…not know… you were Miss Smith's boss… Please come inside and excuse my inhospitality… But we must be like this, you know… Plus, I'm still new…"

"Excuse me, Mrs Grey, but I'm in a hurry. Her address?" I interrupted her ranting, the iciness in my voice as sharp as when I arrived here.

"Oh… Okay. She lives ten minutes from here, by the beach, house num-ber 7."

"Thank you. I will take your leave now." Wrapping this conversation quickly, I turned on my hips to head to my new destination.

"Oh, Sir, wait! Please don't tell the master about what happened here. She will fire me on the spot. I promise I won't repeat this mistake."

"Master?" Her hesitation and statement confused me. For sure, I did not know of any master.

"Miss Smith, of course. She's the master." Mrs Grey nonchalantly exclaimed as if what she had just uttered made complete sense.

"Yes, okay, I won't." Covering my confusion with my short, direct emotionless response, I marched out of there, away from Mrs Grey and her crazy talk. The whole *'master and boss'* reference befuddling me.

Fifteen minutes later, I was still walking around the beach, growing increasingly impatient as I searched for Miss Smith's house. Mrs Grey's explanation led me to a magnificent, enormous two-story house, with brown and white colours, and the number 7 displayed prominently on the high entrance wall, providing a shield of privacy. Noticing the entrance gate open with no form of a security detail to stop me, I swiftly sneaked inside. The house in front of me screamed affluent—the billionaire kind. It was so fabulous even I wanted to buy it, which made me wonder whether the old lady gave me the wrong address or house number.

Miss Smith couldn't possibly own this property, not even with her exceptionally high salary as my Executive PA. Taking in the sight of this extravagant house, which could only be owned by someone of my standard, stature, and affluence, I was even more intrigued than I was this morning. I was sure this place cost more than the average price, given its location by the beach. If, by some stroke of luck, she owned this house, all I can say is that Phoebe was incredibly wealthy.

Completely walking through the entrance, I realised that even though this house seemed like any other wealthy household; it held its own beauty — a personal touch suggesting only someone like Phoebe Smith could own it. Yet, the weird part was that this place had a family atmosphere around it. But I knew for sure that Phoebe didn't have any living relatives. What made it stand out even more from the rest of the properties that screamed self-centeredness was the uniqueness and happy vibe around the house.

With the perfect balance of decorations, the entire property looked both splendid and stylish. On the far-left side, there were hammocks, swings, and a mix of teenage playgrounds in the spacious front yard. The house's front yard, sides, and surroundings were thoughtfully adorned with beautiful flowers in shades of blue and white, of varying sizes, perfectly complementing the house's colour. It would take no genius to guess Miss Smith's favourite colour was blue and white. Overall, it was a stunning place, and undoubtedly, the interior would be equally elegant with her personal style. Everywhere I looked, it was evident that this woman had excellent taste in decor.

But then the unexpected happened when I saw my father at Phoebe's door, hugging and smiling at two young boys. They were all busy with their conversation that they didn't notice my dumbstruck presence. Taking advantage of the latter, I snuck around the corner, where I was at no risk of being seen or found. For some odd reason, those boys seemed oddly familiar to me, but I couldn't remember where I'd seen them before. From my distance, I discerned they were teenagers, brothers who looked almost like twins. I observed the two boys, trying to see if they resembled my father.

Then, out of nowhere, mother nature showed me I shouldn't have been there. Whizzing in a pitch-black Lamborghini Sesto Elemento, my executive personal assistant, aka Miss Phoebe Ziva Smith, made her appearance. As a major car lover, I could tell the sports car she was driving was one of a kind, custom detailed and styled. But this was not the terrifying part… no… this was the cool part. The terrifying part was when she walked out of her garage beside the front door and waved to my dad and the two boys.

Watching her smiling and giving all of them a big hug, it finally hit me where I'd seen those two boys before. Miss Smith had gone on a lengthy lunch with them about two weeks ago, but from my office window, they seemed much older. It wasn't as if I was spying on her or anything as such — I had accidentally seen her when she was outside the building, meeting up with them. Watching her embrace them then made me think they were her boyfriends, and for some unknown reason, I didn't like that idea.

Anyway, this wasn't the issue here. The issue was all of them looking like picture perfect of a happy family. I couldn't understand why my dad was here with Miss Smith and those teenagers. I was highly confused and needed an explanation for the scene taking place in front of me.

As I emerged out of my hiding spot to confront everyone, the two boys headed inside after having their hair ruffled by Miss Smith, as a mother would to her children. But I knew she didn't have any kids — not someone as foreign to feelings and warmth as her. Besides, her personal report in the company database would mention if she were a mother. With each passing second, this situation was getting weirder and weirder. Bringing my attention back to them at the exact moment Miss Smith held onto my father's arm with affection, like her life depended on it, I watched them make their way towards the beach while involved in a deep conversation.

Burying the image of my dad and Miss Smith hand in hand, I stealthily followed them. As I watched them closely, I witnessed all of Phoebe's previous smiles disappear, as if she had just discarded her happy façade. A worried and distraught expression took over her. As I watched them closely, I saw all of Phoebe's previous smiles disappear, as if she had just discarded her happy façade. She seemed torn between seeking comfort, wanting to cry, scream and freely expressing her frustration, while also striving to maintain composure and stand her ground. I did not know what exactly was happening, but Phoebe seemed genuinely agitated about something important. For some unknown reason, I wanted to reach out and comfort her. To tell her everything was going to be okay, but hey, my dad was already there, comforting her and reassuring her.

As a ruthless businessman, I had honed my profiling and analysis skills, but as I watched them, I desperately hoped my suspicion of an affair between my father and Phoebe was wrong. Although I wanted to confront them immediately, I couldn't. I'd only end up losing it. But hopefully, by the following day, I would be much calmer. Revenge is better served cold, after all.

Full of rage and disappointment, I left, craving an escape from the scene of locked eyes and clinging. Giving the lovebirds some alone time for fresh air, I struggled to believe what I had just witnessed. Regardless of my attempts, the images I saw continued to haunt my thoughts like a backdrop.

These newfound revelations regarding Phoebe Smith shed light on the reasons behind her extensive access inside the company, the privacy around her identity, and that damn personalised contract she persistently shoves in my face. For sure, it was because of the relationship she had with my father. But the real question was, what type of relationship did they hold and still hold to this day?

I needed to find out the truth no matter what the cost!

CHAPTER 13
WHY SO ROUGH

PHOEBE

My mind wholly preoccupied by Vanderwill's return and threat that when Tuesday came, I drew a blank on a decent excuse for my absences. Unfortunately for me, I had no choice but to return to work and face the music. Taking deep breaths to calm my nerves, I made a beeline for my office so I could catch up with my work before having to deal with the pain that was Federick Ashton Archer.

With me leaving so suddenly, it wasn't a surprise my current assistant had done little. Her priority, after all, was to make sweet eyes to Federick and act like his pet. The morning had been so busy that I didn't see the time pass by, especially with how peaceful the office was — thanks to Federick's unforeseen absence, might I add. I didn't want to curse my lucky start, but at the back of my mind, I was curious why Federick had cancelled his morning meeting, or why he wasn't here yet. Not that I cared about him. But no words from him could mean he was concocting something dangerous, and I needed to keep an eye out for that.

By midday, however, Mr Archer's absence had become an inconvenience for me. I finished wrapping up last week's paperwork and needed his signature to get the ball rolling for some of our newest contracts. And, as usual, my current assistant didn't have any useful information for me. With my patience wearing thin and nothing much to do, lunch sounded great. And if he still was not here by the time I returned, I'd simply go home or shopping.

Ready to leave for lunch, I walked to the coat hanger by the door that connected my office with Federick's office. With the assurance that no one was nearby, I released my constant hypervigilance. But, dear God, that was a mistake. As I reached for my day coat, a hand shot out from nowhere, tightly gripping my arm, and forcefully pulled me into Federick's office, leaving me startled. My instinctive response was to fight back. I was about to twist the assailant's hand and back-kick them. But before I could give into the Angel in me, I came face-to-face with a pair of cold grey eyes. Intense and staring right through me, his gaze commanded my attention and halted my movements.

In an instant, I found myself forcefully pushed against the door, my words silenced before they could escape my lips. Trapped between him and the door, I could feel his intense gaze dissecting me, while his hands skilfully manoeuvrer behind me and secured the lock. Feeling a searing pain in my back, I realised I had to regain control over myself and the situation.

"Um… Mr Archer… What are you doing here? … I need to head to lunch." I lowly muttered in bewilderment.

"Nice going, Phoebe! Way to regain control!" Taunting me, my inner voice was asking for a big-ass whooping. Regardless of my annoyingly sarcastic inner self, I was going to show Mr Archer he had something else coming his way if he thought he could manhandle, push, or drag me around as he just did.

"If you can't clearly see, Miss Smith, I'm in my office. And last time I checked, I don't need your permission to be in here."

"I'm aware of this, sir. But my question is, why did you drag me in here and lock the door? If you wanted something you could have called me, and I would have seen to it… Also, why the heck are we in this inappropriate position? … Could you please move back? You're invading my personal space."

"Oh, don't flatter yourself, Miss Smith." He said with a sardonic smile. "I'm not interested in YOU in that way — mark the emphasis on you, Miss Smith. I want to look you straight in the eyes while having a serious conversation with you, with no distractions or witty comments from you. Your sarcasm is entertaining, but it won't get us anywhere." He leaned in closer, his eyes locking onto mine with a fiery intensity. "So, let's put the games aside and get down to business —"

"Hold it right there, Mr Archer. Haven't you realised yet that you can't boss me around or control me like you do to others? It's high time you accept this reality. And just so we're clear, I have zero interest in YOU or someone like YOU — mark the emphasis on you. I'm not interested in being your entertainment, one-night stand, or one of your many playthings. And yes, I can cut you off whenever I please. If you have a problem with that, tough luck. Now, back off." My frustration crept in, hiding the pang of hurt

I felt from his words. I kept my voice levelled and steady, determined to show him he couldn't push around or intimidated.

"As much as I would love to continue this argument, let's return to the main point. Unless you would rather stay here with me and bicker all day long," Federick asserted coldly, his eyes a wall to what was transpiring inside his head.

"And your point is? —"

"That's what I thought!" Smug as ever, Federick cut me off. "Where you were yesterday and this entire weekend? Why didn't you accompany me to our abroad meeting?" Federick baked. His arrogance was like a second layer of skin on him.

Locking eyes with Federick, "When you ordered me to accompany you, I told you I had something else going on this weekend. And yesterday I was sick, hence took a day off… Is it illegal or what? — You know what? You have got to learn how to use that bit of common sense you have left." I lightly tapped the side of his head, trying to distract him from his question and give myself some time to think of a clever excuse.

"I specifically asked you to respond to the questions, and drop the atti-tude and sassiness, Miss Smith. Do you really want to stay pressed against this door, caught between my arms? Is this what you're after? Do you secretly crave my attention, Miss Smith? Maybe you even have sex dreams about me and are using your rude and sassy behaviour to cover it." That arrogant piece of shit! He couldn't even stop thinking about himself for a single moment, the egotistical jerk.

With a look of disgust on my face, I retorted, "You wish!" Scowling at Federick, "My behaviour has nothing to do with your fake grandioseness, and I don't owe you any explanation. You can take what I give you, or you can leave it. That's entirely up to you. And as far as accompanying you go; you should have given me a few days' notice — as mentioned in my con-tract. If you have an issue with this condition, you can suck it up, and take yet another beating to your ego from me." Locking eyes with him, a smirk forming, "No matter how much you want to change my contract, you can-not, sir." I enunciated each word, so he understood my stance. "It precedes you, and it's high time you get used to it."

Smug, I bathed in my sense of triumph, but when Federick's demean-our suddenly shifted, I internally took a step back. The iciness in his eyes dropped to a new freezing temperature. It looked like there was a ferocious ice blizzard brewing inside him, ready to unleash its fury at any moment. His body language screamed aggressiveness and tension — someone who was beyond irate. I silently watched as Federick clenched his jaw and ground his teeth, and his eyes narrowed, shooting daggers at me.

If I was sensible, I would have been on alert and taken the step to make sure I was far from Federick. Instead, I let my eyes trail down to his red lips. Luscious-looking, I wanted to bite it until he used his lips for something other than insulting me. As soon as I realised the irrationality of my unexpected thoughts, I instantaneously redirected my gaze to his eyes, hoping to quell the madness stirring inside me.

Alas, I felt pulled by the darkness within his grey eyes. A wave of confusion crashed over me, leaving me disoriented and at a loss for understanding the abrupt shift within me. I felt a stirring in my stomach as his eyes imprisoned me, playing tricks on my mind and body. I honestly didn't know where those weird and unsettling thoughts originated, but I knew I couldn't hold his intense gaze for too long.

This situation was beyond my comprehension. I prided myself on being a fearless individual and the most exceptional spy in the country. I'm not someone easily intimidated or scared by someone's icy stare, no matter how penetrating those stares might be. Although Federick's eyes seemed to have an infinite depth, capable of peering into my soul, I knew he couldn't. Nobody could. Using the technique I learned in my childhood, while training to be an agent, I shifted my focus to Federick's nose, fooling him into thinking I was making direct eye contact with him. This tactic has always proved successful with my dad, Joseph, Alicia, Mia, and my other friends, so there was no chance it would fail me now.

"Yes, how could I have forgotten such an important detail? Your damn special contract!"

Oh, if Federick's words were balls of fire, I would have been burnt by now. Ignoring the fact that his statement was rhetorical, "Because you have the memory of a goldfish — then again, a goldfish is prettier than you." Playing with fire, I cut in and angering him even more.

It wasn't like I loved pissing Federick off every single second of my life. — Oh, wait! Who am I kidding? — That's an utter bullshit and a lie… I relished pissing off *'The great Federick Ashton Archer'*. Serves him right for all I had to go through as a child because of him. I don't care that he doesn't know it was me he used to torture when we were kids. Presently, though, it was different. Federick was actually looking for it and deserved it. There was no legit reason for him to be this mad. That abroad meeting was not even highly important, so his reaction was way over-exaggerated.

Ignoring my art of sarcasm, "Now, you better have a good answer for this next question… And Miss Smith, this question will oblige you to move your gaze from my nose, and look me directly in my eyes, instead of faking it like all the things you've been faking so far… What's the relationship between my father and you?"

Federick was right. As soon as the question popped out of his mouth, my eyes practically jumped from his nose to his eyes. I tried to search for the reason behind his odd question. Unfortunately, the chilling depths of his cold grey eyes captivated me within their infinite abyss. Befuddled by his odd and irrelevant questions, that endless pit that usually draws me in had a different effect on me. A wave of shock and worry washed over me, and inadvertently dropped the mask covering my emotions. My confusion raw to him, I gulp down on my spit.

"Why are you asking? … And why does it matter, anyway? It doesn't have any connection with the discussion we are having." Continuing our intense stare-down, I stubbornly stated, unwilling to let my confidence shake.

As if hovering over me was not enough, Federick moved closer and leaned forward. His face inches away from mine. "I specifically asked you to answer my question clearly, Miss Smith — not to ask another question above mine. Either way, it doesn't matter. Your reaction and statement told me everything I had to know. The initial look on your face proved my suspicions were right. You're not only like the other bitches and gold-diggers around here, but you are also a home wrecker. Heck, you even had me fooled into thinking you were different. At least the women I go out with are honest about their intentions in my wealth, unlike you, who deceive and pretend. And most importantly, they don't destroy other people's families like you."

"What the heck are you blaming me for?" Perplexed and hurt by Federick's venomous words and intense arctic glare, I inquired. I didn't want to show how much Federick's words cut me, but my shock was so intense, and all I could do in that moment was lean on my anger and defensiveness.

"Wow! Miss Phoebe Smith, you are an excellent actor. You even got me to almost believe you. If it weren't for how pissed I am at you, I would order a special award for your talents at deceiving and lying. Now it's clear to me why you don't behave like the other women around me. Why bother when you are already too busy screwing MY FATHER behind my back!? And don't dare deny it. I saw the two of you at the beach yesterday, cuddling with each other. The sight alone made me sick to my stomach. Congratulations, you are a real whore, Miss Phoebe Smith." Federick callously finished; the name-calling from him shattered my heart.

Capable of taking insults like no tomorrow, Federick slandering me shouldn't have done much damage. Yet I found myself unable to digest the sting he was delivering. His accusations hurt me at a deeper level than I ever expected it would. My closed-off heart suddenly didn't seem that impenetrable to me.

Initially, I was puzzled by Federick's constant insults, but everything clicked into place when he brought up seeing Joseph and me cuddling. He didn't hear Joseph and I's discussion. And Federick being Federick, he jumped to conclusion and started blaming me for wrecking his home.

Federick, thinking I was someone this disgusting, infuriated me. He had no right to accuse me of those things, especially when he didn't have solid proof of this supposed *'affair.'* His words got the best of me, and I instinctively slapped him across the face, the sound echoing through the room. His head snapping to the side, Federick clutched his face in shock and pain. Slowly turning towards me, Federick bore his sharp and cold, vicious eyes on me. I stood before him, chest heaving with anger and adrenaline, my hand still trembled from the force of the slap. I allowed the cool silence to envelop us. Not one to cower down, I glanced at the crimson handprint that had bloomed on his skin from my strike and mirrored his scowl.

Federick might have been furious at me, but at that moment, I was far more irked than he could have been. Nobody calls me a home wrecker and gets away with it. Heck, the last person who called me something less offensive, like a bitch, lost the chance to live the next day to ripe the fruit of their sweet words. But this asshole in front of me calls me a bitch with a completely different connotation and still gets to live another day. No wonder I snapped more than usual.

Before he could utter anything else — because I swear, one more wrong word from him, I would have to call the ambulance on him — I opened my mouth again. "How did you find out where I live?" Through gritted teeth, I demanded, trying not to lose my cool.

"Wow… you really are a bitch to the highest degree! I found out you are fucking my dad, of all people, and all you are concern about is how I found your actual goddamn address." Federick ferociously muttered without humour, his posture so stiff and frigid it would put the iceberg that sunk the Titanic to shame.

"You better take back your words, Federick! I'm trying really hard not to snap your neck like a twig… besides, do you even have any actual proof of what you are insinuating?" Shoving him on his chest, I pushed us away from the door and further inside his office.

"I wasn't aware we were on a first-name basis now… And how dare you fucking slap me! You are seriously going to regret this, Phoebe Smith." A promise for vengeance in his words, Federick's eyes breathed fire, "I don't need any proof — I saw both you and my dad together, hand in hand, like love-sick teenagers. I swear, if anything bad happens to my parents' relationship, I'll hold you personally accountable. And I'll make sure you are truly sorry we crossed paths."

"You know what? — Just back the fuck off. I already regret ever crossing paths with you, and I don't care what you think of me… I never did and never will. You, like many other, are in the group of people who constantly misunderstand me, and I have no desire or the time to clear things for your sorry ass."

Filled with indescribable rage, I turned my back on Federick and made my way to the side door of my office to grab my bag before heading home. However, just after taking a few steps, I was stopped in my track. With a firm grip on my arm, Federick pulled me back, swiftly turning me to face him, then forcefully slammed me against the wall. Before I knew it, I was back pinned against the wall, trapped between Federick's arms, unable to escape.

As I stood there in utter shock, a sharp pain coursed through my back. Despite knowing Federick for so many years, I never expected this level of vigour and abruptness from him. The *'Great Federick Ashton Archer'* was always impeccable, composed, calculated, and cold. But for once, he was showing emotions. It was as though he had transformed into a brute, unleashing a side of him he hides from everyone. Although being manhandled by Federick should have angered me, I instead felt an unexpected rush of curiosity and excitement. I felt something ignite deep within me.

Despite my years of training to take hits and blows, I didn't expect Federick's action to hurt me this much — but I was only human. Surprised by Federick's unexpected roughness, a small cry of pain escaped me without warning. Hating myself for this momentary weakness, I quickly got hold of myself and hid how much his gesture hurt like a bitch. There was no way I was going to give Federick the satisfaction of seeing me hurt — it was unbecoming of my nature. The burning and stinging sensation on my back made me painfully aware of how easily I bruised, and I begrudgingly accepted that I would have a visible mark for the next two weeks.

"Where do you think you are going? I want an answer or a reason, and if I am wrong, prove it." His face too close to mine for comfort, Federick stridently voiced with a force that could cower all his adversaries. When our eyes locked, I immediately recognised that his proximity, combined with his brutish behaviour, posed a threat to my mental health.

"If I were you, I would think twice before ever pulling this stunt on me again." With a scowl, my annoyance and impatience palpable, "I've been patient with you, but I can feel my last ounce of patience quickly slipping away. So, let me be clear. This is your last warning before I make you regret it… Let go of me. Or I'll make you let go."

My fire colliding against his coldness, I watched Federick grit through clench teeth. He clearly didn't take me seriously. With a swift motion, I shoved Federick away from me, with a force that sent him stumbling backward. "And don't wait for me to prove anything to you." I spat, "I won't justify myself to you, especially not when you've already judged me for things I haven't done. What I do in my personal time is none of your business."

Readjusting my clothing, "I'm leaving now, and you better not try to stop me." Walking past a stupefied Federick, I felt immensely proud of myself.

But before I twisted the doorknob, I turned to face Federick for one last time. "Oh! FYI, I don't behave like the thousands of women you hang out with — who unashamedly worship the ground you walk on — simply because I'm not like them… Compared to them, who can't see past your outer physiques and title, I know who you truly are. I had my fair share of man-whore, and I'm not interested in going out with yet another man-whore, who, by the way, is a total asshole that thinks with his dick most of the time — which, mind you, is a lot."

With a twist of the knob, I disappeared from the office and ended up at my place fifteen minutes later, in a bad mood. I had to cool off, otherwise I would destroy anything and everything in my line of sight. Water being my relaxing place, I went for a 2-hour swim before calling Joseph to explain what had happened between his annoying son and me. Listening to my voice of reason, I left out the part where Federick was a brute or the weird moment and thoughts that popped inside my mind during that time.

Speaking with Joseph, we quickly concluded we should discuss more about this situation as a team and in person. The reality was I could try to take matters into my own hands and risk making a bigger mess out of this entire ordeal. Or I could take Joseph's help and have an extra helping hand and attentive ears to manage this whole Federick situation.

CHAPTER 14
A DOWNPOUR OF SURPRISE

FEDERICK

The image of Phoebe Smith wrapped in my father's arms left a bitter taste in my mouth and ruined my entire night. No matter how much I tried, I couldn't calm down. There were so many questions around Phoebe, my dad, and those young boys. Even worse, my mind constantly brought up suggestive images of Phoebe and my father going at it with no care in the world. I was disgusted.

Coming morning, I had to find an outlet for my rage and frustration. Breaking my perfect punctuality for the very first time since I took over my father's company, I headed to my suite's gym and immerse myself into some intense and long workouts. I knew that if I didn't release all my anger before entering my company, I wouldn't be able to control myself from punching someone — specifically, Phoebe Ziva Smith.

After a well-deserving re-energising lunch, I marched into the quiet space of my office thinking I could put off confronting Miss Smith. But the instant I saw her getting ready for lunch, I knew waiting would only make things worse. With her departing figure only an arm away, I improvised and instinctively reached out, grabbing her arm. Dragging her inside my office, I swiftly pressed her against the door without thinking twice about my strength or our intimate position and locked the door behind her as a security measure.

Caging her between my arctic gaze and arms, I reminded myself not to be influenced by the cuteness of her shocked face. Or by her sweet scent of vanilla and bergamot. This woman in front of me was beautiful and classy and had an attitude that intrigued me. I could see what my father saw in her. But despite the reality of her being a home wrecker, I internally loved the intimacy of our position. And when she said she hated our closeness, when all women would kill to be in her place, it stung. What made it even worse was that just yesterday, she was cuddling with my father and didn't mind being close to him. Scolding myself for still being charmed by Phoebe, I maintained an angry exterior, and focused on my hatred of her destroying my family.

But God damn it… her sassiness and those full red lip… got the best of me. And when she stared at my nose to avoid eye contact, thinking I wouldn't catch on to this old aversion tactic, it was the cutest thing she'd done in a while.

The magic spell she had me under, however, quickly dissipated when she dared slap me. Never have a woman slapped me. Stunned, hurt and my cheek stinging like a bitch, I was speechless. My mind ebbing with conflicting emotions and a sense of betrayal, my initial mood was far aggravated and sour.

Despite all this, when Phoebe let out a small cry of pain because of my sudden roughness, I immediately and instinctively felt sorry and worried. I had the urge to care for her. But Phoebe didn't even give me the chance to debate my actions. She sucked in her pain and pretended as if nothing happened. In that moment, I realised I had to keep going and lean on my anger rather than that soft emotion trying to bud inside me.

I wanted to keep pushing Phoebe for an answer, but the fire in her eyes told me I would get nothing. As such, I bottled my anger and let Phoebe go. I knew if I had stopped her after she insulted me, I would have done or said something I'd later regret. Not only had this woman disrespected me, but only physically assaulted me and threatened me. If it were any person on this planet, I would have crushed them in seconds. But with Phoebe, it was complicated.

Taking deep breaths to control myself and not explode like a hot volcano, I recognised I had to confront my father to know the truth. Then again, I was sure Phoebe would get to my father for a conversation before I did. It will be extremely stupid of me not to put it past her to run to my father to recount whatever happened between us. After all, they need time to come up with some excuse to save themselves from my wrath.

~~

Seeing Miss Smith's assistant busy at her desk in front of Phoebe's office the following day, it took no genius to figure out that Miss Smith would not show up for the day. I would like to believe it was because I finally got to her, as the very idea of her enjoying herself with my father churned my stomach.

As much as I wanted to go to her place and storm through her door, I resigned myself to let them be — for now. Let them enjoy the limited time they had with each other, because I would not allow this charade between them to continue. My mother's life and happiness were at stake. And when it came down to her, I didn't take any risks.

Yes, I'm heartless, hard-shelled, cold, and indifferent to almost everyone. And that's a choice. I simply hate showing emotions to people who don't deserve it, which, in my case, is everyone except my parents and my best friends.

Oh, maybe there is an exception.

I've shown quite a range of emotions towards Miss Phoebe Smith — usually annoyance and anger. Then again, I've also smirked at her several times, especially when trying not to smile at her innocent sweetness. "Ugh!" This woman was triggering a mixed overflow of emotions within me. It was all so conflicting and frustrating to where I wanted to rip my hair out.

By Thursday, I was reasonably calm and ready to confront Miss Smith. One way or the other, I was going to get the truth out of her, even if it meant using harsh and callous methods. But it would seem she hadn't had enough of the disappearing act she's been playing on me. Even after my multiple due diligence calls over the past couple of days, she still refused to speak to me or show up for work. Finally, having had enough of communicating with Miss Smith through her needy assistant, I left work earlier than usual. It would seem I needed to make another surprise visit to Miss Smith's residence.

I couldn't understand why I couldn't let go of Phoebe Ziva Smith, even after she proved to be like all those other gold diggers circling around the life of wealthy people like me. No matter how much I tried, I couldn't bring myself to hate her as much as I hated the others. Sure, we argued a lot, and I'm annoyed at her almost all the time, but this never meant I hated her. I never did, and even now, when she could be the hand of destruction behind my family's happiness, I couldn't find it in me to hate her vehemently.

On my way to Miss Smith's place, I called her again, and surprisingly, after the fifth ring, she answered. Whispering as if she didn't want someone to hear her conversation with me, I instantly got irritated. Her suspicious tone and action made me realised my father might currently be there with her. And dear God… If my postulation really turned out accurate, I would, with no hesitation, burst through her door and have a *'not-so-tactful'* chat with my dearest father.

"What do you want, Federick?" she asked, her voice tinged with annoyance. "Are you so dumb that you don't understand that when a girl refuses to answer your calls, it means she wants nothing to do with you!?"

Okay, even when whispering, she is sassy and rude. Why was I concerned about her again?

Cold and straight to the point, "Where are you?" I waited for a minute, and when she didn't care to respond, I continued with rising infuriation. "Don't tell me you got so scared you decided not to come to work anymore... Or are you finally embarrassed?"

"Don't dream too much, Federick! I simply didn't want to see your stupid face anytime soon. I'm scared if I do, I might just remodel your face into something I would much prefer seeing every day. Believe me, beating up your face into something beyond recognition has been sounding extremely appealing to me lately. So, I took some days off. In the meantime, why don't you enjoy my assistant? She likes you a lot more than me. And she'll gladly be used as your toy for a few more days."

"Don't worry your pretty head over my enjoyment, Phoebe." Sounding as condescending as I could, knowing it would infuriate her, I bite back. "Your assistant has efficiently been taking care of it more times than I could count. Now, unless you want me to enjoy the entirety of her in your office, on your table, I would suggest you get your ass to work."

"UGG! You are beyond disgusting!"

"I assure you that's not what your assistant would say."

"To hell with you, Federick. Any documents you might need during my absence, I'll send it to my assistant that you love so much. I'm too busy for this."

I was having a great time infuriating Phoebe, almost forgetting why I was angry at her. But then, she had to ruin it for me. "Busy? ... Busy doing what? Because trust me, fucking my dad in your spare time does not count as busy. And why the fuck are you whispering? Are you two in some sort of romantic getaway or what!?"

"I see you still haven't let go of those stupid ideas. Well, you know what? ... I don't care! Think whatever you want of me. You are not my father, boyfriend, or husband, for it to matter to me." Miss Smith finished with a click, ending the call before I could voice out my anger.

Having had enough of her rude and weird behaviours, I sped to her place. Reaching my destination, I stealthily and sneakily made it to Phoebe's front porch and slowly slipped through the already mid-opened door. The hope was to catch my dad and Phoebe red-handed.

Silently standing by the doorway, I watched with awe the most emotions I've ever seen Miss Smith display as she tightly and lovingly hugged the two teenage boys I saw before. Literally gawking and amazed by this unknown side of Phoebe Ziva Smith, I, out of the rare goodness of my heart, willingly waited for her to be done with the teenagers. After all, it was not every day I saw Miss Smith acting like a genuine human being with authentic emotions instead of her usual annoyingly, eerie, unapproachable, and unreachable self.

However, the moment the two teenagers called her mom, all my good intentions faded away. Thrown off guard, I shook to the core of my bone. Compared to the suspicion I had about the relationship between my father and Phoebe — where I agree, I only saw them but heard nothing — this situation with the teenagers was a combination of both, making it even more real. Standing still for God knows how long, I tried to get a grasp on myself and process what I had heard.

"Mom, where are you going again? Is this another one of your plan changes? Because you promised you took the rest of the week off? — Can't your boss leave you alone for once?"

Now, on top of all these mysteries, I also had to figure out what I had done for them to say such a thing. Last time I checked, I left Miss Phoebe Smith alone… Plenty of time.

"Sweethearts, my job is extremely important, and my boss just called for the thousandth time and asked for me. I really need to go, but remember what I told you about the days…"

After that, their words became a distant murmur as my mind wandered elsewhere. I was so stunned that I couldn't accurately discern my emotions in that moment. Questions flooded my mind as I tried to make sense of how she could possibly be the mother of two teenagers. Because unless she had lied about her age too, she must have had them young. And why was this significant detail not mentioned in my company database or her profile? … Or even better, who the heck was the father?

At this, the image of my dad popped into my mind, causing me to feel nauseous and sick to my stomach. Thankfully, just in time, another thought crossed my overly confused and stressed-out mind, saving me from hurling my guts out.

When the fucking heck did I call to ask her to come and meet me, especially during the week? I sure as hell did not do any of the things she was implying. Realising she was lying to them as she had been to me for years, I jumped back to the present with a wave of avenging anger. My thing is, if I was going to get the blame for something, it better be for something I did, and not some fictional tale she was recounting to her kids.

CHAPTER 15
FIRST KISS

PHOEBE

Pissed off and jolted by Federick's insane accusation, I left the office on Tuesday disappointed at Federick Archer and my situation. There was no clear evidence of how Federick got my actual address, but I suspected Mrs Grey, the new caretaker of my childhood home, was the likely culprit.

Inhaling deeply, the refreshing blast of cold air cooled me down as I wheezed on the back road of the city, strenuously convincing myself not to take my anger out on Mrs Grey. Although a word with her was undoubtedly necessary. It was important to brief her that anyone who needed information about me was well-informed, and she had to keep her lips sealed. Mrs Grey was a gentle and kind old lady, but I still had to teach her a lesson. Disobeying my orders, revealing, and divulging secret details about me or my life, and committing treason came with high repercussions.

Amidst all that was going on, I already had a lot going on, and now I had to handle Federick Archer and his wild accusations. Calling Joseph as soon as I got home, I reported how his stupid asshole of a son saw us at the beach and started making crazy assumptions about our relationship. Concluding that the best solution for me would be to take a few days off to let everything cool down, I made plans to enjoy some alone time with my sons. Considering I had been too busy and worried these past several weeks to try acting normal, I suspected my sons were even more suspicious of me, my disappearances, and lame excuses. This *'holiday'* with them might quench their doubts.

However, by now I should have known better than to expect a few fun and relaxing days with my family. As the sick humour of nature would have it, Pierce once again called to destroy my perfect Thursday. Apparently, we got more essential information about Vanderwill. Meaning, I had to be at the agency headquarters to prepare for the next part of *'Operation Couple.'* Under no circumstances was I going to let any more chances pass by, even if it meant cutting short my free Thursday with my sons.

To make matter worse, Federick relentlessly called me for hours, and with the stress from my *'Angel'* life, I couldn't handle it anymore. Knitting their brows at me with a question-filled expression, Wyatt and Teo made it clear they wanted me to answer the phone. With a huff, I withdrew to the far corner of the living room to avoid more suspicion. Mindful of my surrounding, I gruffly whispered on the phone. The last thing I wanted was to take any more chances with Federick, especially now that the bastard knew my actual address.

After my exhausting talk with Federick, I focused my attention on my boys. I knew they were sad about my leaving for the entire weekend, so I tried to explain my over-complicated situation gently. I needed them to see my point without me snapping at their many questions. It was already breaking my heart to know I was the reason for their emotional pain, and I didn't want to add to their pain. They most likely viewed me as the mom who constantly broke promises, and I would completely understand why. Nevertheless, we all had to go with the flow of the situation and do what was required.

Reluctant in their hugs, my sons unashamedly voiced out their dislike of my long trips. Rather than reacting to them, I breathed in an air of patience and crushed them between my loving arms. I, after all, was not leaving without my goodbye hug. However, just as I relaxed in their arms, I sensed an unfamiliar coldness creeping up from behind me. It was like someone was boring into my back. Vanderwill's last words before disappearing immediately played in my mind, forcing me to go on high alert. I was ready to fight — to protect my kids like an angry tigress would when her cubs' face danger. The adrenaline rushing through my veins; I realised I was going to be much worse than a wild, angry animal if this person behind me was a threat to my sons.

To my stupefaction, the person at my doorstep was far more dangerous than Vanderwill. Federick Ashton Archer — the last man I expected — appeared thunderstruck, as if Zeus, the God of lightning, had personally struck him. The shock of seeing Federick freaking Archer at my doorstep froze me in place. It was like I was in a dream — oh no, a nightmare. All the fights in me went *'puff'*... gone out of the invisible window.

Unable to cover up my panic, an unknown fear gorged in the pit of my stomach as Federick's look of disbelief and pure bitter anger washed over me. At that specific moment, I totally forgot about my sons, the mission, Vanderwill, and whatever situation was broiling and waiting for me outside the walls of my home.

In the far background, I could hear my sons repeatedly calling out, "Mom… MOM…", yet I remained motionless and unresponsive. Federick, on the other hand, reacted to their call and snapped out of his trance effortlessly. Rather than doing anything, Federick watched me closely, using his silence to suffocate me slowly, waiting to see my next move.

As my body failed to respond to my brain's insistent and loud commands to act, rather than standing frozen like a popsicle, my sons became worried about my wellbeing. With a slight shake of my shoulder blades, they urged me to react. Normally, this would be a hilarious moment. Unfortunately, I couldn't muster any emotions or reactions just yet.

Having had enough of seeing me stand like a gaping statue, Federick prowled forward. Unfazed by my sons' icy glares, he stood a few inches away from me. If my sons hadn't been on either side of me, glaring at Federick, I would have felt his breath on me, which would have frozen me even more.

"Would you boys stop shouting like frantic little girls!? Go to the back of the house, outside, or somewhere else. Your gawking statue of a mother and I need to have an important discussion. Now." Federick all but ordered my kids around. Piercing them with his arctic glare, Federick stared them down and fearlessly stepped closer to my body and face.

"I don't know who you are, mister, but don't you dare shout at us! And how did you get in here without the guards stopping you!? … Your presence is traumatising our mother, so how about you get going?"

"You go, boy!" I mentally cheered Wyatt while my body remained in a frozen state. A state that was far more petrified than when I saw Vanderwill for the first time after 10 years.

"Look kid, I don't like repeating myself and I don't have time for your frenzied self. Now, will both of you leave or not?"

Even after such inappropriate and harsh behaviour from the great Federick Archer, they didn't budge one inch, making me even more proud of them.

"For your information, I'm your mom's boss. So, you better do as I ask. Now!"

Standing their ground and crossing their arms in front of their chest, they matched Federick's fixed gaze. I, at least, now knew my boys wouldn't take orders from anyone other than me.

As the reality of Federick's audacity to shout at my sons hit me, I felt a surge of electricity course through me, causing my muscle to flex and my fingers to twitch in anticipation. At that specific moment, the idea of beating the shit out of him sounded immensely appealing. Nobody, and I meant NOBODY, could talk to my kids in such a tone except for me. Then again, Federick was impertinent, among other things.

Shifting his attention back to me, his face supporting his infamous arrogant smirk, Federick thrust himself between my sons and me. Trailing his eyes over me, "If you refuse to react, Phoebe, I know a perfect way to unfreeze you."

Federick held my gaze, allowing my sons' curious stares to fade into the background. With a gentle touch, he lifted my chin and, to my surprise, leaned in to kiss me on the lips. Federick's lips were warm and inviting, with a soft yet firm touch that sent shivers down my spine. The iciness I had expected was non-existent — it was nothing like I had ever imagined. I've experienced several kisses in my life, both consensual and non-consensual, and I can confirm that most of them felt the same, but Federick's kiss was different. His kiss felt different and powerful in its own way; almost intoxicating, pulling me in.

My body's temperature rising, I wanted to cave in and give into my fleshly desires. Thankfully, as I felt my body melting to his kiss, I snapped back to reality. In just a matter of minutes, I regained all my energy and reacted. But it was far from the response that Federick had envisioned, given he believed all women easily bowed down to him. Forcefully pushing Federick away, I delivered a resounding slap across his cheek. Given the way things were going between us, I was beginning to suspect Federick enjoyed being slapped.

"Don't you fucking dare put your lips on me again, you asshole! … Especially not in front of my kids! How many times should I tell you, I'm not like the other bitches you fuck whenever you fucking desire and throw away after you have had your fun! You better control your freaking hormones, or I'll make sure you can't father a kid anymore."

His unforeseen public kiss and my internal reaction to it rattled me beyond belief. At that moment, my heart raced at an unprecedented speed, making every aspect of him incredibly irritating to me. I did not care who was around and exploded.

"Wow, Phoebe! So much swearing in one mouthful… Your usual poise self is unbecoming of such behaviour. I would have never expected this. But hey, with all the dirty little secrets I'm uncovering about you lately, it's probably time for me to lower my expectations." Federick exclaimed with sarcasm and disdain.

"Don't you dare interrupt me with all your bullshit misunderstanding and crazy assumptions you have of me!" I exclaimed, frustration seeping into my voice, "Last I checked, I didn't ask you to keep any stupid expectations of me, did I? … NO. I didn't think so… So, stop blabbing about expectations and shit. It doesn't really suit you. Also, who gave you the fucking right to shout and talk to my sons like you just did? You want to shout and insult me, go ahead, but my sons are off-limits, and are always to be treated with respect. Then again, I shouldn't keep such expectations from someone like you. It's no secret you dislike kids, after all." I spat out, the anger within me reaching a new level.

"What the fuck—"

Ignoring Federick's confused tone and expression, there was no stopping this train of havoc inside of me. "I'm the only one who can talk to these boys the way you did. Get that in your thick head. Now, observe and learn how to behave and speak to young children."

Turning towards my lovely and puzzled sons, "Boys, could you please go to your rooms or playrooms? Mr Annoying and I need to continue our brief discussion in private."

"Of course, Mom, but Mom, if you two are a thing—"

"No way in hell!" I cut in way too rapidly, causing them to doubt my words.

"Good, because we don't like this guy. He doesn't have any manners. Never date him until he learns some manners, okay?"

Oh, my sons were too sweet. Especially Wyatt, when he gets so overprotective.

"Thanks for the advice, Wyatt. But sweetheart, rest assured, I will never date such a cold-hearted person as him. Now go play or do something guys your age do."

Smiling at them, I shooed them away until I realised — I had forgotten what I was going to tell them earlier before Teo interrupted me with his questioning. Ignoring the piercing artic gaze that bore into my back, I called out to Wyatt and Teo, bringing them to a stop as they made their way to the playroom, tucked away at the distant corner of the living room.

"Boys, you can go have fun but—"

"Don't step one foot out of this house," Echoing my words, Wyatt and

Teo had guessed why I stopped them.

"No need to make it sound like I say this all the time." I faked a serious tone.

Recognising the trap, my sons chose not to respond. They simply raised their eyebrows, as if saying, *"Really, Mom,"* then dashed to the playroom to escape my comment about their expression.

Sucking in a deep breath, I slowly turned to confront Federick, who had a comically angry expression. There was no doubt he was battling with his emotions, torn between anger and laughter. Raising my eyebrows at him, challenging him to continue, I aided through his decision-making process. Anger and annoyance winning the battle. He sharply glared at me, ready to cut me into several pieces. Refusing to be stared down into submission, I opened my mouth to speak my mind, so I could finish whatever nonsense this was between us, but he cut in — like usual.

"You got the wrong information about me, but same as you, I won't bother correcting you … not now. And even though you didn't ask me to have expectations from you, I did anyway. But I now know I was wrong to do so. I mistakenly believed you were unlike other women, but you proved to be just as deceitful as them — and even worse, lying about not having children when you're a mother. Who is the father, anyway? … Wait, do you even know who the father is? Or is it my dad? Because if they are, then I'm their stepbrother, and you will still get the money." Federick venomously spat out in an accusatory tone, maybe even frustration.

As I felt a surge of pain from his harsh words and resentful gaze, I was ready to respond to his insulting questions and accusations by bitch slapping him, but then my *Angel cell phone'* rang. Noting Talon's emergency number on my phone screen, I had no choice but to ignore this cruel and standoffish man standing in front of me. Since I personally trained Talon and my Elite Team, I knew he would only use this emergency number if it was crucial, and I was urgently required at the headquarter. How could I have forgotten about Vanderwill and my current position? Surely Federick was to be blamed for it.

"Look, I would love nothing more than to answer you," — and smack you to my heart's desire, I mentally stated — "So the two of us can continue playing the blaming game all day long, but I really need to go, like right NOW. So, can you please leave?" Pulling all the pleasant and kind strings in my body, I asked nicely.

Leaving Federick to find his way out, I turned on my hips, facing the direction of where the playroom was. "Boys, I'm leaving. See you later. And remember what you should do in case I'm not back by tomorrow."

Not even peeking out of the room, "Okay," they merely responded. Right now, I couldn't even blame them. Not when it was their way of showing they were still angry at me for running off once again, and then there was this new confusing situation with Federick. Leaving them be, I turned the opposite way to leave the house, only to see Federick still standing in the same spot, clenching his teeth, and eyeing me weirdly.

"You're still here, Mister? I'd kick you out myself, but I'm in a hurry, so lock the door behind you when you leave. You have five minutes after I leave to get out on your own, or my guards will personally see you out."

Without waiting for a response, I walked by Federick, trying my hardest to ignore his cold and enraged glare that was enough to turn anyone into an iceberg. But then he crossed the line. In a swift motion, Federick took hold of my arm and forcefully pulled me towards him. My body crashed on his hard-muscled chest, leaving our faces only inches apart. Looking up at him, the surprise on my face was clear as diamonds.

His piercing grey eyes imprisoned me. "Don't you ever again dare walk away from me! Do you understand me, Miss Smith!? …Wherever you need to go can wait until you give me an appropriate answer."

Federick couldn't have been more wrong. But as the tension between us kept growing, I felt a sudden twirling sensation inside my belly at the hint of an unfamiliar and unnatural authoritativeness in Federick's tone. Draining my well of defiance and inner strength, I resisted the urge to gulp down my spit.

"Or what, Federick! You. Can't. Do. Anything." Pointedly, I spat out, the force of my words punctuating the air. "I'm getting out of here to do something far more important and pressing than dealing with the rubbish that's happening here, so I suggest you release my arm before I make you regret it." I threatened.

Federick cocked one of his fine eyebrows, challenging me, and probably thinking I was incapable of doing anything against him. After all, I looked like a girl who could not adequately defend herself — a girl who needed her knight in shining armour to save her from the big bad wolf.

"You asked for it, so don't you dare complain or blame me afterward!"

Swiftly, I raised my knee and forcefully rammed it into his groin, causing him to release me immediately. Cupping his private part, Federick groaned in pain as he hurled profanities at me and everything around him. God knew how long I've wanted to kick him in the nuts to shut all his bullshit. And I must confess, it felt amazing to give him what he deserved, especially after the past weeks of his nonsense.

I would have done much worse if someone else had pulled this stunt on me. But this guy right here was something and someone else. He didn't know I was a spy; much less knew I could fight like no tomorrow. So, tactics of fighting like a normal inexperienced woman were to be applied.

"I hate to tell you this, but I told you so… Next time, think twice before fucking around with me. And keep your disgusting mouth and filthy hands off me! I hope I made myself clear now." I warned Federick. Looking at his pitiful self, "And despite my better judgment, I'll have my kids give you an ice pack so you can nurse yourself. Afterward, I want you to GET. THE. FUCK. OUT." I spelled it out.

"Wyatt, Teo, drop your games and help Mr Archer. I think his pride just received a blow." Shouting to gain my sons' attention, I summoned them back into the living room. "Again," I lowly mumbled for only Federick and me to hear.

"You are going to regret this, Phoebe. Mark my words." Federick coldly threatened. As a chill ran down my body, I couldn't help but be momentarily astounded by how effective his threats were. Being raised as an assassin, I was accustomed to threats, and they rarely ever affected me, much less shake me to the core. To this day, mainly Cole Vanderwill have managed this feat.

"As if." Sucking it up, I instantly recomposed myself with utmost confidence oozing off me. I was Angel, after all, unbeatable and powerful. Someone as insignificant as Federick Archer should never cause a chill to run down my spine. It was simply unnatural.

Ignoring Federick's intense icy glower, I proceeded to the door and answered Talon's third call that I almost missed. Within an hour, I was back at the agency, marching directly into Talon's office to figure out why he was blowing up my phone and using the emergency number.

✱✱✱

FEDERICK P.O.V

Kissing Phoebe to snap her out of shock was never part of the plan. I was initially going to shake the freaking life out of her, like wringing a puppet. Yet I ignored my wise inner voice and followed my venereal urges. The urges I got pretty good at hiding throughout my years of working with Phoebe Smith.

I couldn't understand how I lost control of myself and my actions. Despite knowing it was wrong, I kissed her and savoured every second, relishing in the forbidden pleasure. But as her hand collided with my cheek with a resounding slap, reality came crashing down with brutal force. While I remained in the dark about Phoebe's true identity and personal affairs, her unfiltered hatred towards me was raw and undeniable. Cutting through the haze of my desire it was a stark reminder that amidst the tangled web of lies and deceit, one truth remained unshakable. And though I half-anticipated her recoil and the sting of her palm against my skin, the pain I felt was palpable. It was a harsh awakening to the reality that this beautiful woman, whom I had just kissed, was in a relationship with my father, and possibly had two illegitimate children with him — thus threatening to fracture my family.

The sheer amount of profanity in a single sentence from Phoebe took aback, yet entertained me. For the very first time, she lacked composure or poshness. I couldn't decide whether to be angry at her bitchy attitude or laugh at the hilarity of her behaviour and this situation. With great effort, however, I buried my absurd mix of emotions and gave her a hard look. But as we were once again arguing, I couldn't keep it together and unexpectedly blurt out all the unspoken expectations I had for her. Clearly, I shouldn't even have bothered. Not only did she act like an ungrateful bitch, but she went as far as turning me into the bad guy in the story.

Peculiarly, midway through our discussion, I noticed Phoebe had a phone I didn't recognise. I observed her glance at the caller ID and swiftly decline the call. Paying close attention to her growing impatience and anxious behaviour as her phone rang two more times during our arguments, I was more than aware something strange was going on.

Allowing my curiosity to get the best of me, especially after witnessing her lying to her kids about who was calling her for *'work'*, I attempted to stop her. Unfortunately for my precious friend, Phoebe freaking kicked me where it should be illegal to kick a guy. Daring to smirk at me with a vengeful cockiness while I succumbed to the pain from hell, Phoebe made herself number one on my list of people to punish.

Taking my threats lightly, Phoebe called up her sons to *'patch'* me up before leaving without a second glance. Despite my pain and frustration, I couldn't help but be intrigued by the urgency in Phoebe's voice as she confirmed her swift arrival to someone on the phone. Now, I just had to decide if I would go with the emotion of intrigue or anger.

CHAPTER 16
METRIX

PHOEBE

"**W**hat's wrong, Talon? Did we receive more information about Vanderwill?" Reading Talon's serious expression, I anxiously inquired.

"I'm sorry, Phebes, we don't have any definitive or new information about his actual whereabouts." Cognisant of the exact piece of information I was looking for, Talon apologised.

"But we have a lead. This morning, we heard through the grapevines that Vanderwill might do business with Metrix. It's currently one of the most famous clubs in the city. Rumour has it that Vanderwill is supplying them with some new drugs formula he created. It's supposed to be more cost-effective and profitable for the dealers, and much more addictive and dangerous for the users. The intel suggests Vanderwill is also providing them with weapons. Although, we've yet to receive full confirmation of the latter. Pierce and I have already deployed Matt, Xylan, and our other top agents over there to cover the bases and learn more about the ground. They are also task to bug each strategic point I mapped out for them on the club blueprint replica, so we can have ears and eyes in all areas of the club."

"Okay. All of this sounds good. What's the catch?" Perplexed about where the problem lied, I questioned Talon.

"The catch, Phebes, is I don't believe in luck. Especially not when Vanderwill is concerned."

"And you think I believe in luck, especially when that despicable slug is concerned!?" I abruptly cut in with my defences rising.

"What I think is, when Vanderwill is in the picture, you don't think clearly. And I don't mean it as an insult. I love you and only want what's best for you."

"Go on." As I gave Talon the green light, he visibly relaxed, reassured I would not bite his head off just yet.

"First off, receiving all this information about Vanderwill's current moves at the club after years of zero news about his existence or plans seems fishy to me. It was way too easy, too quick, and it gave me a sense of exterior planning. It makes little sense why he would carelessly talk of his plans in the open. He must know some of our agents have infiltrated his gang. Besides, he hasn't even received his infamous, most awaited *'Official Welcome-back'* party yet, and he won't risk getting captured so quickly, at least not this carelessly. "

"What are you trying to say, Talon?" Throughout the week, I had weighed all these points. So, I was somewhat confused about Talon's explanation and where he was heading.

"That Vanderwill might wait for you at Metrix."

"And how is that a bad thing? I would say that's an opportunity to end this game between him and me forever."

Deeply taking in a long breath, Talon's face changed. It showed he had indeed done something he wasn't supposed to — as I had first suspected when I walked in.

"Look, I know we should have waited for you, but when Xylan volunteered to disguise himself as a drug dealer for tonight's meeting, I simply couldn't let this opportunity slip by. We had a limited amount of time, and because you've been so tired lately, I assumed you were resting when you didn't pick up the emergency calls."

'Damn you, Federick.' Internally cursing at that inconsiderate son of a gun for making me miss the start of this mission, I was even more frustrated at him. Because of him, one of my best agents had to go undercover on an unknown ground without me or my supervision.

"I assure you, Xylan was barely recognisable by me, so it's safe to say they won't recognise him as one of us. What worries me is that we got little prep time before Xylan jumped right into the lion's den with no second thoughts or real protection. The only thing we can do is wait and see what happens during tonight's mission. After which we can decide if tomorrow is going to be the kill — with your approval, of course." Looking up at me with an apologetic and expecting gaze, Talon waited for my instructions.

Yes, Talon went against my primary rule by conducting a mission centred around Vanderwill without my approval or involvement. I could have been angry with him for that or for moving forward in this case without briefing me beforehand. But, at that moment, I just couldn't. Not only was he my best friend and one of my best agents, but he was also one of the best right-hand men I could ever ask for. And the fact that he was so respectful and supportive, despite knowing how invested I was in him, made me love him even more.

"Your plan and theory have my approval stamp. But next time, make damn sure I'm informed first of anything that has Vanderwill's name written on it. For now, my only order is for you to make sure Xylan and Matt remain safe at all costs. They are my priorities, and if anything should go wrong, they should be the first ones to be rescued, GOT ME!"

"Yes, Ma'am."

"Strengthen Xylan's background by adding imperfections and doubtable situations. If it's too perfect, they will doubt his credibility, and you know better than anyone what the result of doubt is in that kind of world. Make sure we know exactly what is happening over there. We shouldn't miss one bit."

"As you wish, Ma'am." Nodding his head respectfully and assertively, Talon took notes of all my instructions.

"Great. Keep doing your thing. If you need me, I will be in the training room, kicking some asses. I seriously need to unwind, or I'm going to explode."

Paying attention to his facial expression, "No, you can't know why I'm in such a foul mood until everyone is back … See you later." I pointed out, already expecting all of Talon's curious questions.

Now if Talon were Logan, I wouldn't be able to walk out of that room without spilling my guts about what was riling me up so much. He would have made sure of it. Honestly, not having my big brother here with me anymore, fighting by my side, both saddened and pissed me off. I did not like changes, especially this drastic. In fact, I hated change so much that I try to run away from it as much as possible by inflicting the change I want in other people first. But here I was, trying to figure out how to accept and accommodate all these sudden changes in my life. Last week, my life was entirely under my control. And just a week later, my whole universe shifted gear like a racing car picking up speed close to the finish line. It sucked big time.

Through intense training, including kicking, punching, and beating my assassins, I eased some of my tension until I was completely exhausted. Leaving my agents crawling and moaning on the ground, I walked back to my room. Pouring myself a glass of exquisite red wine, I took a 2-hour long hot bath to relax my muscles and soothe the soreness of my abused body. Wearing my P.J. instead of only wrapping a towel around me this time, I went directly to bed.

Around 10 the next morning, Talon shook me awake, screaming incoherent words at the top of his lungs, and making my partly sleepless head hurt. In response to my nightmares, I weakly slapped Talon to silence him, even though it brought me little satisfaction.

"OUCH! What was that for?"

Rubbing his cheek with an over-exaggeration, "You got a powerful hand, lady. You know that, right? So, control your flying hands… Better yet, can't you be like a normal person first thing when you wake up? You could have kissed me good morning like a normal, loving friend. But NOPE, you had to be aggressive and hit me." Talon whined with a cheeky smile.

"Yeah, right, hilarious, Talon … hahaha … I'm dying with laughter, here … Now tell me again, why did you shake me awake like the dog you are?" Noticing Talon's face pale and his expression change, I sat straight up on the bed, fully alert.

"I've got some bad news. The mission was a failure. Xylan got discovered and shot."

"EXCUSE ME! HE WHAT NOW!" I exclaimed in disbelief and shock. "I entrusted you with keeping Xylan safe, Talon! Yet, here you are, saying he got freaking shot." Tears welled up in my eyes as anger, sadness, and fright took over me. My worst nightmare of losing another loved one because of Vanderwill was coming true and I yet again couldn't do anything about it.

Talon started apologising, but I wasn't taking any of it. As my cheek dampened, Xylan burst through my door, his laughter echoing through the room, joined by the uproarious laughter of Matt, Logan, and Talon.

"You assholes, you nearly gave me a heart attack! Don't you think I have enough problems in my life for you guys to be pulling such sick pranks on me!? This has got to be the worst jokes in the library of worst jokes you guys have ever pulled." I coldly glared at them. Alas, they wouldn't stop laughing. Apparently, I didn't quite master the icy glare of Federick Archer.

"Get the hell away … I'm not talking to any of you guys." Pouting, I sat Indian style on my bed and wiped the tears — the evidence of my affection for them.

Annoyed by their hysterical laughter, I began flinging whatever objects were within my reach. They ran around the room like headless chickens and dodged it all. Eventually, there was nothing left around my bed to hit them with, so they jumped onto my bed and gave me one of our infamous group hugs. As good as it felt to be surrounded by them, couldn't forget that I was still harbouring anger towards them. Pushing them away, I marched to the bathroom without saying another word.

"Oh, come on, stop being a cry-baby." All four of them simultaneously called out. But I ignored them and continued on my way, slamming the bathroom door shut behind me.

"I really think we fucked up this time, guys? She's been in that damn bathroom for the past 30 minutes. Xylan, next time you come up with one of your great pranks, shove it up your hole, because I'm not listening to any of your stupid ideas anymore." Talon's guilty tone reprimanded Xylan.

Good, they will learn to never pull such terrible pranks on me ever again. I was going to let them stew longer, but I also needed to know what had happened yesterday. This operation started with hiccups, and I wanted to wrap it up as swiftly as I could before it becomes a disaster. Leaving the safety of my bathroom, I found four pairs of eyes following my every movement, awaiting my decision. They stared at me like I was about to sentence them to death. It was a hilarious scene, and any other time, I would have laughed, but not right now, at least not in front of them.

"Look, boys," I said with a hardened tone, "I'm still furious with you, and there's no way you're getting off the hook that easily. It'll take a lot for me to let this slide. But right now, I need to know what happened yesterday at Metrix. I need to plan my next move for tonight."

"We are really sorry, Phebes, but it was all Xylan's ideas. He forced us to play along."

In a manner that said, "Seriously? Are you trying me right now?" I raised my eyebrows at Talon, leaving no room for additional explanations.

"The mission was kind of successful."

"What do you mean by kind of!?" My alpha tone, commanding and authoritative, sent shivers down their spines as I interrupted.

"Vanderwill never attended the meeting. It's likely that Metrix is part of his strategy to divert our attention from his greater plans or something of that sort."

"What makes you think that?" I rhetorically voiced out my inner question.

"According to the other drug dealers, tonight they will reopen their drug party sessions and trafficking of girls at the back of the club. We need to intervene and rescue the girls before the situation escalates further!" Xylan exclaimed with passion.

If there was one thing Xylan hated with an absolute passion, it was human trafficking, especially ones involving young girls. And if someone wanted to see the devil himself in action, just let Xylan get his hand on someone who was involved with child trafficking.

Despite recognising tonight's event as a distraction, we had no option but to get involved. It was our duty to stop the trade-off and return those girls safely to their families.

"If we're risking walking right into Vanderwill's master plan to save those girls, I need to understand why Vanderwill is going to such lengths and splurging so much money to divert our attention. What valuable and important things do we have against his sorry carcass that we are unaware of? There's no way he thinks I'm naïve enough to not recognise this as one of his twisted plots. — Better question, what is that murderous asshole up to now?"

"Um… Phebes? I know this question doesn't make any proper sense, and don't be worried, but where are Wyatt and Teo right now, and who is with them?" Despite not wanting to worry me, Logan's question both worried and confused me.

"They are home alone. Though there are now a few more bodyguards than usual around the house."

Literally sensing and *'seeing'* the wheel turning inside Logan's head, mine began turning much faster. The mere prospect of having my sons and Vanderwill in the same equation made me want to hurl. Remembering Vanderwill's last sentence before he disappeared once again, I instantly got the answer I needed.

Immediately grabbing my phone, "Wyatt, where are you and Teo?"

Asking in a rush, afraid something terrible might have already happened, and I was too late, my deepest fear kicked in again. Observing my reaction, Logan, Xylan, Talon, and Matt prompted me to calm down by deeply breathing in and out before I get my sons and myself all riled up.

"We are home, mom. What's the matter? You sound worried. Is it your boss who can't keep it in his pants again?"

"No, Wyatt, it's not. Don't worry about him or me. I have everything under control. I just want you and Teo to know Grandpa is coming in about 10 minutes. You're both going to his place today itself. And please don't open the door to strangers. Grandpa has his own key."

Barking my orders, I ended the call before Wyatt could ask any more questions. In a hurry, I phoned Joseph and confided in him my concerns and suspicions. He quickly assembled a team of his own agents to accompany him as they headed towards my place, prepared for any unwelcome surprises. If all of this was one of Vanderwill's screw-ups tricks, then my sons were in grave danger without me.

~~

Later that night, the new team formed for the reopening of Vanderwill's case, accompanied me to Metrix, ready to kick some butt. However, upon arrival, Xylan informed us he wanted to catch the bastards red-handed. Swallowing my disapproval and resistance towards Xylan's sudden change of plans driven by his emotions, we began gathering compelling evidence against everyone in that auction, as we awaited Xylan's cue to crash the event.

Personally, I was more like the Hulk; eager to fight and kill first, then ask questions. In contrast, Xylan was a self-righteous fool. He was determined and persistent about giving those girls — that, mind you, he never met — the justice they deserved. I couldn't care less about them. Regardless, Xylan was family, and I would be darned if I didn't support him in something as minor as saving someone's life. But that was where I drew the line. I could indulge Xylan by letting the civilians — the clients — live to face our court system first, so long they stay in jail. The drug dealers and human traffickers, however, I couldn't let them walk the street again. They had to die.

Startling the members inside the club, I burst through their secret back-door just as they were placing bets on the fate of a helpless girl, instantly turning the tables on them. Those fools, except for the bodyguards, were so heavily drugged up that it was a breeze to fight through their nastiness. Their lack of readiness for unexpected intruders or a raid confirmed Metrix was nothing but a ploy to distract. There was also a possibility that Vanderwill was yet again betraying his new partners, while strategically leveraging my agency and me to clear the way for his business revival and comeback. No matter what his plan was, I didn't want to take the chance. Deep down though, I knew there would always be a risk when Vanderwill was in the picture.

~~

With the dawn of a new morning, it's believed that fresh opportunities emerge, especially with a positive mindset. Given I was finally seeing my sons today, I was definitely positive. But it seemed mother nature didn't get the memo. As I was leaving the agency to drive to Joseph's place, I received a letter from none other than Cole Vanderwill. Reading his bold red name cursively printed on the envelope's cover, I could hardly count that as positive. Sure, it was an opportunity — but one that required more planning and a redo of my list of priorities for the time being.

As I read the letter, where Vanderwill boastfully described his plans, a mix of fury, anxiety, and a blinding red haze clouded my vision. The audacity that Vanderwill had to send me, Angel, such a letter, despite his current failure, boggled my mind. The asshole acted as if I should have felt honoured that he addressed the letter directly to me. Gosh, I was ready to snap and break bones. Changing my plans of leaving, I went to the training room to let out some stem and clear my overloaded mind.

After one hour of excruciating running, I was calm enough to kick some ass. Throughout the entire time, Logan, Talon, Xylan, and Matt observed me with strange and cautious looks, baffled by the unfolding events.

Trying to make sense of the situation, Logan interrupted me, "Are you PMS-ing, Phebes? Two hours ago, you were happy like a clam. And now, you're like a furious hyena, ready to breathe fire on anyone who dares cross your path."

"And yet, here you are, still alive and breathing, not burned to a crisp…"

"Ouch! Definitely PMS-ing," Matt butted in with a low whistle.

"My mood swings don't automatically mean I'm PMS-ing, you jackasses. Also, if I were you, I wouldn't risk my luck by joking around with me right now. I'm still upset with all four of you. The reason, in case you're wondering, is the letter I got this morning." I let out with frustration.

"OKAY! Okay, we got it, girl. What was in the letter that brought such a foul mood?"

"In my room now. I'll explain."

"Are you pregnant with Federick's child or what?" Upon reaching my private suite inside the agency, Matt joked. As I turned around, I saw Talon punch Matt's arm, silencing him without causing harm.

Smiling up at Talon as a thank you, I proceeded inside my room. "Matt, if you're done trying to make me puke and have nightmares that would last me a lifetime, you can proceed into my sanctuary. The image you just put in my head is disgusting and wrong on SO many levels." Feigning a gag, I expressed my horror. "Thankfully, the letter was not as bad as your nauseating supposition, and that's saying a lot given it was from Vanderwill. Our suspicion about Vanderwill's plans was correct — Metrix was a diversion or, in his words, '*a minor competition*' we took out for him — and pray tell, how did Federick come into this discussion!" I exclaimed, successfully jumping from one topic to another.

"Awe… Phebes, you guys are on a first-name basis now." Matt teased, completely ignoring my question.

"Since when? Do share the story. We want to know everything," Xylan cooed like a high school girl, ready for the gossip of the century.

"It's none of your business. And don't you think we have more important matters to discuss?"

"Oh, come on, share, don't be such a party-pooper. Look at the glint in Xylan's eyes, the shock in Matt's, and um … nothingness in Talon's eyes."

I looked at what Logan was pointing at, and sure enough, the emotions he described were on their faces — even Talon's nothingness, as Logan had so awkwardly put it.

"Okay, I'll tell you what happened, but that doesn't mean I'm not still mad at you all."

Without hesitation, I told them what had been happening between Federick and me. Even about the kiss, as well as Federick finding out about my sons, and the satisfying moment of kicking him in the groin, resulted in a collective wince from all the men. However, I felt compelled to leave out the part where Federick forcefully shoved me against his wall, bruising my back. I wanted the man to survive the night, after all.

"Oh, look how she blushes when she talks about the kissing part." Matt teased.

"Did you like it?" Xylan asked with genuine curiosity.

"Did you want more? How was it?" Compiling on Xylan's question, Matt probed.

"Explain. We want more details. Well, I don't know about Talon, but the three of us sure want all the gory details," Logan interrupted Xylan's and Matt's gush.

"You finally got your kiss," Xylan singsung.

Oddly enough, I was expecting a much more mature behaviour from them, but alas, those assholes started cackling all at once. Worst of all was their stupid questions and comments. I swear, sometimes I honestly didn't know why we were still best friends.

"Girls, if you're done, I'd like to take a shower before picking my kids from Joseph's. I'm not telling you more than I already have. It's gross." Pulling a disgusted face, I voiced out. Leaving the room, I got away from their girly behaviours. Alas, not so much from their teasing.

"Oh, she's so going to get laid."

"She's eager to meet her Federick again ... look how fast she's getting ready to leave."

Then I heard three people getting smacked on their heads, and it was music to my ears. I knew it was Talon slapping Logan, Xylan, and Matt. Talon didn't like these types of conversation when it involved me, and I understood it. Along with being my best friend and close to me, like the other assholes I have as best friends, Talon was also my right-hand man. My safety in terms of professionalism was part of his responsibility.

"Weight your next word wisely, boys. You're still not on my good side, and your unwanted remarks aren't helping your case." Slamming the bathroom door in their faces, I warned them.

I realised I didn't get the chance to show them the letter, even though it was our original purpose for coming here. However, despite Federick's absence, he still distracted me and divert the conversation. However, it doesn't take a genius to realise that my best friends intentionally changed the topic of conversation. They were well aware talking about Federick Archer always riled me up to where I stop thinking about anything or anyone else but him.

CHAPTER 17
DEALING WITH MR ARCHER

PHOEBE

Within an hour, I was on Joseph's doorstep, ready to pick up my sons. But first, I had to inform Joseph and Alicia about Vanderwill before even considering leaving with my kids. The more vigilant we all were of his minions, the safer we would be. I took a deep breath and pushed aside the unsettling feeling that surged within me as I imagined Vanderwill getting closer to discovering my true identity. Afterwards, I knocked on the door twice. As Alicia opened the door, her face lit up with a radiant smile, and she greeted me with a warm hug, inviting me into the house.

"Come in, sweetheart." With warmth, Alicia greeted, almost blinding me with her smile, "I haven't seen you in so long." She stated in her usual motherly tone.

"Hi, Alicia. Sorry, I've been busy with work lately." Hugging her back, I relaxed. "I appreciate you looking after the boys while I was away. I hope they haven't been too much trouble for you guys."

"Oh, don't worry, sweetheart," dismissing my statement with a gentle wave of her hand, "These kids are absolute angels. You've raised them well despite your situation," Alicia finished supportively.

"Thanks, Alicia. But you know it wouldn't be possible without you guys and your support." Hugging Alicia once more, I showed my appreciation.

"Thanks, sweetheart, but it's no biggie. Raising you and these boys has been a pleasure —" Alicia hugged me back and then whispered in my ear,

"Despite your secretive spy life."

Not giving me a chance to speak, she grabbed my hand. "Now, let's go to the living room. Joseph has been waiting to have a word with you."

Nodding my head, I quietly followed her to where Wyatt, Teo, and Joseph were watching movies and eating snacks. Greeting all of them with a soft peck on the cheeks, I informed my sons we will leave after I have a talk with their grandfather. Joseph and I then headed to his in-house office.

"So Phebes, the club? Was it a distraction?" Joseph wasted no time and immediately bombarded me with questions as soon as I closed the office door. Not surprised by his impatience and curiosity, I once again noticed how similar our behaviour was.

"Obviously, it was. Years might have gone by, but Vanderwill's trickery manners will never die. Thankfully, Logan's quick thinking saved the day. He identified a probable move that Vanderwill might look to make, which enabled me to take safety actions and be a roadblock to Vanderwill's plan. Otherwise, help me, Lord. I would have torn everything apart." I earnestly exclaimed in an aggravated tone.

"Okay, calm down, my angry tigress. How you are so certain Metrix was a diversion?" Joseph questioned but instantly toned down his musing intonation at the sight of my sharp piercing glare.

"That's how!" Throwing the letter I had received directly from dear Cole Vanderwill on the table, the pitch of my voice increased another notch. As I took a deep breath, I silently watched Joseph as he read the letter out loud, amplifying the reality and undeniable nature of its contents.

'To My Beloved Angel,

It appears you've not only grown more stunning over the years but also remarkably astute. Perhaps even wise, though, only time will reveal the extent of your wisdom, sweetheart.

I regretfully must acknowledge I may have underestimated you, presuming you wouldn't discern Metrix was merely a diversion. Considering your obsession with me, it didn't take a genius to devise a plan to divert your attention away from home and those two brats you call sons. And fear not, my love; I reciprocate with this feeling of obsessive love.

You might wonder why Metrix? What was my goal? Why am I writing to you now? Well, darling, the answer is quite simple. It's high time I get my hands on those pitiful excuses for children you call 'yours.' Alas, with the flawed information at my disposal, I failed to track them down. And although they were not at the expected location given to me, I assure you, my Angel, I remained undeterred.

This unforeseen turn of events, however, compelled me to resort to tracking their cell phones to discover their secret location, and, in turn, yours. But it seems luck was not on my side. Their signals proved elusive to trace or pinpoint. I suspect your enchanting hand played a role in this stroke of misfortune. You've safeguarded those useless brats far more than I ever imagined you would. What happened to hating their guts?

Either way, you've added a thrilling twist to this chase.

And love, worry not, our reunion is imminent. I will soon uncover your exact abode. But until then, keep looking pretty.

Oh, and thank you for eliminating my competition. With Metrix out of the picture, their entire business now rightfully belongs to me.

THE ONE AND ONLY LOVE OF YOUR LIFE,

Forever Yours,

COLE'

Gulping down my seething anger at the audacity of that sick bastard to write me a letter as if he was addressing a lover, I did my best to maintain my composure.

"What are you going to do?" With a calm facade, Joseph's worried voice betrayed his authentic emotions as he asked. The fire burning in the depth of his eyes was vengeful and untameable, impossible to hide.

"At this moment, my utmost priority is ensuring the safety of my sons. I've already arranged for increase protection details around them, as well as an update on the security features on all their techs."

"What happens when they realise the number of bodyguards around them has significantly increased? Because at the rate things are going, it'll happen sooner than later."

Unshaken and unfrazzled by Joseph's dose of reality, I racked my brain for a proper response and solution. "Right now, Joseph, I can't possibly wrap my mind around all of this. I'm taking it one step at a time." I confessed. "My current focus is on finding a valid explanation for my sons' inevitable question about why I sounded panicky when I precipitated their visit here." I anxiously voiced out.

"Although I strongly disagree with this approach and believe you should tell the people you love the whole truth, I will still stand by you and honour your choice, as long as it doesn't cause any harm. If you want to keep your secrets hidden, so be it. But you must stay calm and find more effective strategies to handle the issues arising from Vanderwill's return. I strongly suggest you plan your every move carefully and not play rush like Vanderwill wants you to." With utmost patience, Joseph advised.

"Joseph, I appreciate your support, but your opinion doesn't hold much weight here. I don't want my sons involved in anything that has Cole Vanderwill's mere shadow, just like you don't want your son involved in our world." I retorted with stubbornness.

"You couldn't be more wrong, Phebes. I'm waiting for the day my son will find out the truth."

"Well, this is you, not me. And as far as being patient where Vanderwill is concerned, I can't promise anything. But I sure as hell will try my best."

"Just by promising to be patient with someone like Vanderwill, you're already on the path to success. Now, only time will tell how good you are with it."

"Oh, thanks so much for your vote of confidence and for believing so much in me..." I added with pure sarcasm.

"I'm being serious, Phebes." Giving me a stern glare, Joseph scolded me in a fatherly manner.

"Sorry, Joseph, I know you are. But if I'm to deal with an asshole like Cole Vanderwill and try to keep my patience throughout this entire process, I'm going to need a distraction. There's only so much one person can take. This devil of a man and this operation have been a curse from day one. And I've already lost so much because of him. I don't think I can handle losing more. All I know is I want this situation with him to be over with as soon as possible."

Walking out of the office after making my point, Joseph followed behind, recognising I did not want to continue discussing Vanderwill any longer. "Be careful, Phoebe. Don't let your impatience and need for vengeance cloud your judgment to the point of repeating the same mistake as ten years ago. You have two sons at stake this time. Please put into practice what you've learned throughout the years, and don't let him play you again."

"I know." Turning into the corridor to the living room, I ended the strenuous discussion.

"Boys, bid goodnight to Grandpa and Grandma. We need to leave." Engrossed in my thoughts, I missed the unexpected visitor in the living area, and shouted my order seconds before stepping into the living room.

"Grandpa? Grandma? – What the hell does this mean, Phoebe!?" Eyes bulging out of its socket, and a confused expression decorating his face, Federick Archer demanded in a stentorian freezing tone.

Frozen for a beat, I wished the earth would open and swallow me alive. But I was still here, boring into Federick's frigid stare. Not wanting a repeat of what happened at my house, I did my best to shake off the web of shock. "What do you think it means?" I sarcastically mouthed back.

"Is there any other way for me to interpret this, other than you lying to me all along? … Making me believe my mother was being cheated on and that you and my dad had two kids together. — How could you do this to me? I admit I'm rude and an asshole to you, but going to this extent for payback is pure cruelty."

Aware that Federick would continue blabbering nonsense until I felt guilty, I tried tuning him out. Alas, Vanderwill's letter already got me worked up, and Federick was just adding fuel to the fire.

"Hey there, mister, better hold on! When have I lied to you? And you better use your nut-size of a brain to think twice before accusing me of anything else. It's you who accused me of being a home wrecker, a whore, worse than the bitches you sleep around with. Accusing me of being responsible for your dad cheating on your mother. Did I say something? NO, I didn't! — But wait, let me cut your upcoming response because just last Thursday, you accused me of purposefully having an illegitimate family with your father. Calling me a gold-digger who's after your father's money and using my OWN children for such despicable work. But this wasn't the only unbelievable part of what you've been accusing me of. You had up the game with God knows what kind of expectation you had from me when I didn't even ask you to. Oh, let's not forget how you made MY kids your fucking stepbrothers, and I still kept my mouth shut — so tell me, when the fuck did I lie to you?"

From the corner of my eye, I caught sight of Alicia's shocked expression on the right, while my kids and Joseph's amused faces were on the other side of the room. Taking a much-deserving deep breath, I ended my beautiful recap in a frustrated tone, glad I could show Alicia who his son really was.

"You denied none of it either." Federick quickly added in a composed tone. However, the guilty look in his eyes betrayed him.

"I didn't feel the need to explain myself to you. You wished to throw crazy accusations at me, and misunderstand me like the rest, so be it. I gave you a damn choice! Last time I checked, you are not a baby who still needed to be spoon-fed or an adult incapable of making their own decision. Cause, guess what, even my kids at their young age are responsible enough to make their own damn decision when needed."

"Now, don't be trying to make it all my fault! And how the fuck are my parents, your kids' grandparents? What are you, some long-lost family? — Or better yet, the sister I never knew I had; because this would certainly explain why you haven't fallen for my charm yet."

"Really, Federick! You had to bring up your imaginary charm in this discussion. You're so God damn full of yourself!"

"Babe, you and I both know there is nothing imaginary about my charm. Now, explain the situation you're in."

Okay, so seconds ago, he was mad, and now he had an amused look. Tell me how this didn't confirm my theory of him having a split personality.

Blankly staring at Federick in disbelief as the need to smack him again rose within me, an awesome idea struck me. That idea was not something I would have carried out at this age, as Phoebe Smith. But damn it, Federick was so annoying and, well, deserved it, especially for the unwarranted kiss.

Leisurely walking towards Federick, I drew my lips close to his ear while maintaining some distance between us. Ignoring the people in the room, I leaned in and exhaled warm breath against the side of his neck, my voice dripping with seduction as I softly whispered, "You know why I'm in such a bad… situation, Federick?" As I stretched out my words, I sensually whispered his name, savouring each syllable as my breath caressed his skin.

As I sensed a shiver run through him, a smirk formed on my face. He silently shook his head *'No,'* and I instinctively took a step back, creating more distance between us. "It's because a long time ago, your sweet father had a secret affair. His infidelity brought into the world the most jaw-dropping, gorgeous, kind-hearted, and hot Greek God ever. Also known as my ex-husband and your elder stepbrother. Unfortunately for me, he died a tragic death when I was pregnant with my second child. In other words, I'm your sister-in-law… OOPS! …" I sarcastically finished.

As my breath grazed his face, I watched Federick devour the load of lies I fed him. Gulping without saying much, the perplexing change of emotion in his eyes and expression did all the talking. Out of the corner of my eyes, I caught sight of everyone's faces. It was a mix of shock and suppressed laughter. What got me though, was Joseph's face, which screamed, *'Why target poor innocent me?'*. Not wanting to give myself away, I returned my full attention to the stunned rock that had become Federick Archer. Ah, torturing him was music to my heart.

Concluding that Federick was caught off guard and embarrassed by my sudden and unexpected flirtatious behaviour, I turned on my heel to walk away. However, as the obnoxious, stubborn, and daring person he was, he did the one thing I warned him not to do ever again.

'Oh no, he didn't just do it again,' I mentally exclaimed the moment Federick grabbed my arm, abruptly spun me around, and yanked me towards him. My hands landing on his shoulder to catch myself, I smacked into him, causing our bodies to press against each other like hot iron on wrinkled cloth. Momentarily dazed and lost in Federick's eyes, I completely forgot about the body of people behind me, looking at us with shock written all over their faces. Thankfully, the small mutter of "I hope she doesn't kick him again" from the background brought me back to reality.

"What did I tell you the last time you did this? One would think you would have learned your lesson by now. Remember Federick, I'm your sister-in-law, so behave, young man!" Bringing back our supposed familial relationship, I saw an odd emotion flash in his eyes, but it was gone as fast as it came — as if it didn't even exist, much less happen.

"I remember and understand clearly what you said, but we need to talk in private."

My God, he totally believed all the crap I fed him. Turned out Federick was far more stupid than I had initially thought. Since it was getting harder for everyone to control their laughter, I nodded and allowed Federick to drag me into the office I came out of minutes ago.

I had barely taken a step into the office before Federick forcefully closed the door, locking me in and pressing me against the wall. Not speaking a word and plainly staring at me, Federick's hot breath touched my skin. His face lingered way too close to mine. In a snap, all my laughter was gone.

CHAPTER 18
RESISTING MR ARCHER

PHOEBE

"**N**ow, Phoebe," Federick began, "You may think I'm the dumbest and stupidest guy on earth. But, sadly for you, I'm not."

"Oh shit, Sherlock! You're not." Sardonically acting astonished, I effectively hide the momentary peak in my nervousness. "Anyone talking to you might believe otherwise."

Federick took a deep breath, trying to remain calm and composed, and not get sucked in a round of battering. "I'll agree that, at first, you fooled me with your sister-in-law bullshit. But clearly, it was just another lie. Now, I want the actual truth!"

"This statement just proved my point of how dumb you are."

"It's quite rude of you to make such a comment when I'm being honest and truthful."

"Oh, sorry, did I offend the poor baby?" I cooed as if I was talking to a four-year-old.

"Are you done yet?" Federick exclaimed with impatience and a stormy glare.

"Fine. But first, tell me what tipped you off. I was sure you believed me." Pouting, I surprised him as well as myself.

Scrutinising me, Federick knew I was steering the conversation in another direction. Still, he smirked and played along. "You and the rest of the family trying to control and contain your laughter. Plus, you're not very good at lying."

"Not true. I'm the best at everything I do!" My stubborn side poking its head, I crossed my arms over my chest and stomped my feet. If pouting surprised both of us, the latter left us utterly stunned. Personally, for me, this action astounded me to the core, as the last time I behaved as such was before Mia died.

"While I find you incredibly cute and sexy in this moment, I need you to stop diverting the conversation and give me some answers. Otherwise…"

"Otherwise, what? Have you already forgotten what happened the last time you tried to tell me what I could and could not do? You were cussing like a high school boy. Don't you get it by now? You can't control or order me around. You'll only end up beaten up and with a bruised ego."

"Phoebe, I remember oh too well what you did the last time. Which is why I'm doing what I'm doing right now. If you haven't noticed yet, look down."

Suspicious at his infamous smirk, I looked down and instantly felt my blood boil at his audacity. Though, instead of my anger consuming me, it was my embarrassment that prevailed, turning my face a shade of crimson, like a beetroot boiled to perfection. Beneath my short summer white dress, Federick's right hand claimed a spot on top of my thigh, gripping my knee and securing my entire leg. As I glanced back and forth between him and his hand on my thigh, I couldn't fathom how I had been oblivious to the warmth of his touch.

"Unless you want me to hurt you again, you better get your filthy hand off my thigh." I successfully ordered out with authority.

"Your threats hold no power here, Phoebe. We have a group of people outside waiting for us. Just answer my questions, and I'll remove my *'filthy'* hand. That would be the end of it — unless … you secretly enjoy it dirty and can't get enough of my touch or attention." Leaning forward, his warm breath tickled my ear. "I'll happily make this desire of yours a reality. Just say the word, and I'll gladly give you more than you could have ever imagined." With an arrogantly suggestive tone, Federick let his phrase hang like mistletoe on Christmas.

"Okay! Remove your hand, and I'll try to answer your questions." I uttered. The warmth of his firm hand against my soft skin, combined with his suggestive words, was affecting my mind, heart, and body in ways incomprehensible to me.

Although I could take Federick down and beat his sorry carcass right then and there, he had made a valid point. Harming him the way I wanted while my sons and his parents were outside would only complicate things and raise more questions between my sons and Federick.

"Why do your kids call my parents their grandparents? How are they related to my family?"

"All I can tell you is that they have no blood relation. Next question, please."

"How is this even an answer, Phoebe?" Federick dared quirk an eyebrow at me.

"I don't know about you, but in my dictionary, this is what an answer looks like."

"It's high time to replace your crappy dictionary, then."

"Will do. Can we go now? I'm tired."

"And why are you so tired? You had a pretty long and free weekend. Better yet, where did you go after you took off the day I dropped by your house?" Federick curiously interrogated.

"Last time I checked, you are neither my father nor my boyfriend, or husband, so stop acting like one. You don't need to know where I was, what I do in my free time, with whom I spent my night with, or anything about my personal life, so piss off."

With a slight tilt of his head, Federick silently motioned for me to re-direct my attention downwards. Without thinking, I glanced down and was flabbergasted at how high up his hand had moved on my inner thigh. Any brusque movement from any of us and his hand would easily touch my private area. Not sure what to do, I compelled myself to stand completely still.

"I suggest you drop the sass, Missy," Federick warned, "Your behaviour has consequence, and I'll enjoy myself giving it to you. I don't, however, promise anything about controlling myself."

Turning bright pink from his sexually suggestive tone and comments, "You wouldn't dare… Your mom, dad, and my kids are outside." As I challenged him, a tense silence filled the air, and I watched closely for his next move.

After a few moments of silence and no response from any of us, I let out a sigh of relief, convinced that Federick was all talk and wouldn't actually follow through with his threat. However, my triumphant smirk, which had confidently proclaimed my victory, disappeared in an instant.

Without warning, Federick's lips crashed into mine, leaving me stunned. A whirlwind of emotions swept over me, leaving me both astonished and oddly pleased, but utterly unable to comprehend it all. Never had I had someone ravage my lips with the ferocity he was, and dang, even my body had stopped cooperating with me. Out of nowhere, it responded to Federick's not-so-gentle attack.

Breaking free from the kiss, Federick's mouth moved from my lips to trace a path down to my chin, neck, and the tender hollow base of my throat. Devouring me with the ferocious hunger of a wild animal, his touch on my skin, with the biting, licking, and kissing, left me panting and consumed by sinful desires. Bold and relentless as always, Federick shamelessly dipped even further down the low V-neck of my dress, savouring the forbidden glimpse of my cleavage that had captivated his attention throughout the night. Federick trapped me against the wall, his hands exploring and teasing my breasts, sending waves of pleasure coursing through me. I couldn't ignore my body's yearning for his touch, and as if he knew, Federick's other hand slid higher and caressed my inner thigh, creating a delicious friction that forced me to bite my lips to stifle any sound.

With my back against the wall, I pulled Federick closer, losing track of time as our kisses grew more fervent, communicating a deep desire without words. The fog of passion completely consumed me, and I surrendered myself to the intensity of the moment. Internally swearing at myself and mostly at Federick, I reminded myself to kill Federick Archer later, after I regain my composure. My body felt like it was on fire, the intense heat seeping out until my legs gave way, causing me to cling onto Federick's neck for support. Taking this as his queue, Federick cupped my ass and lifted me up, so I could wrap my legs around his hip. Little did I know it would be this action that would break the spell I was under.

Feeling his erection pressed against my core, it was like a bucket of ice-cold water got poured over my head, drenching me in the reality of what we were doing against Joseph's office wall. We were acting like hormonal teenagers, making out and hiding from their parents. Although I could not comprehend how I lost my self-control to this point, I recognised what we were doing was utterly wrong. With what little sanity I had left, I forcefully pushed Federick away, swiftly landing on my feet. Federick, on the other hand, was caught off guard and stumbled back, falling on his buttocks — and damn, it felt good to see him down and breathless.

My words escaped me as I gazed down at Federick, unsure of how to react. I needed to catch my heavy breathing and shake the crazy lecherous thoughts running wild inside my mind.

"This is the last time I'm warning you, Federick. Keep your filthy hands and mouth off me. Or I won't be held liable for hurting you."

With my heartbeats racing, I consciously slowed them down to calm my nerves and the frustration brewing inside me. "I am NOT like your daily whore girlfriends for you to play with." My eyes filled with intense fire, I exclaimed with a mixture of bitterness and anger before storming out of the office.

I could not believe that asshole was treating me and seeing me as one of his many one-night stands. I had way more value than this, damn it!

Not wanting to raise questions, I momentarily checked my dress and hair in the corridor mirror before walking into the living room, where we had left everyone.

CHAPTER 19
A FAMILY AFFAIR

FEDERICK

Fed up with waiting for Phoebe to answer my multiple phone calls, I was on my last nerve. Grabbing my car keys instead of throwing my phone at the nearest wall, like I so wanted to, I had only one choice left. I hated it, but the truth needed out, and my confusion needed to be cleared. Driving to my parents' house, I readied myself to confront my dad. The idea of him living a double life left a foul taste in my mouth, and no matter how much the truth might hurt my mom and me, this needed done. I couldn't have my dad's mistress working for me or my company.

The chance to break the news to my mom or interrogate my father without throwing a punch at his face, however, never presented itself. Oh, no. I was way too busy being flabbergasted. As soon as I walked into the living room, I heard Phoebe addressing my parents as her kids' grandparents.

Within minutes, a whirlwind of emotions washed over me. An overwhelming surge of happiness quickly overtook my original state of shock, only to be extinguished by a growing sense of trepidation. Learning that Phoebe and my dad were not romantically involved filled me with a strange feeling of hope. But the reality of her somehow being connected to my family swiftly extinguished any trace of hope that had emerged. For the sake of my sanity, I needed to find the truth.

Glowering at Phoebe, I knew my presence had thrown her off-guard. I could read in her eyes that she regretted saying the word grandparent so freely. Taking advantage of the situation, I threw the wildest accusation at her. Internally, though, I was praying she would prove me wrong. After our kiss, I could no longer deny my attraction towards Phoebe — trust me, I tried for years.

However, when Phoebe revealed she was secretly my sister-in-law, the wife, or better yet, ex-wife of my supposedly 'Greek God' of a dead brother, it shook me. That revelation upset me to the core, and without thinking twice, I believed her. How could I not in that moment? The token of their love — as Phoebe put it — was standing in the same room as me. Part of me was also jealous of this 'Greek God' brother of mine because he had the courage to do something I never will. He not only dated Phoebe exclusively for over a month, but he also fully committed to her, married her, and built a wonderful family.

Amidst our argument, Phoebe unexpectedly closed the distance between us, her warm breath whispering against my earlobe, and her body heat merging with mine. Astounded doesn't even begin to describe how I felt. I stood there, speechless and in awe. At that moment, I forgot all about how she's connected to my family or who was around us. Holding her gaze captive, I searched for the truth in its depth. It was then that I caught on the glimmer of laughter in her eyes. Throwing a quick, surreptitious glance at everyone else before focusing on Phoebe's face again, I understood Phoebe was taunting me. For her, this whole situation was a joke.

Aware I might regret it later, I tightly gripped Phoebe's departing hand and yanked her towards me, leaving no room for her to escape. Given our curious audience, and this being my mom's house, I knew Phoebe couldn't physically harm me. As such, I took full advantage of the situation and dragged her into my father's office.

As soon as we entered the office, I pushed Phoebe firmly against the wall. For some weird reason, being close to her felt essential to me. As I locked the door behind Phoebe, the sound of the latch clicking echoed through the room. I leaned against the wall, positioning my arm beside her head, effectively trapping her. Our faces were inches apart and I could feel the heat radiating from her as our breaths mingled in the air. All I wanted was to pounce on her and give into my animalistic hunger. With a deep, internal breath, I reminded myself of the real reason I dragged Phoebe here. I needed to fully investigate this matter and get the truth out of her.

As Phoebe sassily retorted back, I couldn't help but be captivated by her luscious, deep red lips. It was, with no doubt, perfect as the rest of her. The way she looked in her short white summer dress was enough to drive any man crazy. The dangerously low V-neck of her dress highlighted not only her cleavage but also accentuated her gorgeous figure, creating a unique blend of cuteness and sexiness only she could effortlessly pull off.

I couldn't help but appreciate Phoebe's beauty. Practically ogling her, my eyes roamed over her breasts, then down her athletic legs that were a perfect match for her curves. Itching to have my way with Phoebe, I had to fight off the urge to wrap those legs around me and have them open only for me. Thankfully, feeling the velvety texture of her soft and warm upper thigh satisfied my sick, arising desire.

But just when I thought I had my emotions under control, Phoebe blushed, her cheeks turning a delicate shade of pink. Seeing her like this for the very first time, I swore under my breath. It was the cutest thing I've ever seen in my life. Her every action and reaction to my touches and words filled me with a warmth I haven't felt in years. Craving that inner warmth and the sensation of her skin against mine, I was more than happy to ride my hand closer to her womanhood when she refused to answer me.

Unaware of my inner turmoil and demons I was fighting to keep control over my body, my desire, and my actions, Phoebe had to be her stubborn self and challenge me. Locked in her daring gaze, I felt the box that was restraining my composure and animalistic desire shatter.

Pouncing on Phoebe like a hungry lion, I indulged in the feel of her lips and skin against mine. I knew what I was doing was perverse and wrong, but I just couldn't get enough of Phoebe. The way she tasted, felt, smelled, purred, and reacted to my kisses and touches was intoxicating. And despite her many denials of being attracted to me, her actions and hips were saying otherwise. It was criminal how she was moving against me.

Addicted and intoxicated, I wanted more of Phoebe. All reasoning out the window, I tried my shot, and pressed my hard throbbing member against her womanhood. Thankfully, for our future sake, my pursuit for more was short-lived. The moment she felt my desire poking at her, Phoebe's sexual appetite took a backseat, and her senses took over. Regaining power over her actions, she pushed me away from her in one swift motion.

As I sat on the carpeted floor, it crossed my mind that I would have ultimately regretted having sex with Phoebe in this office. For God's sake, this was my dad's office. Not to mention that her kids and my parents were outside, and she had yet to clear my confusion. Yes, I would have enjoyed relishing Phoebe to my heart's desire. But later, I would have felt like an asshole who took advantage of her and the situation.

Honestly, if she were another woman, I wouldn't have thought twice about fucking her in this office, and then asking her to leave or excusing myself. This behaviour, however, would not have been fair to Phoebe. She was not like the other women. I suddenly realised I desired something different with Phoebe — something special.

The notion of deeply and romantically liking Phoebe was both astonishing and disorienting. It felt unreal and like being caught in a whirlwind of conflicting emotions. Relationships and I didn't flow together. Much less emotions around romance. I had to be wrong. Not only was she a mother of two, but a complete mystery to me. Heck, I didn't even know if she was already in a relationship, or if the father of the boys played a significant role in her life. Or worst, what if she was married to someone?

As I pictured Phoebe in my mind, her perfect curves came to life, and I could almost feel her softness between my fingers. The probability of her still being single seemed impossibly low. Yet, I couldn't stop my attraction towards her. Even after I reminded myself that she was the causation of my cluelessness and headaches. That she was eerie, distant, private, surreptitious, mysterious, and fiery. Then again, as I just discovered, she was also surprisingly motherly, warm, and loving. Based on the brief interaction I witnessed between her kids and her, I could picture Phoebe hating and bashing someone to near death if they as much as say the wrong thing about her sons, let alone touch a hair on their heads.

Phoebe Smith was a big question mark.

***

PHOEBE P.O.V

"**J**oseph, I gotta go. Don't worry about anything, I'll keep you updated. Teo, Wyatt, go get your things.". Bidding my farewells as quickly as possible before Mr Annoying could join us, I called out to Alicia, who was in the kitchen. "Alicia, bye, we are leaving."

"Where are you off to, young lady?" Alicia asked, stepping out of the kitchen and drying her hands with a small towel. "You only got here minutes ago. Come on, stay longer. You've been a ghost for so long, and we've missed you."

Alicia's face displayed a blend of seriousness, daring me to disobey or ditch her, and a loving, tender expression that conveyed how much she missed me. Having seen that face for the better part of my life, I knew better than to mess with this motherly side of Alicia.

It was during moments like these that I questioned why I allowed Alicia to exercise so much authority over me and my life. But then I remembered how she had always been there for me when no one else was, not to mention being the mother I never had.

133

"Yeah, Mom, can we stay? Pretty please." Teo pressed, his brown eyes opened wide as a puppy, knowing damn well I was a sucker for it.

Exhaling a caving breath, I began considering the idea when, from the corner of my eyes, I noticed the devil in question. Standing by the living room entrance, Federick smirked at me. And that was the end. I was more than determined to get the heck out of there.

Stealthily stealing glances at the unwanted person, "Look, Alicia, I wanna stay for your sake, but I really can't. Sorry, Teo, maybe next time," Attempting to make the family understand my situation without letting them on the raging tension between Federick and me, I explained with patience and *'regret.'*

However, Mother Nature clearly wasn't on my side. The moment Alicia marked the reason behind my hesitation; she did the opposite of what I expected. She showed no sign of compassion and narrowly examined Federick and me. Reading her like an open book, I realised she was going to oblige me to stay, despite what I had to say. My observations led me to the unmistakable expression in her eyes. It silently screamed her knowledge of a problem between Federick and me, as well as the note of her having something important to say, along with an imminent scolding. I've lived with this woman for years now, and I was no fool to ignore that specific glint. As such, I mentally prepared myself.

"When was the last time you stayed over?" Alicia inquired with seriousness.

"Maybe a couple of months ago?" With a low voice, I answered and bared myself for the inevitable.

"Indeed. So, whatever you have can wait for one night. Right, Phebes?"

Knowing this couldn't be all, I swiftly nodded my head like an obedient child.

"Care to explain why you're contorting your face in such an odd way?" Crossing her arms in front of her chest like a colonel would while scrutinising their army of soldiers, Alicia gave me a funny look.

Instantly avoiding her deep brown motherly eyes, "I don't know what you're talking about … My face is absolutely fine."

"What did you do?" Stretching out her word, Alicia's *'know-it-all'* nature intimidated me more than I would have liked to admit.

"Nothing!" Stretching out my simple answer as well, I hoped to have made my point.

"Then why are you narrowing your eyes at me, just like you did when you were a teenager? It's that infamous look that screams 'I'm getting ready to get scolded because I've done something wrong'."

"Well, I did nothing bad this time!" I exclaimed hastily and with a sharp tone, causing eyebrows to quirk with curiosity. Except for Federick, obviously. He was too busy mischievously smirking at me.

Ignoring everyone's curious expression, I took a mental breath and attempted to explain to Alicia that I was preparing myself for her impending scolding, even though I wasn't entirely sure what I had done wrong.

In slight disbelief, she shook her head gently and let out a small laugh, instantly calming my nerves. "I swear, Phebes," Alicia remarked, "Your talent for reading everyone so well that you can predict their actions can sometimes get annoying."

"Not everyone." Interrupting Alicia, I clarified.

Alicia bounded over to my side in a few swift strides, pulled on my ears as if I were a mischievous child caught red-handed stealing cookies. I swear, moments like these were a reminder of the blessings that came from not knowing my real mother. I could imagine the havoc someone like this would have caused in my already hectic life.

"Did I give you permission to interrupt me, young lady?"

"No, sorry… I won't do it again. Alicia, it hurts…" Holding onto her hand, I spelled out with a hint of pain.

"Mom, stop! You are hurting her." Federick intruded, propelling all of us to turn our undivided attention on him.

Wide-eyed and bewildered, I watched as Federick, of all people, stepped up to defend me while Alicia was in full-on mother mode. The gravity of interrupting her was palpable. That's just how serious it was. His move was equivalent to him willingly taking a bullet for me. And given his newfound tendency to hurt or be rough with me, this action astonished me.

"You, young man, are knee deep in the same mess as her." Alicia scolded, her voice stern. "Both of your earlier behaviour in front of my grandchildren were unacceptable. Looks like you're bringing your ass here, too."

"Yes, mom." Nodding his head, Federick silently stood on the other side of Alicia.

If Alicia's fingers weren't trapping my poor ear — or better yet, if I wasn't under this woman's wrath — I would have burst out laughing, just like Joseph and my kids were.

If my poor ear wasn't trapped between Alicia's fingers or, better yet, if I wasn't under this woman's wrath, I would have been laughing my ass off, just like Joseph and my kids were. Watching *'The Great Federick Ashton Archer'* being scolded by his mother was undeniably hilarious, and it was a delightful sight to behold.

"Alicia, babe, you're hurting her pretty and innocent face. She's gonna need it to seduce all those guys she goes out with every night." Adding fuel to the fire, Joseph successfully made Alicia's demeanour turn further motherly.

Staring at Joseph with wide eyes, I couldn't believe this was how he was returning the favour of me jokingly accusing him of cheating. "Bring some popcorn while you are at it. You will enjoy the show better!" I stated with the utmost sarcasm.

"You better behave yourself, young lady. This is not how you speak to your father."

"Yes, sorry." I apologetically answered.

I swore to God this adoptive family of mine was sometimes unbelievably overprotective and overly loving. For instance, Alicia or Joseph could be cold, indifferent towards me, or my wild escapades. But then, out of nowhere, they would shower me with an outpouring of love, care, affection, and even parental gestures and speeches. It was like they know when I'm about to endanger myself beyond the usual. Thank God, though, that Joseph was laxer than Alicia. From the very first day he took me in, I could see in his eyes that he saw me as his cherished little princess, incapable of doing any wrong.

"Much better. Now, tell me what this thing is between you—"

"Wait!" Federick loudly interrupted, his words hanging in the air as everyone turned to look at him. "When did Phoebe Smith become the daughter of Joseph Archer? And what is this shit about her seducing and going out with several men every night!?". The confusion and displeasure oozing off of him, Federick demanded, his glare frigidly stormy.

✳✳✳

FEDERICK P.O.V

The sound of my mom's voice filled the room as she tried to convince Phoebe to stay the night, leaving me feeling both puzzled and curious by Phoebe's unusual responses and reaction. The woman, who continuously fights me and doesn't listen to a word I say, was calmly taking my mom's scolding. There wasn't one sarcastic or arrogant retort. Phoebe was actually listening to someone with full attention. Watching the strange scene with my mouth nearly agape, I felt like I was in a drama show. Focusing intently on them, my mind was consumed with questions about what was unfolding and the true identity of Phoebe.

Oddly enough, as soon as my mom began tugging at Phoebe's ears for her misconduct, my inquiries suddenly faded into the background. Defensiveness, protectiveness, and possessiveness surged within me, overriding my previous emotions. Watching Phoebe's ears turn increasingly red, my self-restraint evaporated, and I couldn't resist confronting my mother, despite her intimidating *'do-not-piss-me-off'* expression. However, siding with Phoebe came with consequences. My mom, as scary as ever, treated me to the same punishment unless I kept mostly silent.

I silently observed and listened as asked at first, but it only made me more flummoxed. What made it even worse was the bitter truth that Phoebe was constantly seducing and dating different guys daily. Who would have guessed that under her innocent façade hid someone who dated several men at the same time? Bewildered, irritated, and angry that more than a handful of men had had their hands on her, while I kept getting denied, I was at a complete loss. But hey, at least I now knew Phoebe was not currently married.

Blatantly ignoring my mom's orders and interrupting them on several counts, I tried to clear my confusion. But despite my efforts, I got nowhere. Their discussions were baseless and senseless. Not only had my mom mentioned my dad as Phoebe's father, but had also been acting incredibly motherly toward her, as if she had known Phoebe for her whole life. Gawking at them like an idiot, the only plausible explanation was that my father cheated on my mom, resulting in Phoebe's birth, and they had been covertly caring for her as if nothing had happened.

Feeling repulsed by the thought and weighed down by the prospect of Phoebe potentially being my half-sister, a wave of nausea threatened to overwhelm me. My gaze bore into them, silently pleading with whatever higher power might be listening that my suspicion was nothing more than a misguided notion. The mere idea of being linked to Phoebe in such a manner left me reeling, uncertain of how I could possibly come to terms with such a revelation.

CHAPTER 20
ALICIA RULE

PHOEBE

Alicia's icy glare fixed on Federick, she reprimanded to Joseph, "Your son should really learn to respect others more and not interrupt when he's not being spoken to."

"I doubt he's capable of behaving in a manner that doesn't align with his usual annoying self. Prying into people's personal life, even when it's none of his business, has become his second nature by now—OUCH!" I screeched mid-sentence. "Alicia, it hurts." Holding onto my ear, I pleaded with my eyes, "It's not my fault your son is beyond infuriating and is always riling me up."

"As funny as the bickering between you two are, there are lines you two should stop trying to cross." Finally, leaving my ear alone, Alicia stood in front of us.

"If you two can stop being rude and let me finish, I'd appreciate it. Now, Miss Phoebe Ziva Smith, care to explain the reasoning behind your nightly escapades of seducing different men."

Casting a quick, furious glance at Joseph behind Alicia, I silently swore to myself that I would get him back for this low trick. Returning my attention to Alicia, I instinctively rubbed the nape of my neck, my anxiety level rising to a higher degree.

"You're making me nervous. You know that, right?" Intimidated by her stern, motherly side, I muttered with a hint of timidity and nervousness.

"Do I look like I care?" She spat, her voice dripping with indifference, "You better spill the truth, young lady, or I'll ground you. How does being sent to your room for the rest of the night sound? It'll be no going out for the entire week except to work at Archer & Associate."

Staring at Alicia in disbelief, it was impossible to ignore the unwavering seriousness in her expression. However, I also needed to do my job as Angel. This was my priority over everything.

"No fair, Alicia. It's all a lie. Joseph was just getting back at me for the cheating joke — I've been slaving away the whole week with barely any time for myself, much less time to lose on different men every day." Feeling like a teenager again, I passionately defended myself.

"You make a fair point, but if my memory serves me right, I said nights, not days. Did I not?"

As I scanned the room, I observed nods of confirmation from everyone except Federick, who glared at me with eyes that demanded an explanation. Oh, those little shits! They were having too much fun seeing me in this predicament.

"It's just a vocabulary mistake, Alicia. You know how I blabber when I'm nervous." I explained as casually as possible.

"I may not be your real mother, Phoebe, but I'm still your mom. And you're still under my full responsibility. So, go on, tell me with whom you've been spending your nights. Remember, you have a lot at stake here."

"But… my sons are here." I tried my luck again. At this point, I wasn't sure if Alicia was being genuinely serious or pulling my leg and giving me such a hard time because she missed me.

"Oh, come on, Phebes! Who are you trying to fool? Everyone in this room, except my son, knows you speak with no filter around your boys. I'm they know how flirtatious and mischievous you are. Heck, they might even know all the gory details of your sexual life."

"Thank God, not every single detail…" Wyatt voiced out with relief.

"Fine! But not because I'm intimidated by you, but because I don't like being punished or treated like a teenager. I'm 26, for God's sake, not 16. Heck, even at 16, I didn't get scolded for flirting and seducing over a handful of men every week."

"You've flirted with so many guys in a single week. Even I haven't dated so many women in a week. Where did you even meet up with so many guys?" Federick expressed in amazement. However, there was also a hint of discountenance in his tone, which puzzled me. There was, after all, no reason for him to be upset with me for something this insignificant.

"What!? Did you think I was a nun as a teen? I'll let you know, Mister, my dad owned two companies that had thousands of branches worldwide, and with it came thousands of young and well-built handsome men. These men also had similar friends. And let's not forget my dashingly handsome private tutors. Naturally, I would flirt with all of them. Last time I checked, this is exactly what playgirls do." Prideful of my father, his multi-billion companies, and the life we lived together, I let out a valuable part of my past without forethought.

"Alright, Phoebe—"

"Mom, wait…" His brows furrowed. Federick's confusion was evident. "Phoebe just said her dad owned two companies, yet she works in my company as my Executive Personal Assistant. And this time around, she didn't mention you, Dad, as her father." Focusing his gaze at his dad, "And I know for sure that you, Dad, don't own two companies. So, what the actual fuck is going on here!?"

As the panic of my slip and the possibility of Federick discovering my real identity washed over me, my eyes darted towards Joseph and Alicia, desperately seeking immediate rescue.

"Son, I understand you're puzzled, but remember what I said about interrupting me." Once again, answering my scream for help, Alicia came to my rescue.

"But —"

"But nothing! You want answers. You will get them —" Directing her gaze to me for a brief second, "When the time is right."

As those words escaped her mouth, I realised she subtly suggested I was the *'right time,'* which only added more pressure on me.

"Now, circling back to the main point, Phoebe. Let me remind you that all your immature and impulsive behaviours were tolerated because you were a teen. But now, you are a beautiful young woman, a mother of two teens, and someone who has considerably matured up. So again, I'll ask. Who have you been spending your nights and days with?" Alicia demanded.

Blinking and locking eyes with Alicia, the prevailing thought racing through my mind was how shameful it would be if word got out about how Angel was being spoken to. Then again, aside from the Archers and my closest confidants and friends, nobody dared to speak to me in such a matter, less they had a death wish.

Whether or not Alicia was fully serious, I welcomed her question as a distraction from my slip-up. "Alright! I occasionally go around flirting. But I do not seduce them, as Joseph so delicately put it. Besides, these innocent little flirting won't harm anyone. It's only for fun. Otherwise, my life would be so boring." I finally confessed.

"And with whom have you been spending your nights?" This woman really didn't want to drop the ball on this subject.

"Um… Alicia, do I really need to give you with all these details?"

With eyes speaking volumes, Alicia didn't have to say another word.

"Okay, gosh! It's just Talon, Matt, Logan, and Xylan."

"See, not that hard now, was it?"

"Happy now!!"

"Yes, I am."

Whenever I was around them, my childish side would instinctively appear. So, when Alicia turned around to face Joseph, I mockingly stuck my tongue out at her. However, my mischievousness came to a halt as soon as I laid my eyes on Federick. The dude was literally staring at me like a lovesick puppy and making no attempt to cover his unwelcome ogling.

"Don't tell me she just did something childish behind my back?" Alicia asked her husband and my kids, who had been trying to hide their snickers.

My attention refocused. "Of course, not. They just find this whole situation, and your son's face, funny." I responded way too quickly.

"Right!" With disbelief laced in her voice, Alicia called bullshit on my excuse.

"Wait! How can you guys be so easy-going and happy when Phoebe just admitted she had been sleeping with four fucking guys at the same time?" Interrupting Alicia, Federick yet again, stuck his nose where it didn't belong. Clearly, it was he who needed to be grounded, not dear old me.

"It could be worse, you know. I could be like you and sleep around with God knows how many women every other night before kicking them to the curb. Or better yet, inviting them to your office for a fuck before having them escorted out." I snitched with a hint of annoyance. Given what the tabloids said about him and his ruthless habits, Federick had no right to judge me the way he was.

Icily scowling at me, he let out, "The fuck—"

"This is exactly what I was going to talk about next. Both of you need to watch your tongue and what's coming out of your mouth. If you two don't know, people in the civilised world consider swearing this often as bad manners. And I've raised both of you well enough to have proper etiquette."

"Don't look at me. I have plenty of manners. It's your son who doesn't know how to behave and keep his pants on."

"The grounding offer still stands, Phebes, so you better behave. Don't think you are too old to be punished." Alicia carefully warned.

"But I'm absolutely innocent. Why don't you bash on your prick of a son for once?" Giving Alicia my puppy eyes, I tried to turn the blame on Federick. Besides, he had it coming his way. If it weren't for him, I would have had a great evening.

"Alicia, babe, don't you think you're being too harsh on my little princess? Just look at her innocent face. You can't truly believe she'll intentionally do something wrong. I'm certain it's Federick who's pushing her limits." Joseph, ever my defender, attempted to shield me from his wife's claws. "Besides, we can't fault Phoebe for reacting. You know how she gets whenever she feels pressured, ordered around, controlled, or disrespected. I believe we should give my sweet little girl her space to breathe."

In agreement with Joseph's point, I nodded my head like a cute little thing, showing my support.

"Was I asking for your opinion?" With a pointed look, Alicia asked Joseph.

"NO. But it's my duty as Phoebe's official protector and guardian to come to her rescue."

Alicia flatly stared at Joseph with unspoken tension. A heavy fog settled into the room as their mere gaze spoke volume. It was a language only the two of them could comprehend. Uncomfortable with the stretch of silence, I wanted to intervene and break the palpable tension. Yet, as I observed their exchange, I knew there was more to Alicia's demeanour and Joseph's intervention than met the eye.

"Fine. But if our little girl gets herself in major danger again, I swear, Jo, I will hold you personally liable. And trust me, dear husband, it won't be pretty for you." Alicia reiterated, her tone holding a hint of underlying concern and frustration.

Yes, there was definitely more to the story. Alicia's overbearing protectiveness and relentless inquiries, despite her son being here, hinted at deeper discussions between her and Joseph. It seemed my safety, current troubles, or perhaps even deeper worries were at the heart of their unspoken exchange.

Turning to me, Alicia's tone softened. "I'm sorry if I'm being too bossy or suffocating you in my protective cocoon. But Sweetheart, I only have your best interest at heart. The last time was incredibly difficult for all of us, and the thought of it all happening again… it's just too much to bear. It'll crush us." Sensing the pure sincerity, love and fear in Alicia's words, my respect for her deepened even further.

"Don't worry, Alicia. When I accepted you as my mother, I gave you all the right to be and act like my mother. I'm glad you are constantly looking out for me. But, Alicia, I'm a big girl now, not that stupid and impulsive 16-year-old."

Stopping for a moment, my gaze involuntarily shifted towards Federick. "That version of me is very much dead. And I have no intention of bringing her back to life."

Rapidly dismissing this unusual lapse of my gaze, I brought a smile onto my face and focused on Alicia. "Regardless of what's coming my way, Alicia, I'm strong enough to endure everything. You, of all people, should know I can never be in any *'major danger'*. I'm far too good for that." Attempting to relieve her, I allied myself with jokes and funny comments.

"I'm aware of how strong you are, young lady. But as a mother, I'm almost always worried about you. Especially right now, with your situation, and all the pressure and demands it's bringing with it. I fear you will finally completely break down, and we won't be able to bring you back."

"Ali, I will be—"

"No, listen, Phebes. I have this bad feeling in the pit of my stomach. It's screaming for me to lock you up, until this whole situation is over with, and all danger is far gone. But I know I can't do that to you. You are Phoebe Ziva Smith, after all, just as stubborn as your father."

"Thanks, Ali; this is the best compliment you could give me." Pressing my lips against her cheek, I attempted to comfort her and convey my gratitude. I was grateful she reminded me of how much of my father I still was. Out of any days, I needed that reminder now.

Then again, it was moments like these that ignited within me the flicker of yearning to know who my biological mother was. To know if she would exude more, similar, or perhaps less, love and compassion than Alicia. Despite this curiosity, I couldn't fathom my life without Alicia and Joseph. They had been an immense blessing, providing unwavering support, particularly in the aftermath of my father's passing.

Trying hard to stifle his laugh, "Wow, Mom…" Teo chimed in, "Grandma really scolded you like a little brat. If I wasn't so surprised right now, I'd be rolling on the floor laughing." Teo jested soon after I let go of Alicia.

"Agreed with you, bro. It was too damn funny. I never want to be in your place, Mom." Turning to his grandma, "No offense, Grandma, but I never want my mom to become like you. She's perfect just the way she is, even without filters." High fiving his brother, Wyatt pitched in his unnecessary comment.

"OKAY! Before I completely lose the little sanity, I have left. What the fuck is going on here!?"

"Language, young man. I can punish you, too. I won't care how *'Great'* you are."

"You totally should, Alicia. And if you ask me, at least one day without sex will be a big enough punishment for him."

"I'm not a sex addict, Phoebe! Stop thinking so low of me when you barely know the real me," Federick defended himself.

"Oh really, you could have fooled me. Oh, wait! Did you forget you are talking to your Executive PA? The person who takes care of everything for you, even your daily fuck. How is this not knowing the real you?" Rolling my eyes at Federick's defence, "*'Not a sex addict,'* my ass." I mimicked with sarcasm, totally calling his bullshit.

"You only know what I portray myself as, and what I want people to see and think of me. You don't know shit about who I truly am."

"Oh please, don't play the *'I'm so mysterious and complex'* card with me. It may work with your several girlfriends, but I have no interest in knowing more of your annoying self."

"Alright, kids, enough is enough." In a reasonably fierce tone, Joseph interjected. "As amusing as it is to watch you two bicker like a married couple, we've all had our fill for tonight. Especially after listening to Phoebe bitch about you over these past few days, every time your name came up in conversation. If you guys want to keep at it, go elsewhere or wait until you are out of here to do so."

"Come on, Joseph, look at me. How could an angel like me be a bitch?" I proclaimed with a smile. Recognising the underlying meaning of my sentence, Joseph and Alicia gave me a disbelieving grin but said nothing.

CHAPTER 21
TEAMMATES

PHOEBE

"**A**licia, I really need to get home now. I'm starving, and still need to cook. Plus, I have those extra arrangements to make for tomorrow and the days to come."

"If you stay the night, I'll make one of your favourite dishes. Come on, Phebes, I've missed you." Almost begging, Alicia tried to bribe me with food. And God, it was working.

I was strongly considering her offer, especially since I, too, missed spending time with them. But one quick glance at Federick's smirking face reminded me why I wanted the hell out of there. "I really wish I could, Ali, but I can't. I'm sorry."

Not wanting to be questioned any longer and ready to leave, I announced my decision.

Ring *Ring* *Ring*

My cell phone rang, interrupting Alicia before she could dissuade me. Without hesitation, I pulled it out of my pocket. Glancing down at Talon's face flashing on my screen, a smile immediately crept up on my face.

"Who brought this radiant smile to your face?" Alicia curiously inquired.

"Talon." I dismissively revealed as I made my way to the couch and answered his call.

"What do you want, Talon?"

Noticing Alicia softly asked, "What's wrong?" from my peripheral vision, I placed Talon on a brief hold.

"I'm supposedly angry at Talon, so he would learn not to do whatever Xylan ask of him."

"Oh… Go on, then. The rest of us will hang around and try not to eavesdrop."

"Yeah, right…" Stretching my words while giving Alicia a look of disbelief, "Like that's ever going to happen. But I'll take my chances. Now, out, all of you… And Ali, since Talon will take all my time, I'll stay for dinner. Please call me when dinner is ready."

Aware Alicia and the rest would never leave me alone, I turned my back on them. "So, where were we, Talon?" Faking a stentorian tone, I continued my task of making Talon's life miserable. "Oh, yeah, right… You and your hundred faults." Hoping Federick would go away, I focused on Talon and our conversation.

"Go on, tell me what you want."

"Suck it up, big boy." Not having his apologies, I stood my ground.

"Well, you deserve it."

"When did you ever see me displaying emotions, Tal?" Quirking an eyebrow at Talon's accusation of me giving into my emotions, I dismissed his allegation that his actions had hurt me.

"Not taking the chance." I yet again brushed off his plea.

"What lengths would you go to gain my forgiveness?" Playing Talon like a fiddle, and maintaining my serious tone, I finally asked with a smile.

"Phebes, dinner is ready. Stop grinning like a high school girl with a crush and end that phone call before I do it for you." Just as Talon was about to fall to his knees and beg for my forgiveness, Alicia's voice echoed through the dining room entrance as she shouted.

"Okay, Mom. Coming." I instinctively answered, knowing full well my perfect opportunity was gone.

With a smile, Alicia gently shook her head at me before walking back into the dining room. Even though I rarely address Alicia and Joseph as 'mom' and 'dad', there were moments where it was instinct. Gratefully for me, not only did they love behaving like my biological parents, but they also loved it whenever I slipped up and called them 'mom' and 'dad.'

"As fun as this conversation was, Talon, I'm still mad at you. You'll need to work harder for my forgiveness." I disconnected with a small laugh before Talon could respond and keep our discussion going.

"So, what are we having?" I inquired the moment I stepped foot into the dining room.

"One of your many favourites; Steak, salad, soup, and mashed potatoes."

"Yummy! Thanks, Alicia." I mumbled with appreciation as I took my seat between my sons.

My lovely dinner, however, was interrupted once more when my phone rang again, breaking the silence. Instantly looking up at me with a cocked eyebrow, Alicia waited to see what I was going to do. Seeing Matt's picture flashing on my phone screen, I had no choice but to respond to it.

"Sorry, Alicia, it's Matt. I got to take it." Mindful of Alicia's strict *'no phone'* policy at the dining table, unless it was for an emergency, I shyly smiled and apologetically announced my decision.

Aiming for the furthest spot in the room, I ignored Alicia and Federick's momentary glare and walked to the window facing the streetlights. While passing by Teo, however, I caught sight of a succulent cut steak on his fork, its aroma wafting through the air, about to be engulfed in the vacuum of his stomach. This was an opportunity I couldn't miss. Swiftly snatching his fork from his hand, I savoured the succulent flavours of the steak before playfully handing Teo an empty fork and giving him a mischievous wink.

"MO-OM! … My poor delicious piece of meat … all gone." Pouting, Teo exclaimed with exaggeration.

"You got only one mother, mister, humour me." Messing with my baby boy's dark hair, I jocularly voiced out.

"Mom. Hair. No. Touching." Teo spelled out, emphasising on each word. Laughing, I tousled it even more before walking to the window to answer Matt's call.

"Yes, Matt, what's up? Why call so late?" I nonchalantly inquired with my best innocent voice.

"Phebes, you better get your ass to the dining table. Your food is getting cold. And I didn't help my sweet wife prepare food for you to waste it." About thirty minutes later, Joseph called out to me, his fatherly tone making it clear I shouldn't take any more chances with them by staying on the phone. Complying, I walked back to the table with a smile plastered on my face.

"You, too, are not forgiven yet, my dearest." I clarified for Matt before ending the call on him.

Getting an eyeful of Wyatt's food as he was about to take a bite out of it, I aimed to snatch his fork as well. I did it to the other child, so might as well do the same to this one, — just to equal out the love and all. Wyatt, however, was smart and aware of my habits and motives.

"Go on, Mom, have it." Handing me his fork with the food I was eyeing, Wyatt totally outsmarted me.

"Thank you for ruining all my fun with your sweetness." Giving Wyatt his empty fork back, I sarcastically exclaimed.

"You're more than welcome, my lady." Faking an exaggerated head bow, Wyatt cracked me up.

'I know I'm sexy… You … you want me badly ….'

Less than ten minutes passed when my phone started blaring this absurd ringtone. Without looking at my phone screen, I knew exactly who it was. The best was, after all, always saved for last.

"Let me guess, Xylan?" Joseph asked with amusement.

"The ringtone itself screams Xylan. Such a sweet boy he is," Alicia added.

"Definitely." Amused at Alicia's picture of Xylan, I lied. Xylan was the most mischievous one between all of us. Yet pretty much all the female population thought he was this sweet and innocent thing.

I got up from my seat, about to make my way to the same window, when Alicia stopped me and asked, "Where do you think you are going?"

"Sorry for ruining your dinner with all these phone calls, Alicia," I apologised and hoped she wouldn't go all motherly on me again. "But I need to take this one too."

"Sit down, answer your call right here, and finish your meal. I don't know why you are supposedly *'angry'* with them all, but solve it. Quick."

"Okay, gosh" Slumping down in my seat and with a tight smile, I took the call.

"Hey, Xylan. Let me guess. You want my forgiveness, too. But guess what? You, too, are not getting it!" I opened in one breath and hoped he would figure from the tightness in my tone that I couldn't speak as freely.

"No. You're the one responsible for all of this." I countered Xylan's attempt to apologise on everyone's behalf.

"As much as the others had their part in it, you were the evil mastermind behind it."

If Xylan thought trying to change my mind with his million excuses would work on me, he had something else coming his way.

"Well, it was an extremely sick joke."

"I nearly had a heart attack, for crying out loud!"

"Don't you dare sweetheart me right now."

"I'm extremely mad at you."

"You are not the most handsome guy ever." Trying to pretend I just called him handsome, Xylan attempted to move me from my *'angry'* state, with his senseless jokes.

"I take my word back then. You're a jerk, not sexy."

"Is Talon and Matt there with you right now?" Hearing inaudible whispers on Xylan's side of the line, I knew all three were ganging up on me.

"Teaming up on me won't work. Tell them that."

"I hate you. You know that, right?" Mustering as much seriousness as I could in that moment, I vocalised.

"I said hate, Xylan, not love."

"You what? WAIT!" He audaciously disconnected the call on me.

"Asshole."

"Phoebe, language!" Alicia exclaimed, bringing me back to the present.

"Sorry, Alicia, but I need to leave right now. They are crashing at my place tonight without being invited."

"It's not like I have many choices but to let you go, Phoebe. But remember to visit us for a much longer time soon. And please, no mobile phone at the dining table next time. You know the rule."

"Got you, Ali. But you know how important these three are. And ignoring them is pretty much not an option unless you want them to crash your place in search of me."

"Yeah, I'm aware of how stupidly protective they are of you."

"Oh, look who's talking. That's like the pot calling the kettle black, Ali." Letting out a small laugh, I mused.

"Whatever, young lady. Just bring them along next time. We really miss them and their sense of humour. Unlike someone here, who is always serious, they are way laxer." Getting back at me with her remark, Alicia smirked in victory.

"Until they earn my forgiveness, Ali, they are not getting invited anywhere. And Ali, I have a great sense of humour. I've just had to learn to be serious most of the time, and it sort of became instinctive to me. I'm not to blame. Try raising two kids at the age I did, and you will understand." With hands on my hips, I stated with attitude.

Rather than giving me a look of pity or showing sympathy, Alicia held my stare. It was clear she was not having it. "Whatever makes you sleep better at night," Alicia added sarcastically.

Not able to come up with a good comeback as swiftly, my face dropped. Smiling triumphantly, Alicia cracked up, releasing the tension around. Acknowledging I lost this one, I dropped my annoyed look and laughed with her.

"Speaking about sleep, would you mind the boys staying the night with you guys?" Regaining my senses, I asked.

"Sure thing. And Phebes, don't be too wild out there tonight."

"Oh, I can't promise this. Logan is going to propose tonight!" With a little jump, I excitedly and giddily exclaimed.

"Really, to whom? That's the first I'm hearing of it." With sheer curiosity and astonishment, Alicia inquired on behalf of everyone.

"I will tell you more later. I gotta leave. Or I'll be entering a vandalised home."

Hugging and kissing my boys, Alicia, and Joseph goodnight, I totally ignored Federick, acting as if he was invisible. Nonetheless, the image of him clenching and unclenching his teeth and fist etched into my mind, no matter how much I tried to ignore it. His frustration was palpable, but I couldn't care less. That guy was, for sure, bipolar.

'Monday was inevitably going to be awkward. No, getting out of this one, dear Phebe,' I mentally stated.

***

FEDERICK P.O.V

My determination to uncover the identities of Logan, Talon, Matt, and Xylan intensified with each passing second. Though I had no right to feel this way, I couldn't shake the desire to put an end to their extracurricular activities with her. The way Phoebe and my parents spoke of them left no doubt in my mind that these four guys were her most serious admirers.

As heartening as it was to see Phoebe so immensely loved by my family, I was also mind-boggled and conflicted. How could my parents so casually accept her involvement with multiple men? If it were me in Phoebe's shoes, I would undoubtedly face a lifetime of punishment and never hear the end. Yet, Miss *"too innocent"* Phoebe Ziva Smith was exempt from such consequences.

Mother Nature clearly had a huge grudge against me. Just when I thought things couldn't get any worse for me, three of Phoebe's lovers called, taking up all her time. Engrossed in her conversation, she didn't even notice me boiling in fury as I watched her laugh, flirt and make jokes for hours on end. Despite being supposedly mad at them, she unashamedly and openly flirted with them. I couldn't understand how any of her conversations with any of them could be seen as her being angry. If anger meant informing them, with a broad smile, that they were not forgiven yet, then I would gladly endure her rage.

Silently brooding with jealousy and possessiveness, I buried the sudden sadness I felt at being ignored by Phoebe. From the moment she received the first phone call from Talon to the last call from Xylan, before rushing home to them, I was a ghost to Phoebe. Heck, I was lucky whenever she spared me a few fleeting glances for the rest of the night.

With the reality that Phoebe was probably on her way to having a foursome, all my questions since I stepped foot inside my parents' home flooded my mind. Nothing made sense, and no one appropriately completed a conversation. It was an utter madhouse.

I was itching to know more about the mysteriousness of Phoebe Ziva Smith. Why did my mom mention Phoebe was in danger and needed to be locked up for her own protection against something or someone? What was with Phoebe mentioning she was too good for anything to happen to her? Who the heck was even trying to harm her, and why?

More importantly, why was Phoebe working for me if she had always been wealthy and her father owned two businesses? Heck, who even was her goddamn father? Because her brief accidental description didn't appropriately fit my dad's profile. Last I checked, I was the sole heir and current successor of his only business.

On top of that, I was still clueless about who the father of her children was. Logically, she must have had them when she was extremely young, and probably with one of the several men she slept with. It would correlate with what my mom said about *'Mistakes.'* However, with my track record of misjudging whenever it came to Phoebe, it would be stupid of me to make the same mistake and simply speculate. I needed to dig deeper — to do my research and have actual physical proof. Then again, it took no genius to figure out that if I questioned my parents, they would be as silent as a mule. As such, another tactic would have to be in play.

Despite the hundreds of questions buzzing in my mind like bees, Phoebe's excited screech about Logan's proposal tonight echoed in my thought. Like a storm, she rushed out, leaving her kids behind at my parents' house. The thought of her being proposed to tonight filled me with a mix of disturbance, perturbation, and anxiety, intensified by the fact that Logan hadn't reached out to seek her forgiveness like the other guys did. No matter how frustrated I was, or how unsure of where my emotions and feelings were, I sure as hell didn't want Phoebe to marry this Logan guy.

Feeling my migraine increasing with each complicated question and scenario, I needed some fresh air to clear my mind. Better yet, I needed to stop thinking for a while. I needed a release from all these tensions and the hard-on I had got from Phoebe earlier.

Ten minutes after Phoebe left, I said my goodbyes to my parents, Wyatt and Teo, before calling up Lucy Braton.

"Where are you?" I demanded with indifference and coldness the instant the other line picked up.

"At home." Her sultry voice muttered.

"Make yourself free. I'll be at your place in 45 minutes." Sharp and precise, I ordered with power.

"Of course, I'll always be free for you." Her annoyingly bitchy voice responded.

Why did I even bother hooking up with her, anyway? — Oh, yeah, she was a great quick fuck with no dignity.

"Don't make me wait or…"

"I'll be ready. You won't regret it." She promised, her eagerness shining through in every word. From my line, I could literally hear her undressing.

"Better not!" I coldly responded, already irritated, but I needed it.

Good thing Lucy could take it wild, hard, deep, and unforgiving. That was the main reason I hadn't discarded her like the others, even though I had heard she had been attempting to intimidate my other potential double-dates. To her despair, though, I was New York City's most desired heartthrob billionaire, known for my influence and power. I always get to fuck whoever I want whenever I want — For the exception of Phoebe Ziva Smith.

CHAPTER 22
MEETING NADIYA

PHOEBE

The weekend flew by at an alarming speed, welcoming Monday with an unwanted swiftness. With no excuse other than my lack of enthusiasm, I had no choice but to drag my ass to Archer & Associate.

Since Cole Vanderwill was my only case for the moment, I was stuck playing the waiting game. I was hoping one of his devious Machiavelli-inspired schemes would whisk me away again, or that my team would make a breakthrough in the case, but no such luck. As such, the next best thing for me was to check on my less-than-reliable assistant and do damage control. And despite how vexing it was to be Federick's executive assistant right now, I had commitments to fulfil and alliances to preserve.

I was already in hot water for vanishing at important meetings. I cared little about what Federick thought, but because I still needed the support of the rest of the shareholders, I needed to make my many extended absences less conspicuous. Their support was a precious well I couldn't drain just because I didn't want to face Federick after this weekend. And with how furiously my team had been tracking Vanderwill, I knew there was an upcoming long *'vacation'* in my future. When that time come, I would need their vote of support, in case Federick pull a fast one on me. As such, I had to use my resources wisely and do everything I could to limit questions and suspicion from arising in my civilian life.

The best thing about today, however, was my meeting with Logan. His decision to fall in love and leave the spy life behind proved highly beneficial. Not only did it fulfil my plan of infiltrating someone I completely trusted with my life in the highest position at Archer & Associate, but he also conveniently helped me cheat agency's policy regarding agents trying to leave before retirement age. Even more exciting, today I finally meet the lucky woman who captured my big bro's heart. I'll get to find out if she's good enough to be Logan's wife and my sister-in-law.

Walking into work, I caught Federick standing by my assistant's desk, talking — or rather, flirting — with her. The expression on Federick's face said it all. His eyes widened in surprise as he caught sight of me. I'd wager he believed I would be too frightened to show my face again so quickly.

'Ha, take that asshole!' I mentally shouted with triumph. Yet another blow to his ego.

With a quick 'hi', I walked past them and locked myself in my office, under the pretence of catching up with work. The last thing I wanted was a full confrontation with Federick in front of people. Although I was still grappling with the events of last week and trying to make sense of them, I was determined not to let Federick Ashton Archer intimidate me. He would not win this. As such, I ignored the lingering, awkward atmosphere and persevered and focused on my work. However, there was no denying the stifling air on our floor; it hung heavy and oppressive. Anyone who made the mistake of walking onto our floor instantly felt as if caught between the pages of an ancient tome, each footfall pressing down with the weight of centuries-old secrets.

By noon, I was more than ready to scurry out of the office for a much-deserving lunch with Logan. Wearing my big-responsible-girl pants on, I paged Federick, informing him of my departure. Skilfully brushing off his thousand questions and putting a full stop to his inquisitive behaviour, I walked out to the outdoor restaurant in the city, a few blocks away from Archer & Associate.

At the restaurant, I beeline for Logan and melted in his brotherly hug. Gosh, I so needed it, and I didn't even know. I wanted to stay in his protective arms for much longer, but I didn't want him to question me, or learn where my mind has been the entire morning. Not giving Logan the time to stare deep into my eyes, I expressed my excitement at meeting his fiancée. However, I disappointedly found out his fiancée would not make it on time. Her boss was determined to squeeze every last minute out of her before her contract expired. Right away, I found myself unimpressed by her, her inability to stand up for herself, and her complete disregard for punctuality. I hadn't even met the lady yet, and she already made a terrible impression on me.

While we waited for our food, I gently clasped Logan's hand. "You realise I'll be scrutinising and judging your future wife? Looking for any single fault I can." A grin plastered on my face, I playfully warned.

With a supportive smile, appreciative I was giving him this chance, Logan placed his other hand on top of mine, "I would expect no less from you." Lightly squeezing my hand, his voice laced with confidence and understanding. "If the situation were reversed, I would do the same, if not worse."

"In that case, let's be clear. I disapprove of her lateness and disregard for my time. She's going to have to be fantastic to end on my good side." With a tint of seriousness, I informed Logan of how it was going to be.

"Oh, don't worry, Phebes, she's great. Besides, it's her boss's fault, not hers."

"Mister, there's no need to already be taking her side on everything." I playfully tsked.

"Whatever." He answered with a cheeky smile.

"What's her name, anyway? I can't believe I don't even know my best friend's fiancée's name. And you call yourself my big brother. What a shame."

"Her name is Nadiya Amatore. And I don't just call myself your big brother, I am one. But Nadiya was my little secret. One which, at the start, wasn't supposed to become a reality."

I smiled at Logan, my eyebrow quirked, "Embellishing her for me, huh… No need to go that far, bro. The glimmer in your eyes, and the way you made her name sound cute, moved her up my scale" Observing Logan's face lit up at the mention of Nadiya, I had to give it to him. The man was genuinely happy.

"Thank you."

"So, does she know anything about your majestic little sister, or did you hide me from her as well?" I jocularly posed, not really expecting that he talked about me.

As he scratched the nape of his head, his nervousness was evident. "Actually, no."

"What does *'actually no'*, means?" I asked, confused. "How much information does she know, and what should I be aware of? I don't need this lunch to be awkward, Logan. My day with Federick has already been strenuous and awkward; I don't need it here as well." At the reality that I barely knew the woman or what she looked like, nervousness washed over me like a tidal wave. I didn't like it one bit.

"Well, I revealed as much truth as I could about my life and the people in it. She deserves all the honesty I can provide."

"Really now." Quirking my eyebrows, I commented with sass.

"Don't worry, Phebes. She doesn't know about your secret life or that you're Angel. However, I spent a lot of time talking about you, Teo, Wyatt, Matt, Talon, Xylan, and pretty much anyone important around us. To where she can now easily pinpoint anyone of you without introduction."

Worry and surprise overtook me at his words. Tilting my head sideways, I stared at him like he was crazy. "As flattering as this is, why on earth would you talk about my sons with her?"

"Interesting story, really."

"Is it now? Do tell." My tone and expression intimidating him, I turned a blind eye to his nervousness.

"Nadiya had this crazy suspicion about our friendship and closeness. Apparently, I'd mentioned you so much that Nadiya assumed I was actually in love with you, not her. Even though I made it abundantly clear to her, I only loved her romantically. But my declaration of love met with deaf ears."

Right then and there, I broke into a fit of laughter. "She thought what!? Oh. My. God. That's hilarious."

"It's funny now. But trusts me, it wasn't back then. You can't imagine how bothersome it was."

"OH, GOD…" Wiping a drop of tear from my eyes, "She got another point from me. How the heck did you manage such absurdity to rise between you two?" Chuckling, another roar of laughter was building up.

"It's not funny! … Will you stop laughing your ass off now?"

"NOPE."

Anyone watching me right now would undoubtedly think I was having a hysteria attack. But I couldn't care less. This situation was too damn funny. Walking to my side, Logan planted his hand over my mouth to shut me up. He was, however, only able to muffle the sounds.

"Okay! Have it your way. I'm going to the bar to get us a drink and check where my fiancée is."

"Don't get us something too strong. We still have to work." As Logan departed, I called out to him and chuckled at his slight head shake, amused by his reaction.

Just moments after Logan left, I felt a faint tapping on my shoulder blade. Startled, I spun around, half-expecting to see Miss Nadiya standing behind me. In front of me, however, was the extremely pissed-off face of someone I had been trying my best to avoid the whole day.

"What the fuck are you doing here, Federick?" I immediately stood up, positioning myself so that his back was facing Logan, and let out a frustrated hiss.

"Well, I should be the one asking you this. Didn't you have something important to do?"

Could I rip this guy's head off his shoulder already?

"Are you following me now?" I demanded as I reminded myself that I couldn't kill Federick just yet.

"Who knows? Maybe I am." Face to face with me, Federick compelled me to look up an inch.

Why in the world did I have to be shorter than that asshole? Better yet, why was I suddenly thinking he looked hot, standing tall above me, his breath gently brushing against my face?

"So stupid, Phoebe! Get a grasp — we are in public, and Logan could be back any minute." I mentally chastised myself.

"Then I would advise you to stop. I have a life to live." I meant to sound tough and clear, but what came out was a low voice.

Annoyed at myself and the tightness in my throat, as well as irked by Federick, I took a step back. Without skipping a beat, Federick grabbed my arm and pulled me towards him, asserting his dominance. Uncaring of onlookers, Federick shamelessly had his way on the goddamn street.

"Will you stop manhandling me, asshole!?"

No response, only an inexplainable stare.

"People could be watching." Frustrated, I added as my last resort, our closeness riling up my nerve.

"You didn't seem to mind who was watching when you were openly flirting with that guy who went to the bar! Who is he? One of your many boyfriends?" Federick glacially snapped, his volume low for only us to comprehend. Momentarily bamboozled, I could feel the heat of his breath as it brushed against my face.

"My God! Don't tell me you, too, think the same thing." Baffled, I responded in a low voice, questioning why I was even bothering to justify myself to this jerk face. He could think whatever he wanted, and I shouldn't care.

"What do you mean, you too?" Confused, Federick inquired.

"I—"

"Phoebe Smith?"

Interrupted by an unrecognisable female voice, I slightly panicked.

Fiercely holding my gaze, Federick's grip on my arm tightened as he noted an alarming expression wash over me. Shifting his death glare to the woman behind me, he seemed to ponder how to get rid of her. Mercifully, he reconsidered his course of action and let go of my arm.

Slowly turning around, "Yes." My words barely escaping my lips, I found myself trapped in a bear hug.

"Who might you be?" Captive between the woman's arms, I cautiously posed.

"My God, I'm sorry!" The woman apologised while still holding onto me, "I should have known you wouldn't recognise me. I'm Nadiya Amatore, Logan's fiancée. I hope he told you this much." Keeping a death grip on my shoulder blades, this girl had no sense of personal space.

"Oh, you are her," I awkwardly stated.

Beaming at me, "In the flesh." Curiously looking between Federick and me, "Is everything alright here?" Nadiya inquired with concern and an edge.

Noting her worried expression, I realised she was a compassionate woman, ready to jump at the chance of helping her friends — or, in my case, the best friend of her lover.

Momentarily turning towards Federick, "Sure, why wouldn't it be?" I stated, dismissing Nadiya's quirking eyebrow and concern-filled eyes.

"We're not done. This discussion will continue." Completely ignoring Nadiya, Federick whispered dangerously close to my ears, so only I could hear. The threat in his words sent shivers down my spine, leaving me momentarily speechless. Without waiting for my response, Federick turned on his heel and left, allowing me to exhale a much-needed breath.

Immediately giving me another death hug, my suspicions about Nadiya purposefully jumping into mine and Federick's conversation proved correct. Given Federick's death grip on me, any observant person like this woman here would think I was in some type of danger. But few of those observant people would do something about it.

With a broad smile and oblivious to what had happened in his absence, Logan approached us. "Glad to see two of my most favourite women are getting acquainted."

"No, thanks to you." Trying hard not to suffocate from Nadiya's hug, I sarcastically stated.

"Nadiya, babe, if you continue to cut her airflow, I won't have a little sister to make fun of anymore." Jesting, Logan let out a chuckle.

Finally letting go, she said, "Oh, sorry. I'm just so excited to finally meet the woman I've been hearing non-stop about."

"So, I just found out," I said with a chuckle, amused by the revelation and reminded of Logan's antics.

"You ladies can stop making fun of me now." Squeezing between Nadiya and me, a playful smirk gracing his features, Logan casually draped his arms over our shoulders as he balanced drinks in both hands.

"Our food is waiting on the table, so why not go enjoy it? Why did you leave our table anyway, Phebes?" Logan turned his full attention toward me, his gaze locking onto mine as he placed me squarely in the spotlight.

"I—um … Went to the restroom." I brushed aside Nadiya's confused and inquisitive gaze and instantly fabricated an excuse. Thankfully, Nadiya didn't call me out on it, sparing me from further scrutiny.

"Okay." Taking a bite of his food, Logan didn't suspect a thing.

"Now, Nadiya, tell me all about yourself! How did you two meet?" With a warm smile and a curious expression, I leaned forward. "And how on earth did you manage to capture my big bro's heart? I was sure that it had foss-ilised."

As we enjoyed some much-needed quality time at the restaurant, laughing and joking, I learned more about Nadiya and the story of her relationship with Logan. Teaming up, Nadiya and I constantly made fun of Logan, exchanging embarrassing personal stories about him, and making him profusely blush. After all, he deserved all the taunting after the secrecy act he pulled on both of us.

Peeking at my silver diamond wristwatch, "We, unfortunately, must leave. We have a meeting, plus I have other affairs to take care of. Still doing damage control." Pouting, I really didn't feel like going back into that hell-hole with Federick Archer as the master torturer.

"Your assistant again, huh." There was no need for Logan to ask; it was evident from the look on their face and his slight *'I'm sorry'* head shake.

"Soon-to-be ex-assistant, Logan. Very soon." I said with hope.

Calling our waiter over, Logan insisted on paying the bill when it was me who invited them for lunch. I had no choice but to comply after he played the 'apology' card for not informing me about Nadiya earlier.

"Nadiya, would you like to join us? It might be advantageous for you to know where your future husband will be spending most of his days." I said with a smile, extending the invitation.

"I would love to, but I don't wanna pry," Nadiya revealed with hesitation.

"Oh, nonsense! Come, I'll give you two a tour of the office."

"Are you sure, Phebes?" Logan asked for reassurance.

"Just come on, both of you." Setting off towards the office, I didn't give them a choice but to follow.

As Logan stepped beside me, I muttered under my breath, "You chose well, bro. Your fiancée is officially on my good side."

He responded with a grateful smile and a squeeze of Nadiya's hand.

~~

Standing a few feet away from my office's threshold, I turned to Nadiya. "Nadiya, would you mind taking a seat in my office while Logan and I head to the conference room for a private interview?"

"No problem." With a warm smile, she reassured us.

"Great, we won't be long."

Instinctively reaching up to Logan, I readjusted his suit and reattached his tie, not thinking twice about it. Logan, too, didn't say a word. But then, midway through, I realised Nadiya might mind me touching her fiancé in what others might see as an intimate manner.

"I hope you don't mind how I'm touching Logan. He's interviewing for an important position, and I want him to look his best for it."

With a bright and sincere smile, "I'm all good."

"If you haven't gathered yet, Nadiya, Phoebe is the ultimate control freak. She treats everyone in our group the same. There's no escaping it." Logan taunted.

"Oh, shut up, you asshole. Let's go." Lightly smacking him on his shoulder, I shot him a playful glare.

Smiling at us in silence, Nadiya's expression conveyed her understanding of the deep bond Logan and I shared.

CHAPTER 23
JOB OPPORTUNITIES

PHOEBE

With the conference room securely locked, Logan and I found our seats, preparing ourselves for the meeting with Danny. If Logan passes this inquiry-based interview, he will replace Danny by tomorrow.

"Logan, as you know, in Federick's eyes, he's the sole owner of this company, and I'm only the executive assistant with special clearance that he's yet to fully understand. Until I decide otherwise, the truth about me owning half of this company as a silent partner is to remain unknown to him."

"I'm aware, and that's fair." Matching my professionalism, Logan responded, the curiosity to see where I was bringing this conversation shining in his eyes.

"What you might not be au courant of is that Danny has been covertly representing me for over three years. To everyone, including Federick, Danny is one of our major shareholders, and a partner of Archer & Associates. For me, however, his key role has been to make sure Federick never learns about the ownership anomaly, and to challenge Federick when needed." I revealed a part of my business that Logan knew little about.

"Okay." Trying to see I was going with this, Logan answered.

Glancing at Danny for a split second, I could see the spark of approval in his eyes, indicating that he already favoured Logan as a candidate.

"Danny is ready to retire and get away from Federick's tyranny. I'm offering you his job, and all you got to do is say yes. And don't worry about work experience or training. Danny has gracefully agreed to train you before he leaves." Externally, I sounded confident of myself and certain that Logan would take the job. But internally, I was a ball of uncertainty. I hoped Logan would agree, so I wouldn't have to openly violate the agency's rule and play favouritism.

"This is definitely a life-changing opportunity." Gently rubbing his chin with his thumb and forefinger, Logan seriously contemplated my offer.

"It is. You have the experience for it, and throughout the years, you've shown me you have the skills to be a successful and determined business-man." Hinting at the fact that he was my best agent for going undercover as a businessman, I discreetly encouraged Logan.

"If I accept, what would I be doing?" Interested in the offer, Logan inquired.

"You will manage Danny's floor, oversee our lead directors, and attend all executive, shareholder, and partner meetings, particularly the ones Federick would be attending. There will also be specific documents and event planning that would need your exclusive supervision. But don't worry, aside from your training with Danny, you'll have an assistant to help you out and maintain your daily calendar. Given that you'll be covertly representing me and my shares, you'll need to double-check all the documents passing through your office before signing them. Danny will show you which types of sensitive documentation would need my personal signature or direct evaluation. Especially the ones that need to go to Federick for further exam-ination. The concept here is for you to be the middleman between Federick and me."

"Does Federick know of this change in shareholder? If he does, what's his thoughts?"

"Don't worry about Federick. I'll handle everything that has to do with him like I've been doing for the past two years. You simply must make sure you let nothing slip."

"What would be my official role and title?"

"On paper, and to everyone outside of us three, you'll hold the presti-gious title of President at Archer & Associate. And if it came down to it, your vote and Federick's vote would wield the most power. Laddering it, Federick is at the very top. You are beside him, and the rest of the part-ners and shareholders are under you both. Mind you, though, they are all a bunch of vicious share-stealing vipers. You'll need determination, strength, and authority in this job. Although, be mindful not to defy Federick too much. The asshole will end up doing something rash, and it'll be on me to clean up after you two."

"Understood. Can you tell me why the other shareholders want my share so desperately?"

"They are unaware that your share is actually an ownership stake, and no one can distribute or divide it."

"To clarify, since you are part-owner, no one can gain your stake?"

"They can, but only if I allow it. Then again, I would never do such an absurd thing."

"What should I do if I encounter challenges while making certain decisions or changes?"

"Honestly, Logan, for the first year, you'll probably need a lot of my help. So anytime you need it, come to me." I warmly invited. "The power I'm entrusting you with gives you complete autonomy to make a vast majority of decisions without my direct consultation." My words hinting at the trust I had in Logan, I revealed. "Despite that, I'll again point out, be careful to not constantly reject Federick's choices, or butt heads with him in the open. He is, after all, in the public's eyes, the sole CEO and owner of Archer & Associates. Then again, if you believe you have a much better idea than what Federick proposes, and he refuses to listen to you, you can directly tell me. I would see to it and make sure others hear it."

Observing Logan carefully, "Do you have any other question?" I asked with the utmost patience.

"It's a lot to take in, but I have no more questions right now." With a brief smile that didn't quite reach his eyes, Logan responded.

"Don't forget to tell him about your unpredictable leaves of absence, and the protocols around that." Danny jumped in with absolute professionalism.

"Thanks, Danny." Voicing my appreciation, I turned to the man and smiled.

Danny was a great man, but he did not know of my spy life. Despite coming across some of my paperwork hinting at my covert endeavours, he never allowed his curiosity to get the better of him, and continuously showed his unwavering loyalty by turning a blind eye to it all. However, over the past few months, Danny had had enough of Archer & Associate, most specifically of Federick. So, after my initial shock at Logan's request to leave my agency, it only made sense to replace Danny with Logan. Finally, I could work with someone in the civilian world that I fully trusted and whom I didn't have to lie to. With Logan as the representative of my stake, I would have to do less hiding, lying, threatening, and secretive planning. It would take so much off my shoulders and give me much more free time to focus on my family and finding Vanderwill. And as far as Danny was concerned, Logan was a younger version of him who might have more patience with Federick. Danny did not suspect a previous relationship between Logan or me, much less that Logan was the elder brother figure in my life. If I had to guess based on Danny's character, I'll say that he just didn't care. His policy has always been, *'The less he knew about me, the better.'*.

Turning to Logan again, "As Danny pointed out, sometimes I must take planned or sudden leaves of absence, and during those times, you'll have the power of attorney to sign sensitive documents that would otherwise need to go through me. You'll need to step in, know what to prioritise, what to keep locked up for me, and handle some of my most sensitive workloads. You'll also have to deal directly with Federick and my PA without my help. With you here, I'll, of course, make a better attempt to replace the PA I currently have, to make your life easier. Even importantly, you need to know how to keep secrets, and sometimes lie for me. My interest is your interest."

"It seems like there are a lot of responsibilities involved in all of this." Ruminating over everything we've talked about, Logan spelt out.

"Yes, there is." Direct, blunt, and honest, I reaffirmed.

"Okay, I like a challenge. I'll take the job."

"Fantastic. You will receive more information about your pay, medical benefits, insurance, and more later from Human Resource. But right now, come with me." Internally dancing and screaming in happiness, I kept my cool and smiled.

Biding our goodbyes to Danny, we walked back towards my office.

"Where are we heading?" Logan curiously asked.

"To see what you can and cannot do on my laptop." I winked at him.

The technologies and system at the agency and the ones at this corporate business were entirely different. Logan was no longer going through civilian's profiles, blueprints, or databases of victims, assassins, and businesses. The man was now going to deal with numbers, graphs, paperwork, and long hours of reading, and decision-making. This was more than just acting to be a businessman for a couple of weeks. This was doing it in real life.

"Hey, Nadiya, I hope you didn't get too bored in here?" I greeted as I walked into my office, Logan following closely behind.

"No, I had company."

"Really, who?" Curious, since people rarely came to my office, I inquired.

"Your boss." She added, her eyes filled with questions and a need for explanation.

"Oh, Federick. Do you know what he wanted?"

"Nope, sorry. I wasn't interested in hearing him out." Nadiya answered without a hint of regret, and a disinterest clearer than the bright full moon.

"It's okay. I understand." With a smile directed at Nadiya, I commended her for not succumbing to Mr Heartthrob's charm, like the rest of the brainless female population.

"How was your interview, baby?" Walking over to Logan and lightly pecking his lips, Nadiya practically purred. They were like two lovesick puppies.

"Hey, lover boy, come here and show me what you can do with this baby." Logging into my computer, I called out with a sweet smile.

"Do you want me to leave?" Nadiya asked with uncertainty.

"It's not confidential information, so you are welcome to watch your baby in action." Leaving the choice to them, I shrugged my shoulder.

Staying back and standing behind me, both of them leaned in closer as I pointed to my screen, their curious eyes locked on the display. Directing my question to Logan, I assumed Nadiya would not understand a thing.

Big mistake on my part.

"If I emailed you this problem with no additional resources and asked you to provide me with a detailed solution in a limited timeframe, what would be your primary and secondary steps?"

Testing the ground with the most obvious question, I waited for Logan's answer. Nadiya, however, excitedly jumped in and answered the question for Logan, surprising me. Immediately realising she should have kept her mouth shut, Nadiya nervously looked at me while scratching the back of her neck.

"Your answer is impressive, Nadiya. I, however, do not encourage or appreciate interruption in a work conversation." Doing my best to not be my usual cold brute, given her relationship with Logan, I patiently explained.

"Sorry, Phoebe. I knew the answer and got excited." Nadiya apologetically stated.

Silently studying her, an excellent idea crept its way into my mind.

"Nadiya, I'm curious to know, how did you gain such extensive knowledge of business and its technical jargons, given your occupation as a restaurant waitress?" I queried, recognising I still knew little of the woman. "I am not, by any means, trying to insult you or your job. But even my current assistant who studied at a prestigious university had a hard time answering this exact question, much less answer with the precision and detail you just did."

"The dynamics and intricacies of the business world have always intrigued me. And back in Italy, I was a star student in my business classes. However, I wanted more hands-on life experience, and waitressing at a restaurant as big as Asterix provided that. Not to mention, it gave me entry into this country and the chance to study my customers in their natural environment. Their mannerism and tastes surprisingly differ from my fellow Italians."

"That's fabulous and impressive." Genuinely amazed, I praised her.

"And here I thought it was my interview?" Logan interjected with a cheeky smile.

"Gosh, you already got the job, Mister President." I jokingly and dramatically added.

Out of nowhere, like a thunderbolt, Nadiya exclaimed, "You became the President of THIS company! How did this happen?"

"Well, a bit of Phoebe's magic has never hurt anybody." Messing with my perfectly curly hair, Logan winked.

"Hey dude, do not touch my hair. This perfection takes time." Smacking his hand away, I warned him, my tone a mix of playfulness and seriousness.

"See, I told you. She is a perfectionist freak." Logan jested.

Paying no mind to our playful teasing, Nadiya surprised me by sneaking up and wrapping her arms around me while I sat. "Thanks. Your awesomeness surpasses what Logan mentioned."

"Oh — you're welcome." Unsure what to say or do, I sat still like a doll.

"You're making her blush, sweetheart." A grinning Logan voiced to Nadiya.

"Okay, enough of you guys being all lovey-dovey." Breaking free and standing up in front of them, I added, "I just had a fabulous idea."

"Oh, no! What is it now?" Logan added with fake exasperation.

"What's your guys' thoughts about you, Nadiya becoming my personal assistant?" I asked, my voice filled with anticipation.

Looking at each other with shock, the two lovebirds' hesitation was clear. But I could not back down yet. "Look, I desperately need a new PA that's knowledgeable and efficient. I've been searching for one for far too long now. The PA I currently have is complete B.S. and GAGA over Federick. You, on the other hand, are not only talented but, most essentially, not head over heels for Federick. You will be perfect for me."

"Thanks for the compliment, Phoebe. But I'm not sure about this — I mean, this feels like taking advantage of your kindness and our budding friendship." Nadiya stated with doubt and hesitation.

"I think it's a good idea, Nadiya. Your visa is expiring in one week, leaving you with little to no time to go job hunting. Plus, I will sleep better at night knowing my wife is helping relieve my little sister's constant headache. And we can provide each other with a listening ear whenever needed."

My only constant headache was Federick Ashton Archer. And unless Nadiya could help me deal with him; I didn't know how much help she could provide me in that case.

"Logan, you should also know she will often work with you." Instead of saying what I was really thinking, I reminded Logan about an important aspect that could influence their life and relationship.

"I got no problem with it. But it's still up to her to decide." Looking at Nadiya, Logan respectfully gave her the choice.

"Working with Archer & Associates would be a great opportunity. Before I give my answer, though, can I know what my job responsibility as your PA would be?"

"Okay, let's have an interview, after which you can decide. Deal?"

"Deal." Nadiya said with more confidence.

"Logan, would wait outside? And please don't end up in any fight." Aware Federick was still somewhere out there, I joked. The warning behind my tone, however, was very much real.

"Sure. Anything for you ladies." Waving, he closed the door behind him.

"Let's have a seat, shall we?" Going back behind my table, I offered her the chair in front of me.

"So, what will I be doing?"

Surprisingly, just like Logan, Nadiya too knew how to change her behaviour from easy-going to professional in a snap of a finger. Her ability to swiftly change mannerism added more weight to my decision. Her *'yes'* would most certainly make my life much better.

"Are you aware of the basic requirement of a PA?"

"Yes, I do," she replied with a confident nod. "My question, however, mainly targeted the rumours about your and Mr Archer's distinctive and somewhat rigorous approach to managing your personal assistants. And yes, rumours shouldn't be taken at face value, which is why I prefer to ask before assuming." Without the usual unwelcome attitude I often receive from other applicants, Nadiya proved to be further earthly and likable. God only knew how grateful I was for the latter.

"The rumours are mostly accurate. Federick and I expect excellence and will work you hard. Your responsibilities will encompass organising, creating, and managing nearly every document that crosses my desk. Federick himself might directly hand you some documents, and those usually go into the priority box. However, because of the low clearance level you'll start at, there would be certain files you won't be able to read or peruse through. And because of my position in this company, there would be a large amount of these sensitive files. Access to more information hinges on your ability to excel under pressure and earn my trust — a feat easier said than done. Although, keep in mind, the more I trust you, the more responsibilities you'll inherit. So, think carefully before committing."

"Given the company's high standing and the significance of the position you're offering me, your requirements and emphasis on discipline sound sensible to me. As far as trust goes, don't worry about it. I've always been trustworthy, and not just for the people I work for. Either way, you're my future husband's best friend, his baby sister, so earning your trust is essential to me."

"Great. This brings me to my other point. Logan. We are non-blood related, but in our eyes, that doesn't matter. For years now, the man has been my best friend, and my overprotective, annoying, but loving big brother. I utterly respect and love him, but this would not change how I will rate you. Out of work, I would treat you like my sister-in-law, but in this office, while working, you will be my personal assistant, and I will treat you as such. Federick and I might argue and disagree on almost everything but the motto; *There is a time for fun, and there is a time for work*, is the one thing we completely agree on. Also, pay close attention to not bring any work tension home. It isn't exactly healthy."

"I understand and truly appreciate your honesty. What else should I be aware of before making my decision?" Still calm and seemingly unbothered by the challenge in front of her, Nadiya asked.

"You'll primarily work for me, and I'll be your boss. But when I'm not here, you'll be assisting Federick as well. I'm often away on trips, ranging from long absences to short absences, and sometimes spontaneous ones.

Which means your workload would vary, with the days I'm gone being heavier for you, with more on your plate. I'll also need you to be agile, capable of keeping secrets when needed, and doing everything you can to make my life easier. What happens on this floor should not leave this floor. We'll train you on what types of documents and businesses take precedence, and what comes solely to me. You'll have to be mindful to avoid unnecessarily questioning me or my process at all the time. Oh, and often, you'll be working with Logan on my behalf. As my assistant, you'll have all the basic assistant responsibility, you'll manage my calendar and phone calls. Also, Federick and I have a habit of not getting along, so you'll be hearing a lot of that. Because of our dynamic, you must be able to work in our volatile environment while making sure nothing gets to the press."

"I will not lie to you, Phoebe, this sound like a lot of responsibility. But I like this challenge."

"Tell me how you feel about Federick Archer?" Taking her by surprise, I asked the most important question yet.

"Not to be rude, Phoebe, and I'm sure he's great in his own way, but I'm not very fond of Federick. And the way he behaved earlier at the restaurant gave me a sour taste of his character."

"If this is how you really feel about him, I hope you'll say yes. It'll make my day — You do not know how annoying it is to see every single woman endlessly praise him like he's God himself."

"I can only imagine." Matching my smile, Nadiya snickered.

"Unfortunately for you, you'll most likely be the communicator between Federick and I, especially when we have huge arguments. The asshole is always in a bad mood, yet somehow on some days, becomes even more bitter after dealing with me. This is me warning you of his sour mood swings and our destructive dynamics. There will be a plenitude of weird things happening on this floor, including screams and loud banging of doors and walls from both mine and Federick's office. Lately, though, it's been more of suffocating silent treatments. We argue pretty much every day. And don't even think about intervening. You'll only harm yourself or your career." I gave her a fair warning despite really wanting her to take me up on my offer. She, after all, deserved to know the devil that was Federick Archer.

"I can deal with that. Knowing you are kicking Federick's ass behind closed doors is peace enough for me."

"You are an amusing and peculiar person, Nadiya Amatore." I lightly laughed, liking her even more.

"I don't want to pry, Phoebe, but why did you lie to Logan at the restaurant? Why didn't you tell him about Federick being such a brute to you in the middle of the street?" Perplexed, Nadiya inquired, the concern laced in her eyes visible.

"Between all four of my best friends, Logan is the closest to me, and we share pretty much everything. Yet, when it comes down to Federick, there are some things I don't see fit to divulge. You'll soon learn how overprotective Logan is of me, and you'll understand why I keep certain things hidden. In the meantime, I hope you will respect my decision."

Nodding, "I respect it. But, Phoebe, you know Logan only acts like this because he loves you deeply and would die if anything happens to you. In his eyes, you are the sister he always wanted."

"I understand, Nadiya." Lightly chuckling, "You don't need to defend your fiancé." Joking, I appreciated her concern.

"Also, why are your trips so impromptu?" Bringing back her professional tone, she posed.

"The position I'm in requires me to travel a lot, sometimes with little notice. However, if it's not for business, it's for personal reasons, or sometimes, to piss Federick off purposefully. Whatever the reason might be, prepare yourself for Federick's questioning, and to lie your ass off if needed. Also, if you take the position, be careful of Lucy Braton. She'll try to annoy you and make your life hard with all her lies and rumours, particularly during my absence." Suddenly remembering that bitch, I warned Nadiya.

"Lucy Braton?"

"One of the shareholders' assistants and the office slut. Her deviousness, viciousness, and the entirety of her is appalling." My disdain for that slut was visible despite my attempt to keep my tone in check.

"I appreciate the warning, but don't worry about me. Women like her are nothing to an Italian woman like me who worked in a cut-throat restaurant." Beaming like it was no big deal, Nadiya stated.

"Great. If you don't have more questions, and agree with my offer, you can start training tomorrow. I will have a selected mentor ready for you."

Walking to the glass coffee table beside the panorama floor-to-ceiling ballistic darkened window, I poured myself a glass of orange juice. This spot was one of my favourites. High above everyone and with a clear view of the city, it made me feel invincible. There was a safeness here that I didn't feel everywhere, and I yet again understood why my father prized this spot so much. Vacantly looking down at the busy street, I savoured the scene in front of me while waiting for Nadiya's response.

"I'll take it." I turned on my heels the moment I heard the words and was immediately engulfed in a hug.

Grinning, "You're one of those hug types, aren't you?"

"Can't help it."

Laughing, we both tightened our hug before letting go.

"Can I ask you a personal and awkward question?" Studiously looking at me, Nadiya uncomfortably inquired.

With a sense of apprehensiveness, "Sure, go ahead."

"I know you already accepted me as your sister-in-law, but would you also consider me as one of your best friends?" With a hint of uncertainty and embarrassment, Nadiya asked.

"I don't see any reason to refuse your proposition. But, before I accept, understand that I'm not great at friendship. Nor do I have a filter or the capability to trust easily." I warned, not sure how I would do with a girl who was a civilian, as a friend after so long of only having my teammates as my friends.

"I completely understand and respect it." Hugging me again, "You just made me the happiest person on earth." Nadiya unashamedly showed her excitement and joy.

"I'm glad. Now, let's go. We all have businesses to attend to."

Joining Logan outside my office door, we informed him of our great news. Sharing in my excitement, Logan gave us a quick hug. From the look Logan and Nadiya were giving each other, I knew this was a big day for them, and they had a lot to talk about and plan. Not wanting to keep them here longer than necessary, I proposed we do a quick office tour so they could take the day to rest and get ready.

"Hi there, Miss Nadiya. Nice to meet you again." As we were about to start the office tour, Federick, like the ghost he was, popped his unwanted head out of his office.

"Not so nice meeting you," I whispered under my breath, the words barely audible to the three of us, but not to Federick.

"Hi to you too, Miss Smith. May I know who this gentleman is?" Peculiar and still cold as ice, Federick demanded.

Forcing a smile, "Hi, Mr Archer. This gentleman is my best friend." Emphasising the best friend's word, I matched his coldness with fire. The split second of relief that washed over his face after my words, however, confused me. I wanted to enrage him, not to relieve him!

Twisting the invisible dagger deeper, "Oh, he also took over Danny's position as of today. And Miss Nadiya, his fiancée, is now my new PA. I'm hoping you're going to show them respect and tone down your rudeness."

This new information seemed to have done the trick.

"Guys, this is Mr Federick Archer, my boss, and the owner of this fine establishment. Now that you've all made acquaintance, we should get going." I stated, more than asked, pushing Federick's buttons further.

The mere joy I got from annoying him and constantly pushing all his buttons was pure bliss.

"Miss Smith, could we have a talk in my office for a minute?" Federick calmly and stoically asked. The intense coldness emanating from him, however, was palpable, as if he were throwing icicles at me with his gaze.

"Sure. But once I'm done showing them around. We don't want to lose our new shareholder's time now, do we?" With utmost sweetness, I fruitily stated, and even added a fake eye fluttering for Federick.

Scowling, he turned on his back, saying no other word. The radiance of power, coldness, arrogance, over-confidence, and strength followed behind him. It was like his personal coat, flapping around.

"That was your Federick! Dang! No wonder he constantly lingers in your mind. I'm straight — my fiancé can attest to that — and I find him mind-fucking-blowing hot. Talon is SO going to be pissed off when he finally meets Federick." Mischievous as ever, Logan exclaimed with all kinds of exaggeration.

Hitting him on the side to shut him up, "First off, the asshole is not *'my'* anything, and he sure as fuck is not inside my head all the time." My attempts to defend myself, however, went completely down the drain.

Logan rolled his eyes and whispered, "Don't believe her," to Nadiya and continuously gave me his *'I don't believe you'* look.

"Let's go, asshole. I have a bigger asshole than you to deal with afterward." Rolling my eyes at Logan as well, I began walking in front of them.

"Tell me all about how you are going to *'deal'* with him, dear Phoebe."

Completely ignoring Logan, I showed them the most visited section of the building.

CHAPTER 24
AN ENTRANCE À LA AMATORE

NADIYA

From the top floor of the towering skyscraper, I marvelled at the rare sight of the city below through the clear, laminated window, and I couldn't help but feel a sense of awe. From this height, everything and everyone appeared miniature, like tiny specks in the distance. And this office space was no less impressive. It was so massive; it could easily hold two of my generous size apartment room.

The sheer grandeur of her office filled me with admiration rather than intimidation. This woman seemed to have achieved a lot. After talking and befriending her despite our initial hiccups and awkwardness, I couldn't help but admire her. Phoebe was strong, confident, sassy, kind, and, well, a boss. She was so fascinating that now, all my anxiety on the way to meet her seemed irrelevant. Given Phoebe's strictness and the importance of punctuality in her eyes, I thought I had ruined it all after being unable to leave work on time. And even though Logan reassured me that Phoebe would understand — if not for me, then for him — I wasn't fully convinced. But now, my perspective had completely shifted.

Sensing a pair of eyes coolly piercing icicles through my back, I became hyperaware of the present. One minute I was curled in a wave of warm admiration, and the next, I felt a wave of chill cascading down my skin. In that split second, it felt as if I had transformed into a frozen statue, though I knew it was impossible. I would have been beyond pissed if I had turned into stone just moments before my long-awaited wedding.

Slowly but surely, I turned to the source of this sharp iciness, and in front of me stood the ex-hot guy from the restaurant. The same jerk who was manhandling Phoebe as if she was his property. Back at the restaurant, when I interrupted his and Phoebe's conversation, I wanted to kick him in the nuts so badly, but I refrained myself. After all, I didn't want Phoebe to have an even worse opinion of me than I feared she already did.

"Dear God, you nearly gave me a heart attack." For the time being, I kept my behaviour in check and placed my hand gently on my chest, reacting to the shock I felt rather than letting anger take over.

"Wasn't my intention." Without a trace of apology or remorse, the brute glacially stated.

Whoever he was, his assholeness radiated from him like a toxic aura.

After glancing around, he turned his gaze back to me and inquired, "Who might you be?" He asked nonchalantly.

"Nadiya Amatore. I'm waiting for Phoebe to come back." Not backing down, I uttered with confidence.

He leisurely scanned his eyes over me, pausing at my engagement ring. "I saw you earlier at the restaurant?" He asked for confirmation.

Thank God for Logan and his humongous diamond ring. Anyone could see it from a mile. The last thing I wanted was the attention of this man.

"You mean when you were being rude and manhandling Phoebe in front of everyone?" Keeping a stern and sarcastic tone, my displeasure was unmistakable.

"Well, Miss Nadiya," He said with a stern tone, "Consider this friendly advice. In the future, it's best for you to avoid sticking your nose where it doesn't belong."

Pique, his rudeness was like a knot in my shoulder that didn't go away no matter how much I rubbed it. "Duly noted. Who the heck are you, anyway?"

"I'm Federick Archer, Miss Nadiya. The owner of this building, and Miss Smith's boss." Sarcasm laced in his voice, Federick somewhat surprised me.

"Oh, you are him." I've heard a lot about him, but he was so much worse in person.

"Yes, that I am," Federick stated with utter pride.

"I've heard quite a bit about you." Keeping my distasteful comment about his character to myself, I voiced.

"Sure, you have. Everyone hears about me."

"Hope your head doesn't burst through the door on your way back." All my manners were out of the window, and I indirectly threw him out of his own building.

"Oh, don't worry yourself about my head, Miss Amatore. Worry about yours."

"Is this a threat?" Provoked at his bluntness to menace me, I stared at him with narrowed eyes.

"Take it any way you want, sweetheart. I don't care."

"My God! My fiancé was right." Exasperated, I threw my hand in the air. Or I would have strangled him.

"About what, exactly?" Interest other than frigidity flashed in his eyes.

"You, being the biggest jerk to have ever existed. I truly don't know how Phoebe puts up with you!"

"She puts up with me, alright."

Despite his monotonous tone, the suspicious underlying note in this sentence couldn't escape notice. Paying no actual attention to the latter, "Whatever! Could you leave me alone?" Faking politeness, I stretched a smile.

"Gladly. Tell Miss Smith to come to my office once she decides remaking an appearance." Making his demand, Federick Archer turned on his heel and disappeared, leaving me in a sour mood.

Thankfully, shortly after, Phoebe and Logan walked in, bringing with them a sense of warmth and energy. Stepping into my lover's embrace, I felt my frustrations fade away, and the memory of Federick Archer almost disappeared. Despite how much His Royal assholeness bugged me, today turned out beneficial for me and my future relationship with the people around me. Logan received a wonderful job that was more stable than his previous one. Phoebe accepted my friendship, and to my surprise, she also offered me an incredible once-in-a-lifetime job opportunity. Yes, overall, today was a blessing.

What needed more investigating, however, was the actual relationship between Phoebe and Federick.

Based on their earlier encounter at the restaurant, Phoebe's questions about Federick during my interview, and the scene outside her office, something peculiar was in the air. The suppression of unsaid words and emotions was heavy in the air whenever their gaze matched. Carefully and silently studying their interaction, I realised Phoebe was the one doing most of the suppression. Any doubts I had vanished when I saw the unmistakable look of relief on Federick's face as Phoebe introduced Logan as her best friend and me as his fiancé.

***

Phoebe Pov

True to my promise, I marched towards Federick's office as soon as the tour with Logan and Nadiya was over. The two lover birds had gone to spend a happy day together, while I was unhappily walking towards the causation of my recent headaches.

"What do you want, Federick?" Closing the door behind me, I demanded.

"Lots of things you can't give." Dripping with sarcasm, Federick did me the honours of looking up from his documents, "But I'll gladly take an explanation for now."

His initial response and question threw me off a bit, but I kept my composure. "Really! What kind of explanation do you want from me now?!"

"Why didn't you inform me sooner about Mr Logan Virgo being your best friend and already engaged?"

Now I was further thrown off guard. His questions were as stupid as him.

"Perhaps because you were too busy accusing me of being a slut." I declared fruitily and sarcastically.

"Given what my dad said about you flirting with several guys each week, you can't blame me. Still, I made the effort of asking instead of making my usual assumption." Federick exclaimed, not one bit remorseful for his action.

"Just how stupid are you? Your dad was joking, given the awkward position I had put him in."

"I wouldn't call it stupidity, Miss Smith." His sharp glare was ready to dissect me. "Not after finding out my initial knowledge of who you are utterly bogus. I now must take whatever information I get, as absurd as some might be, and explore it." Frosty like a snowman, he coolly stated.

"Whatever. If you had toned down the accusation, I would have told you about Logan and Nadiya. And why the hell am I even explaining myself to you? What I do in my free time does not concern you."

"Why was I not informed about Danny retiring?" Sensing my confusion, Federick promptly moved to a more professional topic.

"I intended to. But you were too busy ludicrously blaming me. So I didn't get the chance to broach the subject."

With each one of his questions, his condescending tone, accusations and icy glare, my patience grew thinner. And the fire within me was tired of continually being pushed down.

"You can't keep holding me responsible for every single bad thing that occurs, Miss Smith. Since you are so fond of throwing accusations, try blaming your inability to speak up and explain yourself accurately when asked a question. Better yet, blame your high temper and secretive ways." Harshly charging at me like a bull, Federick's words were a verbal punch to my heart. The asshole dared hold me accountable.

"Well, asshole, it isn't my fault if I can't properly express myself. Or that I'm unable to tell you every fucking thing that happens in my fucking life." Blowing up in a high-pitch orotund tone, I astounded both of us. I was no longer in control of my emotions, mouth, or self.

"See what I said, hot-tempered." Joshing, Federick attempted to lighten the air.

I, however, was not taking it. I couldn't understand why I was being so defensive, interpreting everything Federick said as offensive and accusing. All I knew was he couldn't air in the caution line after purposefully throwing jabs at me. I felt like I was a pressure cooker whistling stem with fervour.

"I'm not fucking hot-tempered. You're the one who's hot-tempered and bipolar." Scowling at him with fiery eyes, I blurted out louder than necessary.

Intensely focusing on me, Federick crossed his arms on his table, slanting his upper body forward, and away from his big comfy black leather office chair. "I don't know what's wrong, Phoebe, but calm down. I was just trying to lighten the air."

Stupefied and stirred by his deep, calming voice, it took me a beat to recompose from my dazed expression.

"Yeah, because insulting me is not your favourite hobby of the day." Turning an intentional blind eye to his body movement and the flexing of his arms under his tight suit, I took sarcasm as my weapon.

"Okay!" Unsure why I was aggressively attacking him, Federick surrendered.

"Was this all you had to ask?"

Federick's words and accusation of my virtue weighted heavily on me, causing a sense of unease within me. I didn't like that sensation one bit. I shouldn't care what that jerk thought of me. Yet, I felt irritated, angry, and irked at how low he thought of me.

"No, I had more questions. But given your weird attitude and behaviour, you can come back when you feel a bit more normal." Recomposing himself in a wink of an eye, he returned his stoic gaze to his papers, his tone way too casual.

"WHATEVER." Refusing to let myself be affected by his bipolar jerkiness, I spelled out my word in a stentorian tone.

Marching out of his office, I couldn't comprehend how much Federick could stir my emotions and reasoning. All it took was one hungry kiss and make-out episode at his parents' place, and the man got the capacity to mess with my head. But I couldn't let that continue. I had to pretend like the kiss never occurred, erasing it from my memory.

I had to do my best to keep everything simple between us while keeping him at arm's length. My sanity was at stake.

CHAPTER 25
DISTANCE AND GOOD NEWS

PHOEBE

For two weeks, Federick and I used emails as our primary form of communication. Besides the occasional greetings and necessary interactions during meetings, we were like strangers walking the same road. Not that I was complaining. I relished the peaceful silence that surrounded me. And Federick's frustrated grumbles whenever I took my sweet time to answer his emails were music to my ears.

The unspoken distance felt necessary. But as time went by, the tension between us kept increasing. To where it was even transparent in our emails. Still, I didn't want to have a face-to-face encounter with Federick and expose myself to his psychological games. And I sure as heck did not want him to witness the impact his tricks have on me. But I ultimately had to suck it up. We were set to present a pivotal project to Alpha Group tomorrow — a company that Federick had been relentlessly pursuing for months. And as Federick always says, works comes before feelings, and I too adhere to that.

Armed with my resilience, I stormed into Federick's office without bothering to knock, causing him to jump out of his skin. Swallowing my chuckle, I reminded myself to maintain distance and a straight face.

"My apologies for scaring and disturbing you, Mr Archer, but we need to finalise the materials for tomorrow's presentation." Feigning an apology, I innocently stated.

With a gaze fixed on me, Federick leaned back in his chair, his arms folded across his chest. "You didn't scare me," he said confidently. "Your presence is a surprise, though. I thought we were still playing the *'let's ignore each other'* game." Sarcasm laced in his words, Federick maintained his granite features.

"Well, I can go back to playing that game. But before that, I want to make sure we have everything for tomorrow's meeting." Using sarcasm as well, I retorted.

"Don't worry about the meeting. You have been little help this past month, so I made myself a set of all the needed data for tomorrow's entire presentation." Pointing at the stack of paper with his eyes, Federick nonchalantly revealed. "And Miss Smith, if you intend to keep that useless assistant, do her the favour of handing her all the documents I'll be needing when you make yourself unavailable. All she does is ogle at me and spread her legs around." With a look of disgust on his face, Federick commented without humour.

Repressing my laughter at how the mere presence of my current assistant irked Federick, I quickly revisited my decision to replace her with Nadiya. The idea of keeping her slut-ass here for my amusement and torture weapon against Federick was tempting, but not advantageous in the long term. Not for the projected growth of this company and my future need with my several leaves of absence.

I was a word away from telling Federick he shouldn't have fucked my current assistant in the first place, but I restrained myself so not to prolong my stay in Federick's office. To say I was proud of myself would be an understatement.

"It seems you got everything handled, and I'm not needed. I'll see you at the meeting tomorrow, then." Turning on my back, "The less time I spend with you, the better." I mumbled under my breath.

"What are you mumbling?"

"Nothing that concerns you."

Federick scowled, his lips tightening into a firm line. "Where do you think you're going, Miss? Your job is not over yet. You still need to work with me to finish the presentation."

Scowling at him, I was tempted to smack his arrogant smirk off his beautifully annoying face. Wait! Why was I even thinking his idiotic face was beautiful? What was wrong with me?

As Federick rose from his throne and walked towards me, his commanding presence demanded my full attention. His upcoming closeness causing my heart to pick up in pace, I momentarily panic and instinctively took a step backwards.

"You better stay where you are, Archer! I want you as far away from me as possible." Projecting the anger from my action onto Federick, I brushed off the momentary flash of hurt in his eyes. I couldn't believe that he once again got a reaction out of my heart and bodily function. It was frustrating, and I wanted to hurt him for that.

Instead of reacting, Federick swiftly regained his composure and returned to his usual standoffish demeanour. With a sharp and cold glare, ready to slice me and the entire universe, Federick wore his aloof coat like a second layer of skin. This version of Federick I was used to, and given our current dynamic, I welcomed it.

"If you want us to work together, go back to your seat, and I'll take the seat in front of you." My legs itching to bolt out of the room, I compelled myself not to run away.

My order, however, seemed to have fallen on deaf ears. Like a predator closing in on its prey, Federick swiftly closed the gap between us, and within seconds, stood tall in front of me. His breaths fanning over my face and his lips hovering only a few inches away, Federick's dark aura engulfed me, trapping me in place. The sight of him pressing his lips together sent my mind spiralling into a whirlwind of vivid fantasies, catching me off guard and leaving me momentarily breathless. Simultaneously, something at the back of my mind was screaming for me to put some distance between us, and to stop him from searching the depth of my eyes. But I stood still. Studying his eyes, shifting from icy to an almost blank stare, and then switching into a glower, a shiver travelled down my spine. At that moment, fascination overcame me.

"You think too highly of yourself, Miss Smith." Leaning in close, he coldly whispered into my ear, "What are you afraid of? Sharing another kiss with me? If that's the case, don't worry. That kiss meant nothing to me. It was fleeting." Federick's tone was almost mocking, but before I could react, he stepped back and arrogantly stated, "Now, unless you want me to teach you how to really kiss a man, I would suggest you tone it down. No need to act all high and mighty when we both know you too think I'm irresistible and acting out because of it."

Even though his words stung, I was determined to confront him and give him a piece of my mind. I wasn't one to cower down to his glower or viciousness. But just as I opened my mouth to retort, Federick seemed to expect it and interjected right away.

"Let me remind you. I give orders here, not you." Stroking the back of his forefinger on my left cheek, "You, my little assistant, work for me. You do as I say, sit where I say and when I say." Federick's comment shook me to the core, his strident tone carrying a palpable iciness.

The combination of Federick's audacity, demeaning words, and the heat of his breath, lingering inches from my face, left me rooted to the spot. I couldn't believe the cruelty in his words and the callous tone in which he spoke to me. Yet, I shouldn't have been. I have seen him trample on people and treat them like insect with no remorse. But despite all our fights and arguments, he has never used this specific tone with me. He had never outspokenly treated me like I was beneath him or call me his little assistant.

Without uttering another word or sparing a second glance, Federick swiftly spun around and returned to his throne. Following his every movement, I saw a flash of regret in his eyes. But it was so quick, I almost missed it. And, if I didn't know any better, I would have easily thought it was a product of my imagination.

The shock in me boiled down to rage. I wanted to beat Federick to a pulp. Unfortunately, I couldn't physically harm the guy I was assigned to protect — at least not to the extent I wanted to. Taking calming breaths, I watched Federick focus on the document in front of him, as if I was not in the room. Slowly, I unclenched my fist. Even if I couldn't break his bones, I would make him pay for his words in other ways.

"The one who needs to stop thinking so highly of themselves is you, Mr Federick Ashton Archer. I'm not sure what lies your brain has been telling you. But let me clear it up for you. Your weak ass kiss meant nothing to me, and it sure as heck did not affect me. A virgin can kiss better than you. So, no. I don't want to learn anything from someone as incompetent, talentless, arrogant, and mannerless as you." Glowering at Federick, I had the pleasure of seeing the fury in his eyes sparkle like a diamond, and his jaw flexing with anger. The satisfaction of his reaction made up for my lie because God knows how his surprise kiss affected me. And his skilled tongue, gosh! It created a burst of magic inside my mouth.

Marching to his side of the table, I stood in front of him, and thrusted the blade deeper, "If not for your parents and the future of this company, I wouldn't be sticking around your bullshit, much less, around you." Leaning forward, "You, Federick Ashton Archer, disgust me. You're a womaniser without a heart, and a calculating asshole with an arrogance as big as Mount Everest."

Our breaths were so close, almost touching, as I leaned in towards him. The anger emanating from me was almost tangible, like a pungent odour. "Never talk to me the way you just did." Planting my hands on his armrest, "I'm not your little assistant or someone you can walk on. I might work under you as your personal assistant, but I have as much of a say in this company as you. If you've forgotten, let me remind you of my contract created by your dad." I watched as a mixture of surprise and annoyance swirled in his eyes, creating a strange darkness. I could tell my words were pushing his buttons, and that made my heart dance. "Your tricks and intimidation tactics may work on everyone else, Federick. But not on me. Now, if you're done trying my patience, let's finish this project so I can go home and relax."

I thought I was winning this round of arguments, but dear God, I was wrong.

In an instant, Federick's hand shot out and grasped the back of my head, his fingers entwined in my hair. With a forceful motion, he pulled our faces together, his lips smacking against mine. Taken aback by his actions, my hands slipped from the armrest, nearly causing me to fall forward. Gripping Federick's shoulder for balance, I further leaned into his kiss without meaning to. I had no clue what was happening or why Federick was kissing me. But the force and passion in his kiss left me wanting more. My mind was foggy and confusion as the forefront thought, all my common sense was out the window.

Federick, seemingly aware of my confusion and heightened emotions, wrapped his other hand around my lower waist as he stood up. Towering over me with ease, his firm grip held me in place as I lost my footing. Frozen in the darkness swirling in his eyes, I welcomed the moment to catch my breath. Within a few heartbeats, however, Federick picked me up by the waist, swiped all the documents off his desk, and pinned me down on the desk. I had no time to react or understand what had just happened. All I heard was piles of paper dropping on the floor. Then my back hit the hard surface of the dark wood table. I laid there, under his domineering self, like a dessert for him to devour. Recapturing my lips before I could mutter anything, Federick was no gentleman.

Effortlessly manoeuvring my body, Federick wrapped my legs around his hips and kept my hands firmly pinned above my head. It was as if I was putty in his hand. My inside boiling up with need rather than anger, I lost control of my body. And Federick knew it. The bastard licked my bottom lips, ordering me to open my mouth for him. I wanted to refuse. I truly did. But as he licked that same spot for the fourth time, I opened for him and welcomed his tongue inside my mouth. Showing his dominance with the simple laps of his tongue, I knew Federick was singing a victory song inside.

My breathing quickened as my chest rose and fell. And without thinking about it, I arched my hips upwards as a small moan left my throat. I wanted to smack myself for it, especially when I felt Federick's smirk against my lips. With one hand, Federick held both of mine in place, while his other hand traced a tantalising path along my body until it reached the hem of my dress. Breaking away from the kiss, Federick trapped me with the power in his dark grey eyes as he slipped his hand under my dress. As Federick's warm hand moved closer to the intimate space between my legs, I couldn't help but hold my breath. I had no clue what he was going to do, and logically, this was my time to put a stop to this insanity.

In the blink of an eye, Federick yanked down on my G-String, leaving it tightly wrapped around my knees. Shock doesn't even begin to describe how I felt — my heart raced, and my breath caught in my throat. My eyes bulging, I had no words. I never thought I would find myself in this intricate situation with Federick, and now that I was, I felt completely stunned. This Federick, here, was someone I had never encountered.

Leaning forward, his eyes swirling with danger, "It seems my weak and virgin-like kiss can make you breathless." Federick huskily taunted as his fingers unashamedly stroke my womanhood.

Just as I was about to retort — not that I realistically could, given the blankness that covered my mind the moment he touched my private area — Federick's firm hand clasped the back of my head, his lips meeting mine in an unexpected embrace. Tugging on a fistful of hair, Federick kissed me fiercely, with an explosive blend of anger, passion, arrogance, and dominance. His fingers went from lightly playing with my entrance to rubbing my clitoris. A part of me wanted to feel disgusted so I could push him away. Instead, I found myself irresistibly drawn to him, returning his kiss as I ground against his hand in a slow, deliberate rhythm. My body, not my own, seemed to move on its own accord as my heavy and loud breathing filled the air. At that moment, it all belonged to Federick.

Federick, fully aware of his power over me, broke off the kiss and leaned in to whisper in my ear. "Tell me again how I don't affect you?" Raspy and husky, Federick lowly whispered. "You're so wet, your lies can drown in it."

With each stroke, Federick's fingers traced a path of ecstasy along my womanhood. His touch on my clitoris was a perfect balance of intensity and gentle caress, building up waves of pleasure that left me longing for release.

"Look at me, Miss Phoebe Smith." Federick commanded.

Directing my gaze to him, I witness the sharpness in its depth and a danger I didn't dare to play with.

"Don't play games with me, Miss Smith!" With a teasing touch, he glided over the entrance of my vagina, never fully inserting his finger inside me. "You'll fail," he taunted. Without giving me a chance to respond, he resumed his touch on my clitoris, increasing the pressure. "I never intended to go this far with you, but your disrespect has been over the top. From now on, I expect you to do your best to behave."

With a swift motion, Federick ended his torment by sliding my G-String up, the sharp snap against my heated flesh reverberating in the room. As the standoffish expression returned to his face, a gush of frigid air wrapped around him. Lifting me off his desk. "Now, let's get back to work. Pick up those scattered papers while I pull up the slides for the presentation."

Every part of me stunned by Federick, his words and actions, I quietly did as he asked. The Angel in me that usually steps in to protect my pride and honour was conspicuously absent, leaving me feeling defenceless. I felt slightly hurt, exposed, and shaken up by the way Federick kissed and touched me to prove his point, and in that moment, all hopes that he might have liked me died. As I set all the documents back on the table, I realised there was no compassion inside Federick. The way he used and controlled my body for his own benefits showed me just how dangerous he really was. There was a side to him that even I didn't know. For once, I was getting a taste of my own medicine, and I did not like it at all.

I needed to recompose myself and retake control. This speechless girl who did as she told was not me, and if Federick thought I wouldn't make him pay for his action, he was gravely mistaken. As I sat beside him, working through several slides for tomorrow's presentation, the fogginess that had captured my head slowly cleared. On the surface, I appeared calm and composed as I collaborated with Federick to iron out the crucial details for tomorrow's agreement. But inside, I was seething. I wanted to make him pay, and no longer cared about that dangerous, unfamiliar monster inside him.

But first, I needed to distance myself from him. As soon as I finished examining the last slide, I quickly snatched my laptop from beside him and briskly made my way to the opposite side. Without saying a single word, I sat down in front of Federick and opened the word document I had meticulously prepared for the meeting. I knew my action confused Federick, but I didn't comment on it.

"What do you think you're doing?" Eyes sharp, but mixed with curiosity, Federick asked.

My head held high. "Keeping my distance from you." I said with confidence.

My eyes blazed with fury, meeting his piercing gaze head-on. "Your actions, carried out solely for the sake of proving your point, leaves me feeling disgusted. Today I learned you are viler than I could have ever imagined. And since you didn't adhere to my request to stay away from me, I'm taking matters into my own hands."

Without uttering a word, Federick maintained a collected and calm demeanour as he observed me for a beat. Then when I least expected it, "You are right." Federick said in a clear and confident voice, taking me by surprise.

This was the very first time that Federick admitted I was right, and with such composure.

"I've never been this vile to you, and I never intended to. No matter how many times I try to talk to you, you consistently cross my boundaries, pushing me to my limits, and testing my patience, always provoking, and challenging me. You've brought this on yourself, Phoebe. Since you didn't want to listen, I had to show you the side of me I had always kept hidden from you and teach you a lesson." Federick stated with a calmness that awed me. Boring his dark pool of greys into mine, "The rule is simple, Phoebe. You respect me, I respect you back. But if you disrespect me and act the way you've been, I'll punish you the way I deem fit." With a finality in his tone, Federick returned his attention to his computer.

Even if I wanted to say something or refute him, I couldn't. I hated how he placed the blame on me. He had no right to do so. Then again, there was a truth in his explanation. I had been pushing him beyond his limits for months now, and ever since his discovery of my kids, I became even more errant. And I'm sure the discovery of my relationship with his family, or the new VP, had not been easy. Still, I couldn't let him win this one. The sensuous ways he touched me and owned my body were criminal, to say the least.

Without acknowledging his explanation, I redirected our focus back to the task. But being the infuriating jackass, Federick disregarded my demand for distance. The halfwit found an array of excuses to get close to me. Out of nowhere, there were issues with the notes, the editing, and even the damn presentation — when I had just gone over them with him. The worst excuse yet was the sudden issues with the computer that required my fixing, as if I was part of the damn IT team and had the skill set to fix it.

The worst part, however, was his breaths on my neck sending shivers down my spine, and the ever-increasing incomprehensible tension in the air. And each time he would ask me to examine something, he would lean in, brushing his fingers against me, seemingly accidentally. The asshole was head bent on reminding my body of his touch.

Feeling a storm brewing inside my belly and a throbbing in my head, I cracked. "You know what, Federick!? I'm done!" My voice filled with frustration, I exclaimed. "You and your stupid behaviours are annoying. My assistant has already booked a nearby hotel for our guests from Alpha Group. You, and your ways of trying to teach me a lesson, can go to hell!" Marching out of his office and into mine, I snatched my handbag and sped-walk out of the building.

Frustrated and wanting to punch something, preferably Federick, I drove home like a madwoman.

~~

Today was an important day for Archer & Associates. After months of negotiation, we finally booked a once-in-a lifetime introductory meeting with Alpha Group. For over a year now, Federick had been trying to work closely with Alpha Group, but they hadn't responded to any of his offers — until recently. I was curious about their sudden change of mind, but I dare not ask.

For good reasons, I had kept my distance from that company and anyone that was affiliated with them. But Federick wanted to partner with the company. And what Federick wanted, Federick got. Then again, despite my initial reluctance, the numbers spoke for themselves. Still, Federick had not secured the deal yet. Today was the first round of meeting, and it would dictate how long the initial round of negotiation would run. Given Federick's domineering and calculating nature, and his tyrannical approach, I anticipate a lengthy process of negotiation and cooperation with Alpha Group before our companies reach a mutually beneficial agreement.

On my way to Archer & Associate, however, Xylan called, requesting a meeting with the team. Part of me wanted to jump at the opportunity of not having to deal with Federick given what happened yesterday. But the other part of me knew how important my presence was in today's meeting with Alpha Group. Xylan, however, did not take no for an answer. Insisting that he had some new information that would be best to hear in person, he left me with no choice.

Yes, Federick and I worked tirelessly to secure this initial meet-up with Alpha Group, and this deal could make us millions by the end of the year. But I couldn't dismiss anything connected to Vanderwill's name. I had to remind myself that eliminating Cole Vanderwill took priority over everything. Besides, from Xylan's tone, I had a gut feeling that his new information would bring me a step closer to Cole.

With a few quick taps on my phone, I messaged Federick that I would be late to work. Not knowing what time I'd return, I warned Federick that our pitch and presentation might be all on him... Needless to say, his dissatisfaction was palpable. This time, I could fully understand him. Given how much this deal could blow our annual profit, I'll be irate too if my assistant and partner dropped out on me at the last minute. Sincerely apologising to Federick for ditching via text and at the last minute, I silenced my phone and strode into my agency.

Sitting in my private office with a view of the bustling milieu and other offices, I watched my three best friends completely absorbed in their phones. Spotting me as I silently stood at the threshold, Xylan jumped with excitement, like a kid in a candy store.

"Hey, Phebes, guess what?"

Raising one of my brows in curiosity, Xylan's excited outburst nearly cracked me up.

"Guess… Guess what I found?" Trying to make me guess, Xylan repeated, with a grin as big as a Cheshire cat. Whatever it was, I was sure it was great news.

Talon and Matt both lightly slapped the back of Xylan's head, causing him to shout at them. Rubbing the nape of his head, Xylan whined and childishly complained.

"Stop taking all the credit, asshole." They simultaneously cussed Xylan.

My arms crossed in front of my chest, I patiently stood in front of them. After all, I had all the time in the world to stand there and wait for them to be done arguing. Rolling my eyes at them as they threw blows at each other, I took another step inside the office. Their childish behaviours were amusing, but today was not the day for it.

"Okay, boys! Stop fooling around. I don't have the whole day." Looking up at me with a wide grin, I captured their attention.

"There's an important meeting I should be at right about now. So, if you wouldn't mind, spit whatever is making you all giddy like a bunch of schoolgirls."

"You're no fun, Phebes. But after hearing our fabulous news, you'll be just as happy."

"I highly doubt it, Tal. But go on." My patience considerably decreasing, I stated with a clear voice.

Smacking the back of Talon's head, Xylan glared at him humourlessly. "I'm going to tell her, since it was my life that was at risk," Xylan exclaimed, determined to share his story. As childish as he was, however, he couldn't help but mutter *'nerd'* under his breath — his attempt to be unheard, unsuccessful.

"I can hear you mumble, stupid. But carry on. You got a point." Letting Xylan take the reign, Talon sat back.

"Why, thank you…" Rolling his eyes, Xylan turned his attention to me, "Like I was saying before being so rudely interrupted, I discovered something interesting with the help of these two morons here. Remember those girls we saved at Metrix?"

"I do, Xylan. Please, carry on." My business tone matched his enigmatic tone.

"Okay, Ma'am… So impatient. Good God."

Paying no attention to his dramatic tone, "Believe me, Xylan, I'm very patient and limited in time. So, how about you share the good news?"

"Whatever you say, Miss Busy pants." Xylan teased. "The good news is that one of the women we rescued has detailed information about Vanderwill's location. So, my dear Angel, we now know where Vanderwill currently is."

A mix of shock, disbelief, and elation consumed me all at once. "We found that son of a bitch!" I muttered, struggling to believe we were finally ripping the fruit of our labour. "Oh, my God… I can't believe it… Gosh, I love you guys so much." Forgetting my business posture, I openly professed my elation and happiness, hugging them until we all fell to the ground.

Pushing aside the faint voice of doubt and suspicion at the back of my head, I savoured this moment and all its possibilities… After years of looking for something that would propel me a few steps ahead of him, I now finally had an advantage. So no, it wasn't too soon or too easy. It's been 10 fucking years. I was going to enjoy every victory, as small as that might be.

"What are we still doing here? We should check if the address is true or just a bluff. Then I will knife that asshole until he bleeds like the pig he is." Sweet vengeance swirled in my eyes and mind. I was like a starving wolf. Already salivating at the sight of my prey.

"Calm down, sweetheart. I'm already on it." With a firm grip on my shoulders, "Our finest trackers are going above and beyond, as if their lives depended on it. And I'm personally overseeing the strategies to approach the location." Talon reassured me. His voice was a calming balm to my spirit. "Now, don't you have a meeting to attend?"

Trusting Talon's judgment, I was relieved that he had personally taken charge of the operation, sparing me the need to give him explicit instructions. Calming my heartbeat, "You're right. I don't want his royal assholeness on my ass again." Smiling at Talon, I kissed him on the cheek.

"Thanks, guys, you all made my day." Going around, I kissed the other two on their cheeks. "Especially you and your information-extracting method, Xylan." Winking, I ruffled his hair a bit.

"You got no idea how excruciating and tiring it was. All these women… God!" Mischievously grinning, Xylan gave away the underlying meaning of his words.

With a slight shake of my head, I bid them goodbye and made my way to Archer & Associates. Even though I was most likely going to get reprimanded for missing the start of the meeting, Federick would not ruin this perfect day for me.

My dreams of vengeance were finally coming true. Even from this distance, I could taste the unmistakable sweetness lingering in the air.

Special edition art - credit to Professionalillustration(pixabay).

CHAPTER 26
WHO ARE YOU

PHOEBE

Cheered by Xylan's exhilarating news, my usual anxiety over tardiness
evaporated. On any other day, my professionalism would have gnawed at
me for being late for such an important meeting, but today was different.
With Xylan's revelation still dancing in my mind, nothing could dampen my
spirits. I felt like a character in my own fairy tale, the heroine triumphant
and untouchable.

With confidence in my stride, I entered the conference room, politely
excused my tardiness, and beeline for the seat beside Federick. Curiosity
shining in everyone's eyes, they followed my every move. And, for a split
second, I felt like I had stepped into the wrong room. It was like I was an
alien in their world. Worse of all, were the men from Alpha Group. Unlike
the male population in Archer & Associate, who knew not to eye-fuck me,
the males from Alpha Group openly checked me out, lust written all over
their faces.

Sensing Federick's penetrating stare beside me, I felt a pull to give him
my undivided attention. Usually, ignoring his obnoxious ass was second
nature to me, but this time, I found myself unable to turn a blind eye. With
just a glance at his furrowed brow and narrowed eyes, I could tell that Federick was eager to hear the explanation for my tardiness. He wanted it right
after this meeting. Fortunately for me, this meeting was the first day of
briefing, and was likely to run for hours without breaks. This meant I had
all the time in the world to come up with a good excuse. And if luck was
truly on my side today, I might have the chance to escape without facing

Federick.

Ignoring all thoughts of Federick, I focused my attention on the presenter standing confidently in front of the projecting screen. Studiously watching the presenter's every move, I couldn't shake the feeling that I had seen him somewhere before. He was handsome. Caucasian, tall, fit, and dark-haired, with a beautiful pool of brown eyes, he possessed a captivating aura of self-confidence. Probably slightly older than me, the man could have been a model if wanted to.

Whenever his eyes met mine, he would flash a sly smirk, as if he held some secret. He knew I was staring at him. The mischievous glint sparkling in his eyes hinted at the latter, and at a hidden side of his character. That intrigued me. The complexity oozing off him, however, also increased my wariness. For all I knew, he was one of my enemies — someone aware of my identity as Angel. Or worse, someone sent by Vanderwill.

The moment that horrid thought wholly registered, I stiffened. Rigid as a rock, I was tensed out of my mind. Considering where I was, part of me knew this possibility was hardly probable. But that dark thought already had me tightly in its grasp, suffocating me. Being on the verge of victory against Vanderwill, it wouldn't surprise me if mother-nature decided to play dirty tricks on me.

Gosh! Vanderwill was not even in the room, and he could make my mind go wild. I hated the control Vanderwill still had over me. Every fibre in my body demanded to be cleansed of Cole Vanderwill.

Nudging my thigh with his own, "What's wrong?" Federick stealthy whispered.

Striking off the hint of concern I heard in Federick's tone as a figment of my imagination, and what I call a *'Vanderwill after*-effect,' I discreetly shook my head, showing I was okay. Federick, however, did not buy it. Going the extra mile, I briefly glanced at him, and sweetly smiled, letting him know there was no need to worry — in case he had the capacity for such an emotion towards others.

Nodding in response, Federick shifted his focus back to the presentation, feigning indifference and masking his earlier concern. Not thinking twice about it, I directed my attention to the guy presenting, racking my brain to recall where I had seen him before. With my mind racing, I paid no attention to the guy's deliberate smirk and lingering gaze whenever his eyes landed on me. Federick, however, ate up each one of them. From the corner of my eye, I saw Federick shooting a sharp glare back and forth between the presenter and me, as if I were to blame for the presenter's leering gaze. But whenever I turned to Federick, his usual standoffish posture would welcome me. It was as if the dark aura and pissed-off glare I sensed from him was a figment of my imagination.

My attention captured between these two men throughout the entire meeting, I completely overlooked the absence of Mr Ambrosh. Earlier, when I walked into the meeting, I assumed the old man had either stepped out to use the restroom or was attending via conference call. I did not expect his complete absence. But since my liaison with the Ambrosh family was now near to nothing, I was clueless who ran the show within the Ambrosh establishment.

It's been ten years since I last spoke to any member of the Ambrosh family. I had purposefully turned a blind eye to them and their dealings. And when Federick brought them up, I acted like I knew nothing about them. Despite all this, I figured I would have heard if Mr Ambrosh sold his company to the young man presenting today. Glancing at the stranger as I bid my goodbye to everyone else leaving the meeting room, I wondered if Mr Ambrosh sent him here to speak on his behalf. The old man was busy, and if history serves right, he loved making other people do his job. Besides, if this man did work for the Ambrosh Family, it would explain why he looked familiar.

In the closed conference room with Federick and Mr Suspicious, I directed my attention towards the latter, his every gesture and expression analysed by my curious gaze. Federick's palpable displeasure emanated from him, but I brushed him off.

Staring back at me, gaze unfallen, Mr Suspicious folded his arms in front of his chest and stood at attention. An exemplary posture all my spies had perfected. Competitively holding my gaze, I was relieved his stare was not as intense and pulling as Federick's. Giving me a much-deserved break.

Switching his neutral expression into a cocky smirk, his knowing grin grew more substantial than the ones he was giving me throughout the meeting. The man had an unfair advantage over me — he knew something I did not. I was not in a good place, and Federick's irritation beside me was not relieving my confusion.

Why the heck was Federick even irritated at me? Him and his complicated and bipolar facet was worsening my situation. What if I was openly staring at the guy for way too long to be considered proper? Federick had no right to be irritated at me for the latter.

Or was it because I was losing his time by standing here instead of going back to work? — YES, that must be it. I was losing his precious time. And I'm sure he was waiting to question me on my late arrival.

Dropping my mystification of Federick Archer, I concentrated on the stranger in front of me. "Hi, I'm Phoebe Smith. You are?" With a fake wide smile and my guard never down, I stretched my hand out to the guy, offering a professional handshake. I was giving him the benefit of the doubt. But just in case, I positioned myself so I could easily use his arm as support to flip and toss him over my shoulder before pinning him to the ground to get my answers.

"You don't remember me?"

'If I did, I wouldn't be asking now, would I?' I mentally retorted with sarcasm. Outwardly, however, I maintained a straight face. "I'm sorry, I don't. Could you please refresh my memory?" Doing my best to stay calm, I posed. My inside wanted to go into attack mode, but given where I was, I had to maintain a professionalism. There was no need to let my anxiousness and worry mind cause damage to the company's reputation and dealings.

"If that's the game we are playing. Hi, Miss Smith, I'm Damien."

The name brought me on edge. Instantly, I narrowed my eyes at him. As coincidental as his name was to my childhood best friend, and as logical as it was for me not to recognise him after 10 years, I could not jump to conclusions. But I sure as heck was going to thread with caution. Especially since our base in Rio didn't notify me of Damien coming here. My Damien left at age 22, and back then he still had that gentle look to him. This guy in front of me had a roughness to him I didn't recognise.

"Excuse my ignorance. But Damien, who?" I asked, as I maintained an air of confusion.

"I'm hurt, Phebes." Feigning hurt and taking a step closer to me, "And before you freak out and kick my ass for knowing your nickname, allow me to reintroduce myself to my sweet angel."

Understanding the underlying meaning of his words, it was clear the man knew of my life as a spy. The Angel in me was ready to come out if he wasn't the Damien I grew up with.

"You better have a good explanation, Mister, or else!" Letting my phrase hang, I threatened. Given Federick's presence, I couldn't openly threaten to end his life. Nor could I reach under my dress, draw out the dagger strapped to my thigh holster, and press it against his throat.

"Oh, Phebes, swallow that suspicion. I'm the most handsome and sexy man that you could not take your eyes off. Never have and never will." For some inexplicable and unsettling reason, during his descriptions, I found myself stealing a glance at Federick.

"YOUR Dami-poo." He exclaimed with a cheeky smile.

Instantly redirecting my gaze to the man, I was thunderstruck. I now knew who he was. Federick, however, was further puzzled. Scrunched eyebrows decorated his face, replacing his earlier annoyed look. It surprised me how Federick hadn't accrued a major headache yet. The weight of all these confusions, deceptions, and constant feeling of being deliberately kept in the dark would have done it for me. If I were him, I would have already lost my mind.

"Have you finally realised who I am? Or have the years made you so dense that you need more clues to help your goldfish brain to remember —"

SMACK

The whip of my hand cracking against his skin echoed off the office walls. Twisting his head back in my direction, the red mark of my palm was glowing like a traffic light on his cheek. My hand stinging, I watched both men's jaw drops as shock washed over their faces. Outside the office, we could hear whispers and gasps, but no one dared to step foot inside.

"This answers my question." Holding onto his reddened cheek, "But WHAT THE HECK, Phebes! Is slapping with such vigour your new way of welcoming someone who's been gone for 10 freaking years?" Battling the tears of shock from his eyes, Damien exclaimed.

"Oh, Damien Ambrosh, you deserve at least this much, if not more." Feeling good after whacking him, I stated.

"Right. But this hurt, woman. Next time you want to practice your slapping skills, swing your hands at someone else. Perhaps your *'boss'* or Fran-"

"Don't you dare finish saying that name!" I cut in threateningly. "Actually, never dare uttering that name again. Or I swear on my kids' lives, you'll regret it." With a fire burning inside me, I warned Damien.

Holding his hands up in surrender "Got it, girl."

The person Damien almost named was a significant part of my life. But that was the past. I never wanted to see him again, much less hear his name. He was an asshole in a whole different way than Federick or Vanderwill. But, as luck would have it, my name still somehow remained linked to his.

Willing myself out of the incoming memories of that God-awful man, I focused on Damien, giving him a slow once over. A feeling of content washing over me, my excitement rose, and I impulsively threw myself at Damien, catching him off guard. It took a few seconds, but he eventually reciprocated my embrace, crushing me with a bear hug that showed just how much he missed me. Needing a breath of fresh air, I pushed myself off of him and flashed him my genuine, rare smile.

"Wow, girl. First, you slap the fuck out of me, then give me a bone-crushing hug, and now this breathtaking smile." Damien teased with his own smashing smile.

"Gosh, I've missed your smile." Ignoring his teasing, my happiness was unmatched. "I've missed you," I revealed with honesty and love. "I can't believe you're standing right here in front of me." Checking him out from head to toe, I lowly voiced out.

In that moment, I fully forgot about Federick and what he would think of my behaviour. Damien was the centre of my attention. And I didn't care if others saw me being my old, giddy self. This sudden sight of Damien brought me back to my teenage years, where I could fully rely on him.

"Dare to dream, Phebes. The love of your life is back." Damien stated as he dramatically faked a bow. "And he's loving you checking him out. Who would have thought that the great Phoebe Smith would lose her mind over me? Now, that's an ego booster." Damien jested.

"You're done yet." Faking impatience, I rested my hands on my hips.

"Nope. How can I when you literally jumped on me? I knew you couldn't resist me or my charm."

"Oh, whatever." I tried to shush his tease.

"What? It wasn't me who stared at myself for hours. It was you who couldn't take her eyes off me throughout the entire meeting. Just admit it."

"Shut it, smartass. Just be glad I've missed you so much." Smiling like a cheshire cat, I retorted.

Our eyes locked in a moment of silent contemplation, we marvelled at the fact that we were finally face to face again after so many years apart. "You've been gone for far too long. But now that you are back, don't think I'm going to let you go so easily. I'll make sure I have a tighter grip on you this time around."

Giving him another quick hug, I held onto his shoulders. "God, you've changed so much. No wonder I was having such a hard time recognising you. But despite your major makeover, the time apart, and everything that happened, I still love you."

"Is it good or bad change? Am I still hot like I was ten years ago?" Damien jokingly inquired, faking deep concern.

"Humm…" Cocking my head to one side, I gently tapped the side of my temple with my index finger. "Let me think about that?"

In response, Damien's hands firmly gripped my hips as he effortlessly lifted me off the ground and twirled me around. Glimpsing Federick's annoyed face from the corner of my eyes, every time Damien would spin me in his direction, I discerned jealousy in his eyes. Momentarily curious, I wanted to know why he was behaving this way. However, at that moment, I couldn't be bothered by Federick's complicated self.

"Okay. Okay. Put me down. I would really like to keep my food inside my stomach." Giggling, I gave in.

Happy about his win, Damien gently set me down and playfully tousled my hair. With a swift motion, I pushed his hand away, realising yet again that it seemed to be a common occurrence for the men in my life to tamper with my hair.

"It's a good change. Happy! You look more handsome, still hot, better built, and older. And these stubbles, it gives you more character. You know how I have a thing for men slightly older than me."

"Wow, another compliment. I think I should more often pull a disappearing act, then come back. Just imagine the mountain of compliments I would get from the Almighty Phoebe Smith."

"Oh, just shut it." I said with a smile, hiding the hurt I suddenly felt at the thought of him living me again. "Besides, don't you mean run away again and then come back?" I joked.

At this, Damien's face fell. Instantly feeling bad for making such an insensitive joke, "Sorry, I didn't mean it this way." I quickly apologised for my stupid slip.

"It's okay," Damien uttered with a sad smile.

"Either way, I don't think you'll leave this time." Smiling to erase my slip, I feign confidence. "Because next time I see you after you pull this trick again, it won't be a compliment waiting for you, love." Smacking his chest lightly, I tried to wipe his sad smile.

"I know, sweetheart. I was just joking. No need to get all serious. You need to loosen up a bit and enjoy yourself." Letting out a small laugh, we hugged again.

"Now that you're here, I'll completely let loose." Looking up at Damien, the uncertainty of his plans to stay eating at me, "You're staying, right?"

Cupping my face into his palms, he confessed, "These past 10 years without you have been miserable. Not being able to reach out to you, much less able to physically see you or hold you, and offer comfort when you needed it, was horrible. I've missed you so much, Phoebe. And I'm truly sorry I wasn't there when you needed me the most. I feel useless and like I've cheated on you. But … I still can't promise my stay. I will, however, for your sake, promise to stay as long as I can."

"Shh…" Gently placing my forefinger onto his lips, I leaned in and kissed Damien on the cheek.

"I understand. It was all my fault, Damien, not yours. Not in a million years." I said emphatically. "Nobody was in control of the situation back then. But I promise I'll fix all these past mistakes, and everything will be fine again. What counts is that you are here now. And you'll never guess how much I'll be needing you. If you genuinely want to help me and be a part of my life again, support me and be here for me this time around. But please make sure you don't fail me this time. For now, though, let's forget about all this. Come home with me tonight — you'll get to meet the kids."

Quietly studying his reaction to my mentioning meeting Wyatt and Teo, the look of uncertainty was clear on his face. After a while of complete silence from both Federick and Damien, I stubbornly added, "I didn't want to bring it up, but you did, in fact, cheat on me."

"Okay, Phebes, I get it. But let's schedule that meet up for tomorrow night. I need to rest from my flight and this meeting. Plus, I have to wrap my head around the idea of meeting the boys for the first time since they were toddlers."

"Okay, as you wish." Pouting, my efforts to change his answer remained unsuccessful.

"Umm… Phebes, you're sure about this, right?" Damien asked with uncertainty. "I mean, it's going to be awkward. Do they even remember who I am? More importantly, will they willingly accept me back into their lives? What if they hate me for leaving them—"

"My God, stop worrying and rambling so much. You're acting like you just found out you fathered a child. I mean, you just left them. Maybe they will kick your ass or hate you with a passion for a while."

"And this is supposed to relax me. How?"

"Sorry. Just joking, Damien."

Looking directly into his eyes, I cupped his cheeks in my hands. "Everything will be fine. The boys have grown up and would understand very well."

Faking a cough, Federick pulled our attention back to him. Glaring at Damien as if he was the villain in a movie, "Sorry to cut your reunion short, but how do you two know each other? You look damn intimate to me."

Damn, I had almost forgotten about Federick's existence besides us. Quite like a mouse only minutes ago, he now was a lion demanding attention. Narrowing his eyes dangerously at poor Damien and suspiciously scowling at me, he waited for a response.

"Est-ce qu'il sait ta vrai identitée?"

"Non, bien sûr que non! On travail juste ensemble. Je jure, il est si emmerdent."

"Oh ok, alors. Qu'est que tu vas lui dire?"

"Regarde et apprend."

Winking at Damien, I turned towards a furious-looking Federick. Glaring at us like we had each grown another head, it was obvious he didn't understand a lick of French. Another point for me.

"You were saying?" With as sweet a voice as I could muster, I fruitily asked Federick.

"I was asking, Miss Smith, how do you know Mr Ambrosh's son? And speak English this time."

"Oh, Mr Archer, I'm sorry," I feigned an apology. "But I don't need to tell you shit about my personal life. All you gotta know is we are very close." With an emphasis on *'very,'* I hinted in a sultry tone. "Now, if you would excuse Damien and me, we are going to do some catching up. See you tomorrow." Seeing Federick's eyes flash with something I couldn't quite understand or recognise, I clenched onto Damien's hand harder than I had intended.

My goal was to annoy Federick, and from the looks of it, I had succeeded. With nothing left for me to do, I briskly dragged Damien out of the office. The last thing I wanted was to pull Damien into my and Federick's daily routine of arguments and fights.

Drawing his hand from my smashing hold the moment we stepped out; Damien rubbed his wrist. "Easy, girl. There's no need to abuse my poor hand with your solid death grip."

Dismissing him, "Oh, stop whining, Dam."

"Not true. I do not whine." He added both defensively and jokingly.

"You know, with the way you all behave, it won't be long before you, Logan, Talon, Matt, and Xylan become the best of friends. After, of course, a bit of pushing on my part — given your terrible history with Logan and Talon."

"Yeah, sure. But for right now, let's go out, listen to your stories, and eat. I'm starving." Completely redirecting the conversation on purpose, I did my best to respect his decision.

"Sure, there's a fine restaurant nearby." My stomach grumbling at the thought of food, I realised I had eaten little today. "And filling you in on what you've missed these past 10 years would be delightful. Unfortunately, I must warn you, fucking Vanderwill is also involved in the narration." Getting in the car with him, I expressed.

"You don't need to if you don't want. I know how much you hate this guy." He compassionately commented.

"And you don't?" I rudely bit back.

"Oh, I do. I despise him with every fibre in my body. But I know your level of hatred for him is way out of my league. In all reality, your venom for him is the only thing that helps me sleep better at night. Trust me, if you keep growing your amplitude of hatred, we'll soon catch him, and finally get justice."

"I can't help but agree with you. However, not talking about him is not optional. Because guess who's back?" I spat out sarcastically.

"Vanderwill." He stated with hatred.

"The devil himself," I added dryly and vehemently.

"And you, my dear, are welcome to help me kill him before he does us."

~~~~~~

Translation From the French Phrases:

"Does he know your true identity?"

"No, of course not. I just work with him. I swear he's so annoying."

"Oh, ok then. What are you going to tell him?"

"Watch and learn."
~~~~~~

CHAPTER 27
UNNERVING À LA DAMI-POO

FEDERICK

Today marked a significant milestone as we embarked on negotiations with Alpha Group, after years of relentless efforts. With my hard work paying off, I felt content and ready for whatever the day had in store. The stakes were high, and I knew well that any significant mistake on the first day could have dire consequences for the partnership. But I was also confident that Phoebe's and I's diligent work was going to pay off and capture Alpha Group's heart. And most importantly, capture a huge percentage of what's inside their pocket.

However, halfway through drinking my morning coffee, my mood darkened. We were an hour away from the meeting of a lifetime when Phoebe texted me her apologies for bailing on me. Even worse, her excuse was subpar. Thrown off my game at the most impromptu time, my confidence about everything going to plan for this meeting dissipated. In a blink of an eye, it felt like my months of preparation went down the drain.

Just as I was about to give Phoebe a call, my phone lit up with a notification — another apology from her. Apologies were a rarity for Phoebe, making the weight of her latest message even more significant. Yes, recently my trust in Phoebe had decreased. But despite all the surprising discoveries about her, I still believed there were some facets of her she couldn't have faked. For instance, her overconfidence, arrogance, and annoyance towards me was one such facet. Another one was her rarely taking responsibility for her actions. This time, however, as I re-read her message, I knew she was ready to take responsibility for this misstep. A part of me was glad about that. The other part, however, felt displeased by Phoebe's lack of respect towards me or the hard work she put into this project. Huffing an air of annoyance, I left Phoebe on read.

~~

Halfway through the meeting, as my presentation ended, Phoebe breezed into the meeting, her heels clicking on the floor. Seeing her, I couldn't help but feel a wave of relief wash over me, a feeling I hadn't experienced in a long time. But this feeling didn't last long. The minute she set foot inside, she became the centre of attention for every man in Alpha Group. Their lustful expressions gave away their intentions as they shamelessly ogled her, never taking their eyes off of her. The men from my company, however, did their best to lower their gaze and fondle with their stack of papers. Unbeknownst to Phoebe, all the men in my company knew I would tear them apart if they as much as dared to look at her with lust. Much less try to ask her out.

Then again, the short black body-hugging office dress Phoebe wore wasn't helping. The outfit hugged her killer curves, accentuating her figure while also showcasing her long, tan legs. And the low 'v' cut of the dress showed off her full cleavage.

My blood seethed and my possessiveness rose as I watched all these men ogle at Phoebe. All I could think about was shielding her from the lecherous gazes of these men. I wanted to lock her up somewhere so no one other than me could look at her so lecherously. The moment this idea crossed my mind, images of us making out at my parents' place and in my office flooded me. Realising that I was the only person in the room who had touched Phoebe in such an intimate manner gave me a unique peace of mind.

By the time Phoebe made it beside me, she was profusely blushing, worsening my situation. Her little act was so cute I felt my friend showing its excitement under the table. How the heck could the mere sight of her blushing excite me? It made no sense. I was a grown-ass man, not a high schooler. Then again, from the look on the other men's faces and their shifting, it seemed they were experiencing the same dilemma as me.

However, unlike with them, it was not just about lust for me. Lately, I've felt a range of emotions whenever I think about Phoebe. She single-handedly messed up my emotional and mental state — to where I often act in ways I otherwise wouldn't. Coldly glaring at all the men from Alpha Group, my expression warned them not to mess with me, and to keep their dirty minds and eyes to themselves. Phoebe was mine.

Phoebe, however, didn't seem to notice her surrounding. Oh, no, she was too busy fixating on Damien Ambrosh — the son of Mr Ambrosh and the interim CEO of Alpha Group. Then, out of nowhere, she went rigid and tense up. A wave of worry flooded my senses, and I wanted to stop the meeting to comfort her. True to her stubborn personality, however, she pretended like nothing was wrong and once again lied to my face. But as I observed her through my peripheral vision, her body language, and furrowed brows spoke volume — she was anything but fine. In that moment, however, there wasn't much I could do other than quietly let it slide.

This whole meeting was a disaster. Phoebe's shifting mood and restless body language made it impossible for me to focus during the meeting. Continuously glancing between a furiously blushing Phoebe and a smirking Damien, my blood was boiling. There was something fishy about Damien and the peculiar stares between them. Briefly sparing me a few questioning glances, the asshole was aware of my possessive demeanour and glacial, sleeted glare. But he continued to smirk flirtatiously at MY GIRL. Breathing through my annoyance, I had stopped giving a damn about the major profit he would bring to my company. He was majorly pissing me off, and I didn't like him one bit.

Intensely focused on Damien and Phoebe, I initially missed that I had internally been referring to Phoebe as 'Mine' and 'My Girl'. But as my thoughts caught up to me, it felt like a torrent of gravel pelted my mind. This was not good. I shouldn't be thinking of her as mine without her consent, especially when I barely knew anything about her. For heaven's sake, I didn't even know who the father of her children was. Was she still in contact with him? Did she still love him? And more importantly, did they still have a good connection and could get back together?

As I blankly stared at Phoebe, my mind turned into the Olympics, with thousands of questions racing like their asses were on fire. Then all at once, the questions stopped dead on their track, as if someone had just doused them with a fire extinguisher. The fire it was using as fuel ceased the moment Phoebe looked at me with confusion. Instead, my usual neutral standoffish expression and demeanour took over.

As the hours passed, my anxiety, anger, and frustration grew exponentially. I wanted to hit something hard. And my irritation was itching to poke its face out. The people in the room sensed the darkness oozing off me and fidgeted with nervousness and anxiousness. Phoebe, however, was so engrossed in her admiration of Damien that she didn't even notice. She was unashamedly gawking at Damien like he was her next meal. A delicious piece of meat she wouldn't think twice about eating right then and there.

Steaming with fury in my seat, I was itching to grab Phoebe by the arm and drag her out of the room, away from all prying eyes. I wanted to show her just how much I wanted her — to where she'll never look at any other men this way again. Only I deserved this hungry look from her. But our situation didn't allow for these fantasies. This feeling of helplessness, especially when a woman was in the picture, was infuriating. I hated being so out of control. But I also recognised this feeling wouldn't go away anytime soon. The more I push it down, the more it was increasing.

When the meeting finally ended, I was ready to drag Phoebe out of the office and away from Damien. She deserved another round of punishment for her behaviour today. And if I was lucky, get my answers from her. However, my feeling of relief once again lasted only a few minutes. Complicating matters for me, Damien stayed behind. In a matter of seconds, it was like I didn't exist. Phoebe maintained eye contact with Damien and gave him her full attention.

For the first time, I detected a different tone in Phoebe's voice as she introduced herself to Damien. It was unlike her usual professional tone. Heck, she even willingly gave her full name rather than her usual brief introduction whenever she talks to any new associate. Even, I, her boss, had to search for her full name when I first took over the company. This woman had acted cold, professional, and distant since day one.

All I had got was, *"Hi, I'm Miss Smith, your Executive personal assistant,"* along with a copy of her insane contract with my dad about her high level of clearance and out-of-the-ordinary job responsibility shoved in my face. She didn't even have the decency to ask for more details about me.

Seeing her act so differently towards Damien made the green monster inside me do another twirl. Silently breathing out, I had to restrain my animalistic instinct from attacking Damien and dragging Phoebe out of that room. As each minute passed, the conversation between them turned weirder, which only increased my confusion and headache. Staring between them, I felt genuinely surprised that Phoebe hadn't lashed out at Damien yet. He was cocky. His introduction, or lack thereof, revealed his self-absorption, overconfidence, and tendency to flatter himself. And who even called themselves Dami-poo? — A weirdo, of course.

That nickname, however, seemed to have awakened Phoebe's memory. A wave of shock and disbelief washed over her face as she finally recognised Damien. Or should I say, Dami-poo?

But then, Phoebe stunned both Damien and me.

Instinctively flinching and holding onto my left cheek, my brain screeched in pain. Gaping at Phoebe's palm imprint on Damien's red cheek, I could imagine the many occasions she could have slapped me this hard.

Despite the pain I felt for Damien, I still hated him. His mere presence disgusted me. Even more so when Phoebe jumped into his arms and clutched onto him for way too long. She was acting as if he was her lifeline, and if she let go, she would instantly combust. The green monster in me was raging. I even dismissed the strange annoyance in Phoebe's voice when she warned Damien not to take a particular person's name — which could have been a valuable information-extracting tool. But Damien's cocky smirk and the liberty he was taking to touch my woman were beyond frustrating and clouding my judgment.

I felt shocked as I openly gawked at Phoebe, who was laughing, being compassionate, easy-going, and showing her embarrassment. For years now, I dreamt of squeezing out any sort of positive emotions from her, but all I got was a cold-hearted person. She was always so fiery, bossy, with a constant state of irritation and anger, it seemed like she had forgotten how to feel any sort of positive and happy emotions. Yet here she was, happy and twirling around in someone's arms in my conference room, her laughter filling the space.

To say I felt infuriated would be a major understatement. I was beyond boiling, nearly erupting like a volcano. This asshole had no right to make Phoebe feel so carefree that all her guards had magically dissipated. It was me who profoundly and passionately liked Phoebe — not him.

Yes, it just dawned on me I had been crushing on Phoebe for a long time now. I romantically liked that woman, and I would not freak out openly about it. Not yet anyway. For the moment, I was going to be mature about it and own it.

Behind Phoebe, like the mere shadow I was in her life, I couldn't believe how much she was praising Damien's physique. Even more baffling, however, was her open-heartedly allowing him back into her life. And worst of all, was Phoebe professing her undying love for him after he left her 10 years ago, without as much as a word throughout the years. Each of her affectionate word towards Damien were a verbal punch to my heart.

In all reality, I couldn't recognise this woman in front of me. Adorned with the utmost beautiful and bright smile, this woman was allowing herself to be run over with — and that too by a man. Where was the strong, over-confident, sassy, cold-hearted, and powerful woman I knew and admired? Where was that annoying *'I am almighty'* attitude that I came to love?

Who was this woman who easily forgave a man who cheated on her and left her stranded with two kids to raise on her own? What the fuck was their current relationship status? And did I just brought one of her exes back into the story by accepting this deal?

Damien was a conniving bastard. He stood there all high and mighty, and instantly got my sweet angel to admit her love for him. What he didn't reveal, however, was that the only reason he even showed his arrogant face here was because I had personally called him up and requested his appearance. This cheating, lying bastard was blatantly taking advantage of Phoebe's innocence and kind heart. Heck, he even got Phoebe to blame herself for his mistakes and poor choices. For Christ's sake, he was a grown-ass man who chose to leave Phoebe when she most needed him. It was his decision, and thus his fault.

Why couldn't Phoebe see the sick side of Damien? This man should have been on his knees, apologising for her forgiveness. But there he was, making one lame attempt at apologising while audaciously pointing out he couldn't promise his stay. Still, Phoebe remained swooned by his cheesy and well-crafted line of 'undeniable love'.

Silently standing, I was seething with rage for Phoebe and her kids. I had heard of and experienced being blind in love, but in Phoebe's case, she was also being stupid in love. Did she seriously think her kids would welcome and accept this asshole back into their lives as she was, just because mommy said so? What even was her plan to explain that *'daddy'* left them as toddles and never bothered to check in on them their whole life?

After talking with Phoebe's kids while icing my precious friend at her house, or after she rushed out of my parents' house to meet all her *'friends,'* I had got a good sense of them. These boys wouldn't be taking this news as lightly as Phoebe was thinking. I needed to talk to them, and Phoebe, before Damien goes over her place. I knew my intervention in her family matter was unnecessary. But the pull demanding I shove my nose into her personal business was too powerful to ignore. Besides, somehow, Phoebe and her kids were involved with my family, and I always protect members of my family — no matter how annoying or stupid one might be.

However, at that moment, a much more pressing matter needed my attention. I needed to clear my suspicions, so I don't repeat my previous mistakes of overthinking and jumping to crazy assumptions. I had heard enough and needed to put a stop to their cheesy reunion. There was only so much a possessive man like me could take, and I was most definitely reaching my peak. Damien seriously needed to keep his hands to himself before he could not use them again.

To my astonishment, I discovered little Miss Phoebe Smith knew how to speak French; a language I clearly did not understand. To make it worse, Damien also shared this skill with her. I swear this guy was a real pain in my ass. Damien, 1; me, 0 — I mentally swore. Yes, I was scoring both of us. Any problem with it?

As they engaged in their little French session, I anxiously awaited the opportunity to have my questions addressed. Studying Phoebe, I noticed a different level of confidence emitting from her. It was like she got a significant confidence boost — not that she wasn't already overconfident. She appeared more relaxed than what she had been these past few days, or when she was in my arms in the office. If I had to guess, Phoebe's change in demeanour was likely caused by her old flame being here, which allowed her to depend on someone other than herself.

This thought, my friends, didn't do any good to my already sour mood. With each passing second, my desire to find the truth about those two became more of a necessity. Most importantly, I needed to know if I still had a shot at winning her over. I wanted her to rely on me and not on another man, much less a man like Damien.

Giving me one of her *'Phoebe full-on-sass answer'* — which doesn't even answer the question — she grabbed Damien's hand and pull dragged him out of the office to God knows where. This woman truly frustrated the fuck out of me. Still, I couldn't help but like her. She differed completely from the others. A rare specimen, if you ask me.

Watching those two take off hand in hand felt like a hot iron rod was burning my soul. The sight of her touching another man was hard enough. But seeing her letting another man touch her in ways only I should have the right to, that was torture. The green monster in me was ready to burst and hulk out.

I had to vent out all the fumes built up inside me. But, at the same time, I had to cool down before I completely explode. So, I did the only thing possible. I showed no remorse as I destroyed the conference room, throwing chairs and files in every direction. After I was done, the only thing existent was the cacophony of mess left behind by my rage. Staring at my handiwork with satisfaction, I knew this entire room would need repair and replacement that very night so Phoebe would not get wind of this.

I was feeling two emotions I had never felt simultaneously before. Jealousy and genuinely romantically liking someone. I was super jealous of Damien — of how Phoebe seemed so carefree with him, but not with me. I was furiously jealous, to the point of killing someone.

CHAPTER 28
DOWN TO MEMORY LANE

PHOEBE

As I tightly gripped the two-frame portrait with my dad and Mia's picture, the weight of the day's event came crashing down on me. Damien was back, and I was finally closing on Vanderwill. With two wonderful news back-to-back in one day, I almost didn't know how to react. It almost seemed too good to be true. But I would not let my fear deny me this joy.

Stroking both pictures of the two people who died because of me, my mind slowly drifted back to *an 'oh-too-familiar'* memory lane.

~Flashback - Ten Years Ago~

Finally, after months of research and cover work, I found one of Vanderwill's henchmen who held the key to leading me directly to the lion's den. Discreetly tailing the unsuspecting henchman, I infiltrated Vanderwill's newest hideout and hid. Every now and then, the monster's voice echoed through the air, barking orders. I needed to wait for the right opportunity, but as the hours ticked away, my impatience grew. And it didn't help that his voice was itching my desire to finish him.

Despite that, I patiently waited until all his men had exited the building. As Vanderwill locked his office, I seized the opportunity and pounced on him. He was the unsuspecting gazelle to the ferocious tiger. My fury and sadness melted together and poured over Vanderwill with each of my blows. I saw red, and my brain turned to mush. All that mattered to me was hearing Vanderwill's pained grunts and turning him into a pile of bruises.

My blind and uncoordinated fighting, however, soon became my disadvantage. Somehow shaking off his shock while I was trashing him, Vanderwill effectively blocked one of my kicks. Holding onto the leg that tried to kick him, Vanderwill grabbed my arm and in a blink flipped me over his shoulder. Leaving no room for a breather, Vanderwill kicked me in the stomach, momentarily knocking the air out of me.

Taking advantage of my daze, Vanderwill pinned me to the ground, his entire weight on me. I should have called upon my years of training and used one of my many strategies. But I still wasn't seeing the big picture. My anger and frustration combined with my disgust at being this close to Vanderwill completely messed me up. Writhing underneath Vanderwill to get out of his stronghold, I was seconds away from biting him like a deranged dog.

"GET OFF MY DAUGHTER, YOU FUCKER!" a loud menacing voice bellowed from behind Vanderwill.

It didn't take a genius to know my dad was beyond furious. After all, I betrayed his trust by coming here tonight. But I had to do what was necessary for Mia and for my promise to her.

"Father." Unable to control my tongue, I muttered in surprise as I tried to twist away from Vanderwill's crushing weight. My headless action compelled both men to turn their heads towards me. My gaze solely on my dad, I saw the sadness in the depth of his eyes, but the anger for Vanderwill was predominant.

"I'm not repeating myself, Vanderwill!" He growled dangerously as he approached both of us. "You have five seconds to get off her before I end your miserable life."

"As you wish, old man. No need to get all riled up." Vanderwill snickered as he stood up. "You might end up breaking something." With his hands raised in surrender, his palm open and directed towards my father, he cautiously retreated from me.

Rather than responding to Vanderwill, my dad walked up to me and offered me his hand.

"What are you doing here? I was clear with my order for you not to follow me!" Taking his offered hand and standing by his side, I tried not to act on my anger.

"Technically, sweetheart, I followed your order to the letter. I didn't follow you. I just had someone else keep a tab on you." My dad noted casually. Giving Vanderwill a quick and weary glance before turning to me again, "You should have known that I would never again leave you alone with this monster. No matter what you think, sweetheart, I'm still your father, and I'll always do what I think is best for you. So, yes, I've had you followed for months now, and I can't believe you didn't notice it."

"Sorry to cut in your father and daughter bonding time, but I got places to be, people to kill, so if we could hurry this up."

"Shut the fuck up!" My father and I simultaneously shouted.

"In just a minute, you and I will pick up where we left off. Stay where you are, and I will happily resume beating the crap out of you." I threatened with arrogance and annoyance.

"Sure, sweetheart, anything for this hot and gorgeous body of yours."

"Shut it, you psychopath." Boiling with fury, my father barked.

My focus on my dad, I placed my hand on his chest, "Father, I need you out of here. I can handle Vanderwill and this situation by myself." Trying to keep my voice down, I commanded with a gentle tone.

"I know you can, sweetheart. But I'm not leaving you alone with him. We can't underestimate how dangerous he is. This monster didn't even think twice before killing the mother of his own children. You of all people should know he wouldn't hesitate to hurt you if he needed to." My dad tried to warn me of the danger ahead.

"But…" I tried with as much stubbornness as I could.

"You may be the best. But you're not thinking straight right now. And he's taking full advantage of this." My dad cut in firmly.

I knew a lecture was incoming, but right now wasn't the time for such banality. This was the time for one thing and one thing only — killing Cole Vanderwill. Boring my stern gaze on the two agents behind my dad, I ordered them to escort him out. At first, they seemed hesitant given they came here with my dad. But after they saw the glare that said, 'Do not mess with me', they reluctantly obeyed and, with gentleness, attempted to drag my dad out.

However, after a few unsuccessful attempts, they resigned and finally said, "Sir, I need you to come with us. We apologise, but Angel is the boss now. And we must follow her direct order." With their eyes glimmering a sad expression, they gingerly informed, seeking forgiveness and understanding for their actions. Despite everything and how bad I felt, I found satisfaction because they followed my orders. I tested their loyalty, and they passed with flying colours.

I needed to deal with Cole Vanderwill on my own. He was my business, and nobody else. More importantly, I didn't want my dad getting hurt, just like Mia did. I had enough guilt already. With the latter in mind, the safest option for my dad was to stay as far away from here as possible.

Assuming the other agents had successfully taken care of escorting my dad out, I refocused my attention on Vanderwill. But I should have waited. At that moment, however, I was too anxious and wanted to eliminate the *'Vanderwill problem'* as quickly and as painfully for him as possible.

Smugly smirking at Vanderwill, "So, where did we leave off before we got interrupted?" It wasn't actually a question, but more of a straightforward statement.

But given Vanderwill's stupidity and arrogance, he just had to answer. "Me on top of you, love. About to have my many ways with you, just like old times. Maybe even go as far as I did with your dear useless fragile Mia. That bitch was a fine piece."

"You know, you didn't have to answer. It was a rhetorical question, yet you chose to. And you even had the audacity to insult Mia after mercilessly killing her in front of me."

My fury rose to a critical level by his comments, and the little rationality I had flew out the window. In a matter of seconds, I swiftly retrieved the concealed dagger from under my shirt and hurled it towards Vanderwill's leg. As I watched the shock and pain take over his face, a bud of happiness sprout within me.

"Fuck! Bitch! I'll make you pay for this!" Vanderwill screeched in agony.

Not thinking twice of his obscenities and petty threats, I took advantage of his shock and pain. Sprinting towards him, I kicked him hard on his wounded leg, propelling the dagger deeper into his flesh. This, however, did not seem enough to me. I was out for blood, and he needed to suffer more. Pulling my leg back, I ferociously kicked him in the stomach. With almost a thud sound, he fell back, his one hand protecting his leg and the other attempting to protect his face. My smirk grew wider at the sight of him cowering in front of me as I persisted in my relentless kicking, striking wherever I could. Suddenly, I felt a strong, reassuring embrace from behind, as if someone was trying to comfort me. If I didn't know better, I would have grabbed the person's arms and thrown them over. Fortunately, I recognised my dad's touch. Allowing him to calm me down, I watched Vanderwill take laboured breaths as he spat blood and struggled to sit up.

"Calm down, sweetheart. You've trashed him enough for today. We'll deal with the rest of him later. But for now, let's bring him back with us. I bet Damien wants to see his stupid face, too. Then both of you can take turns to beat the crap out of him until he stops breathing. Remember, slow and everyday torture is the best type of punishment." Even though my dad's words were not successfully calming me down, it made sense.

Vanderwill probably presumed my dad was going to propose handing him over to the authority, or sending him away to our personal jail, not the *'beat him to death'* part. However, as soon as those words left my dad's mouth, clear disbelief shadowed Cole's eyes as they widened with horror. I wanted to finish Vanderwill right here itself, but after seeing his facial expression, I found my dad's idea quite appealing.

"Okay, Dad, if you say so."

Turning to my dad, I gave him a much-deserving, bone-crushing hug. "Sorry for before, Dad. Not just for today, but for every single day since you rescued me from Vanderwill's grip. I've been extremely rude, and I'm really very sorry." I apologised, feeling a wave of relaxation wash over me after such a long time.

'It was finally over!' My brain screamed with happiness.

My dad returned my hug with so much fervour, I had to tap his shoulder lightly to let him know I had to breathe.

"It's okay, sweetheart. You were hurting, and I understood." My dad, however, didn't get to finish what was on his mind.

"Look at you two, father and daughter reunite. It makes me sick to the stomach." Cole venomously cut in.

Spinning blood on the ground, Cole caught his breath again. "I still can't believe I bought the lie that you were Lainey and Mia was the actual *'Angel,'* — the sole heir of Robert and my father's murderer." Gripping his side, his breath still heavy, "It's a shame that Angel's sidekick took my challenge. Against my better judgement, I accepted her as Angel, even when it was clear she didn't have it in her. Her lack of authority and control was too evident. I guess I killed the wrong person." Slowly scooting backwards on his buttocks, Vanderwill recounted between breaths. "I hate having to do this to you, Angel, but you have left me with no other choice."

I knew Vanderwill was trying to irritate me, so I would finish him right there, and he would not have to go through several days of torture before dying. It took all the self-restraint I had not to walk right into his trap. His last cryptic statement, however, puzzled me. It made little sense, just like him killing Mia made little sense.

"What are you going on about, Cole?" I demanded, confused and angry as heck.

"Dad, can't I go back on my words and kill him right now? We don't need to wait, do we?" Not even waiting for Cole to respond, I turned to my father and asked with almost pleading eyes.

As my dad gave me a genuine smile, I could feel the warmth of his love and anticipation. However, before he could utter a word, a thunderous 'BANG' shook the entire room. It was the sound of a gun being fired from behind me. Thunderbolt, I squeezed my eyes shut and waited for the pain that should have followed. But when I felt nothing, my confusion grew.

If Vanderwill didn't shoot me, then who did he shoot? Don't tell me he shot himself because that would be pure cowardliness. A big, dangerous man like him shouldn't be afraid of some torture before dying. It was his own pill being fed to him.

Pushing away my startlement, I whirled around to assess the situation. To my horror, Cole was without a bullet wound. Struggling to stand a bit, Cole slowly rose to his feet, the dagger still embedded in his leg. A gun ominously clutched in his hand, a twisted and sadistic smirk etched on his face. This further increased my confusion. With a casual nod of his head, he silently gestured for me to glance behind me. And that's exactly what I did.

My breath caught in my throat as I watched my father fall backwards, his hands pressed over his heart. His hands and shirt were both covered with blood, and I immediately realised Cole was not aiming for me, but for my dad. In that moment, it occurred to me that Cole Vanderwill was never directly aiming for me, but always going after my dad. He wanted to avenge the death of his father. First, by kidnapping my dad's most precious treasure — his only kid. Then step it up with torturing said daughter for months, before leaving her marked forever. And for the final touch, kill him in front of his own daughter.

In shock, my dad's words played in my mind. *'Real torture is prolonged and never-ending'.*

I wanted to run after Vanderwill and kill him before he could escape. But I didn't want to leave my dad in this state just to catch that bastard. Letting my emotion win, I dropped to my knees, tears streaming down my face, and applied pressure on his wound. At this moment, I didn't care that my agents could see my vulnerable side. Glancing up at the agents amidst my bouts of distress, I saw them standing there. I couldn't believe it. None of them took the initiative to get help or follow the asshole that was Vanderwill. Sitting on that cold and hard floor, with my dad's head resting on my lap, my anger, worry, and sadness became one.

"What are you all still doing standing around!? Fucking call 911!" I bellowed.

Watching them scurry around and doing as ordered, I shook my head at them before returning my attention to my dad. These people were a disappointment. But right now, I didn't have time to focus on them. As I looked at my hands, stained with my dad's blood, I couldn't ignore the sinking feeling in my gut, though a sliver of hope remained. Whispering encouraging words to reassure him, I tried to keep my dad awake while the ambulance came for us.

I wanted revenge. I was thirsty for it. And eventually, I was going to get it. Finally, killing and eliminating the curse of Cole Vanderwill would be the sweetest victory. I promised myself this.

"Get the fuck out of my life, Cole!" I faced Vanderwill, who stood surrounded by my agents. "Run, Cole Vanderwill! Find your best hideout while you can. From now on, it's my life's mission to hunt you down like the unworthy beast you are and destroy your miserable life." I vociferated my challenge. "And trust me, when I track you down and see your despicable face again, I'll make you regret ever being born." With venom and a promise in my words, I declared my act of war.

As I said those words to him, I saw a fleeting glimpse of sadness in his eyes, but it quickly vanished. Regardless of this little show of emotion, I was angrier and sadder than ever. With a single nod and quiet for the first time, Vanderwill swiftly scampered away, his quick footsteps resembling small hops.

Bringing my attention back to my father, I watched as he fought to stay with me. My eyes and face showing my concern. "Hold on, Daddy. Fight this! Do you understand me?" Trying very hard to remain composed, I exclaimed. But when I saw his eyes closing, I panicked all over again.

"Dad, please fight it. Keep your eyes open. Please… I'm sorry for everything… Please…" I pleaded. "If not for yourself, then do it for me… Please, don't leave me … I love you. I need you by my side…" Seeing him struggling to blink his eyes and not responding, "Shit. I'll even marry Franco before my 21st birthday, like you wanted. Just please… fight this!" Fully letting my guard down, I pleaded and promised the one thing I didn't want to do.

Rushing into the ambulance as soon as it reached us, we blared to the closest hospital. Holding onto my father's hands, I wanted him to know I was there with him as promised. Despite my resistance, one paramedic held me back as another one tore open my dad's shirt. I was in shock as I watched him put an oxygen mask on my dad's face, injected something in his chest, and attended to his wounds as best as he could. However, when my dad started muttering almost incoherent words, I immediately got out of the young man's hold and scooted closer to my dad.

"Baby girl, I don't think I'll make it this time." My dad whispered in a croaky voice.

"No! You're going to fight it! You're stronger than this." I persisted with a brittle tone as my tears freely streamed down my face again.

"Listen to me… you should know… I love you more than anything in this world… and … you've never been a disappointment to me. Promise me you're going to live again after I'm gone…" Choking up in his words, some splatter of blood hit my face. I wanted to stop him, but I couldn't do much.

Clinging to his frail hands, "Dad," I whispered, my voice quivering, "Please, don't talk like that." The fear was clear in my tone and face.

"Baby… Promise me… You won't lose yourself in sorrow and live alone. You won't let the memories of Mia or me shroud your heart in darkness…" He coughed, crimson staining his lips, but he persevered. "I need you to be strong for Wyatt and Teo. … They're your sons now… Your responsibility… and no one else."

As he tightened his hands around mine, I could sense the frailty in his grip. Yet, I couldn't utter any other words. The chaos of the loud sirens and the cold, sterile atmosphere of the ambulance were too much. Instead, I nodded as my heart ached with the possibility of losing my dad.

"Oh, sweetheart…" he continued, his breath shallow, "You're the pride of any parent. I know your mom would have been proud of you, too."

Watching him breathing with difficulty while saying all these bittersweet things were too real for me. I couldn't take it anymore. I breathed out my sadness and placed the oxygen mask back on him to *'shush'* him.

"No, Dad, everything is going to be okay. You can't leave me. Not now… not yet… no, no, and again, no. You can't do this to me. Please DON'T." I implored, my cried more intense than before.

"Phoebe. I'm sorry. Just… go to Joseph, he's your Godfather—" He stopped and deeply inhaled from the mask. I could tell his breathing was struggling as he continued to speak. But no matter how much I tried to stop him from talking, he just wouldn't stop.

"Room … Search … Your … Mom." He mumbled those incoherent words. Although the word *'your mom'* caught my attention, I pushed it at the far back of my mind and concentrated on the matter at hand.

He struggled to speak, his words a desperate plea, until suddenly, he fell silent. In that moment, the world froze, and the only sounds that pierced the engulfing silence were the relentless, rapid beeping of the monitoring machine, serving as a relentless reminder of the impending danger. The ambulance, once a chaotic symphony of sirens, now transformed into a cramped chamber of uncertainty.

I felt a reassuring hand holding onto me, grounding me as the paramedics worked frantically. In any other circumstance, I might have recoiled from the stranger's touch, but at that moment, I welcomed it. Denial had taken hold of my heart, and I clung to the futile hope that this was all a terrible dream. Desperation overwhelmed me as I continued to shake my father's shoulders, tears streaming down my face. I begged him to wake up, but he remained unresponsive. With a heavy heart, I surrendered and let the paramedics do their jobs.

As the ambulance parked at the hospital's entrance, the doctors and nurses rushed him to the emergency operating room. Their sense of urgency and tension was evident, turning their hushed conversations into a sombre backdrop. I overheard their words — words that echoed my own fears, "A faint chance of survival", "Near impossible". Yet, I held onto hope, even as I lightly shook my head in disbelief. After all, hope was the only anchor in this sea of uncertainty.

I waited for what felt like an eternity, the agonizing silence of the hospital room stretching on. Hours passed with no news, leaving my heart heavy and my mind haunted by dark thoughts. Just when my despair threatened to consume me, Damien rushed in. His presence was a reassuring anchor in this sudden storm. He tried to comfort me, assuring me that everything would be fine. However, deep down, I knew the future was a canvas of unknown colours, and I couldn't paint it with his false hopes. Changing the topic to shift our thoughts away from the looming shadow of tragedy and death, I asked, "Where are the kids, Dam?"

"They are safe. Don't worry too much about them. I'm sorry about what you're going through."

"It's okay. It's all my fault, anyway. I just hope my dad is fine and survives this."

Before Damien could utter a word, I noticed the doctor emerging from the operation room, his expression revealing the sombre verdict. The unspoken weight of the news hung heavily in the air, and I knew, with no need to hear the harsh words, what had unfolded. Jumping from my seat, unwilling to hear the painful confirmation from the doctor's lips, I ran. Even though my legs felt weak, I forced it to carry me far from the unbearable reality as swiftly as possible.

Eventually, I found myself beneath the sheltering branches of a tree on the distant side of the hospital. There, the tears flowed freely, my cries echoing my anguish and the unfathomable loss. Overwhelmed by the day's emotional turmoil and physical pain, I succumbed to exhaustion and drifted into a dreamless sleep beneath the comforting tree.

To my surprise, I awoke in my room the next day, with Damien seated beside me, his face etched with sorrow. As our eyes met, he moved closer and enveloped me in a tight embrace, confirming the unspeakable truth about what had transpired.

"I'm really sorry for what happened, Phebes. I feel your pain." Damien sympathised as he shared my sorrow. "And as much as I regret doing this to you right now, I have to," After a span of silence between us, Damien uttered in a soft blue tone.

"What are you talking about?" Locking my gaze on him, I asked, perplexed.

"I can't be here anymore. And I can't look at those boys — let alone try to look after them. I'm very sorry. But they are a constant reminder of what I lost — of what has happened twice now. And I can't keep torturing myself like this."

"But—" Suffocating the blow to my heart, I began advocating for myself, but Damien stopped me.

"Take my advice, Phebes, give those kids away… Or just throw them out… They are a curse."

As I took one long look at Damien, I felt baffled. I was in pain too, but I still couldn't believe those words came out of his mouth. The look on his face, though, told me everything I had to know. I knew this day would eventually come. But so soon, especially when I desperately needed him. That was a shock to my system. Nonetheless, I had to accept the fact that he couldn't bear to look at the kids' faces or live here any longer — especially when I caused all his sorrow.

Despite Damien's untimely departure, I was grateful that he had waited at least two weeks and took care of the funeral and burial process before leaving. September 21st was the last time I ever saw Damien. That day also marked the day I turned far more heartless, cold, and emotionless towards everyone. It was the day the real huntress in me awoke and Cole Vanderwill became my ultimate prey.

Even though I had sworn to never care for anyone again — much less love someone — my sons, Alicia, Joseph and my four best friends fought and crushed my defences. It took them several years, but they never stopped.

Through them, I discovered the love of genuine friendship, and the love of a mother for her sons, a sister for her brother, and a child for her adoptive parents. And even though the trio had died, my four best friends made their special place in my heart. I couldn't imagine my life without them all.

However, beyond this inner circle, I made sure that I was both feared and respected me by others. I projected an aura of strength and determination — a veneer that shielded the precious love I held close to my heart. I was untouchable and a force to be reckoned with.

~Present Day~

As I opened my eyes, the sensation of dampness on my cheeks made me chuckle at my state. It would seem that night after night, I was in a perpetual state of shedding tears. Honestly, I didn't even know where my eyes found this endless well of tears every night.

If my agents knew how much of a cry-baby I actually was, it would be a total shame. Then again, the shock on their face at my masterful display of emotional vulnerability would be hilarious. But thank God I mastered the art of silent crying. Otherwise, the household would hear my nightly serenades. As I wiped away another tear, I chuckled as I wonder if my constant crying made me certified to offer lessons on the finer points of weeping — if, by some miraculous chance, such a class existed.

With a determined grip, I clung to the frame that had Mia and my father's picture as I found myself transported back to the pivotal moment when my life took an irrevocable turn. I was reliving those painful memories, desperately yearning for a different outcome. Yet, amid those painful recollections, I also scoured my mind for the precious, fleeting moments of joy, hoping to clutch onto them like lifelines.

After a few hours of indulging in self-pity and crying until my tears had run dry, I inhaled a deep, steadying breath and exhaled slowly. With newfound determination, I placed the frame back on my bedside table, and rose to prepare myself for bed. I had to be strong, if not for myself, then for my sons. They were my joie de vive. If not for them, I would be all alone in this cruel world.

Despite having some of the most formidable best friends and non-blood family, there remained a void in my heart that even their love couldn't fill. It was aching and craving for something else — something more dangerous that I still couldn't quite define. It was this enigmatic yearning that often left me feeling lonely and isolated.

In addition, I felt an undeniable burden of the world's responsibilities resting heavily on my shoulders, making it impossible for me to back down. I had to always be on my guard, especially now that my curse had resurfaced. There was no choice. I had to protect every single person I loved and held dear.

Being the top spy came at a steep cost, and I regretfully had to learn this lesson the hard way.

THE END

(To Be Continued in Book 2)

Hey there, thanks for sticking to the end of this story. My hope is you loved it and are looking forward to the next installment in the series. There are so many questions that still need to be answered and so many things to be discovered.

Before you leave here today, please review this novel on Amazon for me (or the place where you got this book)?

I would really appreciate it. Not only will your small action encourage me, but it would also help other readers to discover this novel. And who knows, it might make their day, and that would be all thanks to you.

Scan the QR code to access this book's website & choose where you want to review:

If you prefer the link, here it is: https://laviniadasani.com/the-spy-within/

If you liked this series and my style of writing, or just want to know more about me, sign up for my monthly newsletter. I promise to keep you up to date and even give you teasers when it's available.

Scan this QR code to sign up to my monthly newsletter:

Again, if you prefer link, here it is: https://plumitifpress.ck.page/65f165d271

READ MORE FROM LAVINIA DASANI

Standalone novel:

AFFAIR OF THE HEART

'There's a Pleasure in Pain' … Renowned Cognitive Behavioural Psychologist, Dr Angelica Buar, soon learns this while working in partnership with Detective Storm Ives in the State Law Enforcement Special Branch.

Non-Fiction Book:

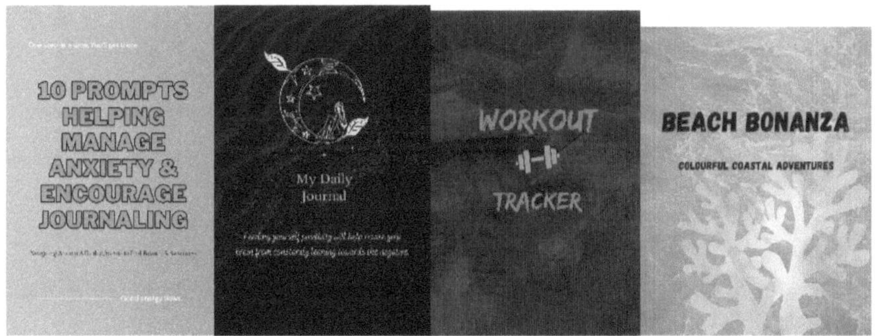

Ж COMING NEXT Ж

UNMASKING — BOOK 2 of Tame Series

Unmasking is the second part of the Tame Series, and it follows the story of a ferocious spy, Phoebe Smith, where the extent to which she will go to protect her secrets is tested when she accepts her boss' friendship. A friendship that was never supposed to exist.

https://laviniadasani.com/books/

ABOUT AUTHOR

Lavinia Dasani is a Self-Published Author and Founder/CEO of Plumitif Press, LLC. Originally from the beautiful island of Mauritius, she migrated to the United States at 16 and began her path in the psychological industry. She enjoys travelling, reading, fashion, animals, the beach, connecting with people, and her readers.

She started writing at 10 years old and published her first online novel on Wattpad in 2013, around the age of 13. Her favourite genre to read and write is Romance fiction.

"Days in & days out, I want to create stories. It's my way of relaxing and expressing myself without speech. Fictional romance novels have always been a source of escape for me, which is why I write in that genre. I also throw in a mix of humour, family, drama, action, dominance, psychology and eroticism in my wiring. My dreams, ideas that pop into my mind, and my emotions inspire most of my stories."

She goes by Lady Lavinia Dasani on all social platforms and has other books under that name. Connect with her on any social platforms now:

https://laviniadasani.com/contact/